ILSA MADDEN-MILLS

Annie ~
Be filthy!
Ilsa xoxo

Filthy English
Copyright © 2016 by Ilsa Madden-Mills

Cover Design by
S. K. Hartley with Luminos Graphic House
Model: Quinn Biddle
Photography: David Vance

Editing by
Rachel Skinner of Romance Refined
and Katherine Trail of KT Editing

Formatting by
Christine Borgford, Perfectly Publishable

Series Interior Design Concept by
JT Formatting

Little Dove Publishing
ISBN-13: 978-1535193337
ISBN-10: 1535193336
First Edition July 2016

"Give me my Romeo, and, when he shall die, Take him and cut him out in little stars, And he will make the face of heaven so fine That all the world will be in love with night . . ."

-Juliet, *Romeo and Juliet*

CHAPTER ONE

PLAIN AND SIMPLE, this night sucked.

Sadly, it was my honeymoon.

I sighed heavily and gazed around Masquerade, an intimately lit London nightclub where everyone wore black domino masks, some elaborate and some plain, to hide their identity. A few die-hards even sported medieval-type clothing and long, loose cloaks.

Not me though. I'd gone modern with a slinky little number and three-inch heels, putting my height at nearly six feet. Yep, I'm the masked giant in the blue dress, towering over every girl and some of the guys at the bar.

My teeth dug into my bottom lip as I gazed around the smoky club, my eyes bouncing off random faces. I felt terribly alone—not surprising since my groom was MIA.

I'd been dumped.

That's right. Hartford Wilcox, aka Mr. ~~Nice Guy~~ Douchebag of Whitman University in North Carolina, had jilted me two weeks before the big wedding day as we had dinner at our favorite Italian restaurant, Mario's.

1

We were over. Like pay phones and mom jeans.

He'd been everything I wanted on my *Perfect Man List*—except for his fast-paced intercourse and overly hairy chest, but I'd overlooked those things because slow, passionate, mind-blowing sex isn't all it's cracked up to be.

Trust me.

I'd had that—a long time ago.

That kind of passion can cut you open and rip your heart out with a spoon.

I never wanted that kind of ~~love~~ lust again.

My bestie Lulu, who'd come with me to London at the last minute, poked me with her finger as we sat in front of the heavy wooden bar of the club. "Hey, Earth to Remi, get that glazed look out of your eyes and order a drink already. I'm thirsty."

Alcohol. I nodded. Time to get wasted.

"Dang, the men in here are hotter than a billy goat with a blowtorch," she added in her southern drawl. She fluffed her pixie-cut pink hair and straightened her black tutu.

Clearly, she was on a manhunt—as I should be.

I half-heartedly agreed, more intent on scanning the bottles behind the bar. "I want tequila," I said.

Her face snapped back to me. "*What?* I know what happens when you drink that crap. You either eat a ton of tacos and puke, or you wrap yourself around some cocky bastard with a well-developed backside."

I grimaced. Hairy Hartford had a great ass—which was probably plowing some sorority girl right now.

A short laugh burst out of me—one of those I'm-miserable-but-pretending-to-be-okay laughs I'd been doing a lot of lately. For the past two weeks, I'd vacillated between a sobbing mess and an angry woman who periodically became so incensed that "fuck" was the only word that seemed appropriate in any given situation. Going to the post office to mail *he dumped me but thank you anyway* cards. Fuck. Going to the wedding venue and not getting the ten-thousand-dollar deposit back. Double fuck. Realizing I was homeless fall semester—which was in two weeks—holy fuck.

Of course my mom said it was all my fault.

Looking down, I realized I'd resorted to my nervous habit—twisting my diamond tennis bracelet around my wrist like rosary beads.

You have to move on, Remi.

The bartender swaggered over to us, a tall, lean guy with a beard and a sleeve of rose tattoos down his arms. He introduced himself as Mike and asked what we wanted. Lulu stuck with her usual, an apple martini.

I ordered an entire bottle of Silver Patrón. Oblivion, thy name is Remi.

"Your funeral," Lulu muttered as I tossed back the first shot and sucked on the lime Mike had left. I shivered as it went down, my face scrunching up from the bite.

"What does it taste like?" she asked, eyeing me.

"Like bad decisions," I said, wiping my mouth with the napkin. "But it gets me where I want. Give me fifteen minutes and I might even attempt to dance."

She half snorted, half laughed. "Liar."

Yeah. Me dancing resembled a goldfish flopping on the floor.

I sucked down another drink as two guys came over and struck up a conversation with Lulu. I barely looked at them. She practically swooned when they asked us to dance.

"Let's go have fun, Remi," she implored as she gazed longingly at the dance floor and then back at me. The guys were already out there, motioning for us to join them.

"I'll join in a sec." I probably wouldn't.

She pouted. "You're lying."

"Yes. But don't worry about me." I shoved down my no-good horrible mood and indicated the bottle of tequila. "Besides, this guy and I have a date."

She gave me a rueful smile. "Okay, but if you see someone you want to get cozy with, go for it. Don't sit on that stool all night and think about Hairy Hartford. You know what they say—'Sometimes you have to get under someone to get over someone.'"

After she left, I fiddled with my bracelet and mulled. I grumbled under my breath, remembering how Hartford had sworn he'd love me forever—only to break up with me over a plate of lasagna. My mind drifted to better memories. I thought about his kindness and sweet nature, his penchant for anticipating my every need, his all-American good looks—

Oh, for heaven's sake, stop the sentimental crap, I yelled at myself.

Lulu was right. I needed a man, someone so spectacularly different from Hartford that—

My mouth plopped open at the beautiful male who strode past me, and by beautiful I mean drop-dead sexy with a body like a brick house.

I snapped my lips shut and adjusted my velvet half-mask—the annoying feathery plumes on the sides kept sticking to my red lipstick—and turned ever so slightly to check him out. He slid into the seat next to me, tall and broad with rippling shoulders and a massive frame.

"Whatta Man" from Salt-N-Pepa came to mind.

I checked my appearance in a mirror behind the bar, mentally analyzing the odds of an overgrown, average girl like me snagging a hottie like him.

Although no one had ever called me beautiful, I did have two—okay, maybe three—things going for me in the looks department. My golden-brown hair that hung down to my shoulders, my fluffy "pillow lips" as Lulu described them, and, lastly, I had an itsy bitsy space between my two front teeth which were otherwise white and perfect. Lulu claimed the gap lent me an exotic look, like Madonna or Sookie Stackhouse. Whatever. I was a True Blood fan. I went with it.

The guy turned his head in my direction.

Then promptly looked away.

Dammit. I had about a one in a gazillion chance of catching his eye.

He shifted on the stool, leaning closer to me. His cologne swirled in the air, the smell of expensive Scotch and musk mingling together to create a heady, slightly dangerous scent. I paused, goosebumps rising when the spicy whiff triggered a distant memory.

I knew that smell . . .

But whatever my nose recognized, it didn't connect with my brain.

As slyly as I could, I studied his profile from top to bottom. Like me, he wore a black mask, although his was more masculine, not hiding his chiseled, movie star jawline. His lips were carnal and luscious, the bottom more plump than the top with a slight indentation in the middle. As I watched, his tongue swept out and caressed it, his top teeth biting it as if he were deep in thought. He raked a hand through his dark, longish, messy hair, held it suspended above his head for a few seconds, and then released it, letting it swish back into its tousled yet perfect place.

Choreographed male perfection.

I tore my eyes away.

Something about him sent loud warning bells ringing in every atom in my body.

Danger, danger. Don't touch that.

You will be annihilated with an M16 rifle straight to your heart.

But my gaze would not be denied as I took in the tight black shirt and sculpted chest that was obviously used to the inside of a gym, right down to an arm that looked like it could snap a board in half—or me.

Nice biceps, Mr. Beautiful.

The *pièce de résistance* was the dragonfly tattoo he sported on his left arm—it was bigger than my hand and in vivid blues and oranges. My gaze traced the contours of the design from the papery wings to the multi-faceted eyes. A bold black color outlined the insect, giving it a masculine feel.

Gorgeous.

Of course, I didn't have any tattoos—my mom would flip her lid—but secretly I'd always wanted one. The artistic side of me admired them on people, especially when they featured anything with wings. Probably because I'm a bird girl, as in someday I'll have a doctorate in ornithology.

Him tonight?

Yes, my body said, g*o for Mr. Beautiful! Make him yours!*

He *was* the polar opposite of Hartford, who was blond, lean, and tattoo-free.

I nibbled on my fingernail. *How do I get him to notice little ole me?*

Just then a redhead with fluffy Farrah Fawcett hair strode up to his stool, bold as brass, wearing a tight, white mini-skirt that barely covered her booty.

She flicked her hair over her shoulder, casually stroked her finger down his arm, and struck up a conversation. Her fake, black lashes—which she'd somehow managed to get outside the eyeholes of her mask—batted. She puffed out her well-developed chest.

I saw it for what it was. *Classic mating ritual.*

Even flamingos toss their heads around and take little mincing steps toward their desired mate. A red-capped manakin bird courts by moonwalking on a nearby branch. It's pretty much the coolest thing ever.

So why couldn't I do that?

He leaned into her and grinned wickedly, his body language telling me he was confident he was the hottest thing in the room. She whispered in his ear, boobs right in his face, but whatever he said back wasn't what she wanted to hear because a few ticks later she crossed her arms, gave me a nasty glare, and stalked away.

I blinked. *What had I done?*

Then he turned and pointed his devastating smile at ME.

My heart flip-flopped inside my chest.

Shit, he'd made eye contact—as much as you could with a claustrophobic mask on.

But wait . . .

Was he crazy?

Because if he'd turned down *her* flirtation, I didn't have a shot.

I didn't know how to do the fingers-tiptoeing-up-his-arm thing and sexy hair flicking. I didn't know how to make my boobs sit up that high.

Everyone knew I wasn't a flirt. Not in a million years. Heck, Hartford had only asked me out because I'd tripped over his legs as they stuck out from a study carrel at the library.

And that memory pricked at my heart.

Stupid, stupid, stupid. This entire night and all men.

Forget Mr. Beautiful. Forget Hartford. *Forget everything.*

I rapped on the bar and tried to get someone to bring me more limes.

Mike with the beard and tats finally noticed me waving. I held my ravaged lime up for him to see. He smiled, gave me a thumbs-up signal, and as soon as he'd finished his current drink order, he brought several over to me in a nice bowl.

"So . . . American?" he asked as he leaned over the counter.

"Kinda obvious." I nodded my chin at him. "You British?"

"Kinda obvious." His lips twitched.

He poured my next shot and I tossed it back, sucked the lime, and slammed the glass back down on the bar. A drink later, I was swaying to the crazy techno music, which I didn't even like.

"Perhaps you should sip it," Mike murmured, still hanging around.

"If you'd had the past few weeks I'd had, you'd chug it too."

He let that go, running a hand across his beard, his eyes skating across the V-neck of my dress. Lingering. He met my eyes. "What's your name, sweets?"

I squinted. "Are you flirting with me? It's okay if you are. Just sayin'."

"Absolutely. You're bloody gorgeous." Hooded eyes raked over my chest. Again.

I laughed. Feeling loose.

Maybe my rebound guy was right here in front of me.

"When you're done hitting on the clientele, barman, we'd like a drink," Mr. Beautiful snapped out in an authoritative British accent that demanded to be heard, causing Mike to flip away from me and focus on him. He scurried over and took his order.

I scowled. Wait a dang minute . . .

I *almost* knew that accent—deep with soft, rounded vowels, the kind of voice that made you want to hop into his bed and ride him like a cowgirl.

At the sound of it, chills had gone up my spine, and part of me wanted to jump off my stool and run away screaming, but the other side wanted to trace my fingers over Mr. Beautiful's lips and ask him to say something else.

My name.

My phone number.

Romeo's monologue outside Juliet's window.

I pivoted on my barstool and found that Mr. Beautiful's eyes had zeroed in on me once more, as if he too recognized the strange pull between us. Weird.

What was going on? Why was he staring at me?

My heart played hopscotch, jumping against my chest. My skin prickled.

Did I know him?

Did he know me?

It clicked, everything sliding into place. *Dax Blay?*

My breath hitched, and I swallowed down the emotion that zipped up my spine whenever I thought of *him*. He was my one HUGE mistake; the time I'd tossed inhibitions and carefully laid plans aside and went with my instincts (lots of sex), only to have it tossed back in my face.

But the man next to me *wasn't* Dax. Thank God.

Last spring at the campus-wide end of the year fraternity party with Hartford, I'd seen Dax, and he'd had shorter hair, like always, and zero tattoos. Yeah. No way.

Plus, last I heard, he was in Raleigh where his father lived.

Yet . . .

Dax was British. He could have family here. Maybe he got a tattoo?

Nah. I mean, what were the odds of us both being at the same club on the same night in a country where neither of us lived?

Move on, Remi, forget faux-Dax. Focus on the bartender. He likes your cleavage.

Determined to get Mike's attention back as he poured drinks for someone else, I slyly attempted to tug down the neckline of my dress with my right hand—*check this out, Mikey*—but the lace bodice snagged on my tennis bracelet in the process, leaving my wrist dangling like a wet dish rag in a most inappropriate place.

I wiggled my arm.

Jiggled it.

Sweat popped out on my forehead.

Holding my breath, I twisted and tugged the bracelet, forcing the delicate material in my bodice to stretch into the danger zone.

"Well, hell," I breathed, pausing to assess.

Skin-tight with a plunging neckline, the dress was mostly a blue stretchy fabric held together by sequined straps and a zipper on the side. Slated as part of my honeymoon wardrobe, it was a Tory Burch and had cost four hundred dollars, the most I'd ever paid for a fun outfit, and no way did I want to damage it. I might have to return it to rent an apartment at Whitman.

Lulu. I needed Lulu. She was a whiz with wardrobe malfunctions.

I spun around on the barstool and used my free hand to wave at her, but she was slinging herself around dancing, having a great time and completely oblivious. I resorted to flapping both hands at her, one high and one low. Several people waved back with baffled expressions, but Lulu didn't notice. *Dammit.*

I groaned and slumped down in my seat, ready to scream. Now what? Go to the bathroom and repair it there? Good plan.

But the club tilted when I stood, the strobe lights making me squint as they flashed in my face. I wobbled in my leopard-print heels—that Lulu had insisted I wear—and grabbed the stool to keep my balance.

I sucked in a breath to gather myself, but I couldn't think

straight. The room spun, and I was suddenly queasy, and why did I slam all that tequila, *and oh my God, my wrist is currently attached to my tit like a T. rex arm.*

"Hey, my shift ends in an hour or so depending on the crowd. You want to grab a drink?" Mike said.

Eeek. I'd forgotten all about the nice bartender.

Go with it, Remi. Be cool. Don't be a wacko.

I pivoted *carefully* around to face him, using my captured hand as a chinrest, forcing me to lean my head down at an odd angle.

His brow wrinkled. "You okay there? You're kinda pale."

"Uh, maybe? Not really. I just—uh—need to go to the ladies' room first. I—I'll be back in a minute." Trying to be stealth-like, I reached across the bar to get my beaded clutch, but because it was my left hand and not my right, which I used most of the time, I got off balance and stumbled—and my ankle folded in on itself. I yelped as my shoe catapulted off my foot and vaulted off toward who knows where, while I fell forward, straight into Mr. Beautiful's lap.

CHAPTER TWO

Fifteen Minutes Earlier

MY COUSIN SPIDER (real name Clarence) and I walked inside the nightclub.

I had one goal this evening: Alcohol and a lot of it.

I hadn't had sex in eighty-seven days, five hours, and a few odd minutes, which seems strange for a handsome and charismatic guy like myself who was used to getting a different flavor each month, but when my twin brother Declan had dared me to be celibate in order to clear my head, I'd accepted his challenge.

Besides, it wasn't proper for a Blay male to turn down a dare. It was on.

But today before we'd left for the club, I'd had to deal with my father, Mr. Winston Blay, a former United States ambassador who'd gotten my English mum pregnant with my twin and me, married her—then promptly divorced her a year later.

He'd called me earlier from his mansion in Raleigh to demand I go to graduate school after I graduated from Whitman.

School hadn't even started and he was already on my back. As usual.

I'd said *"hell no."*

As a fifth year senior, I was a huge disappointment to him.

But this year—*this year*—I had to get my shit together and figure out what I was going to do after graduation.

Which meant not living at the frat house any longer. Done. So come fall semester, I was homeless.

Wearing his standard gray leather jacket and skinny jeans, Spider adjusted his mask around his bright blue hair and nudged me, reminding me to put mine on. With his penchant for getting tossed in jail for brawling and using heroin, I'd officially been his babysitter this summer in London until his bandmates, the Vital Rejects, reunited for their tour. What can I say? I'm a good cousin, and it gave me the chance to get out of Raleigh for the summer.

We waltzed inside the main area of the club where a fifty-foot bar lined the back of the room and a sizable dance floor held a shit-ton of writhing bodies.

Spider smirked as he looked around the place. He loved the masks because he could hide who he really was. "Any bets tonight?" he asked, rubbing his hands together.

"Dude, if you want me to take your quid, I will."

All summer, we'd made silly bets for miniscule amounts of money.

Who could last the longest in an ice-cold shower? *Me.*

Who would stand up in the pub and sing "I'm a Little Teapot"? *Me.*

Generally stupid stuff, but Spider needed all the distraction from trouble he could get.

"I'm feeling lucky tonight," he said with a grin.

I nodded. "Sure. What do you have in mind?"

His brown eyes gleamed from behind his mask. "Who can get a quickie shag in the loo first?"

I grimaced. "No."

Normally, I'd be all over a random one-night stand—even in a bathroom stall—but no one had felt right in a while. But, if the perfect girl came along, I'd ditch my celibacy in a heartbeat.

"You sure? You are the self-proclaimed Sex Lord of Whitman. Hmmm?"

I arched a brow. "You're really going there—you're throwing down the gauntlet?"

"Yeah. You're a pansy who needs to get laid. You're not gay are ya?" He squinted at me. "You are a tad pretty if I say so myself, plus all those bulging muscles."

I snorted. With Declan's encouragement for me to stay busy, I'd worked out this summer at the local gym, let my hair grow longer than normal, and had gotten my first tattoo. Spider was covered in them, the main one a black widow on his neck, and seeing his had given me the bug for ink.

"Not gay," I said.

"But you have to admit, you like to moisturize and exfoliate. Plus there's the hair products and clothes—oh, and we can't forget the man-bag."

"It's a *messenger* bag."

"Bollocks!" He slapped me on the back. "I love teasing you. But seriously, what the fuck is wrong with you?"

"Nothing, arsehole. Maybe I'm setting my standards higher."

"Tosser," he chuckled. "Come on, pick a wager already." He tapped his fingers against his legs—a sign that he was antsy.

"Give me a minute," I said as I surveyed the bodies gyrating on the dance floor, then scanned the bar area. Nothing interesting. Same music. Same girls we saw every time we came here.

Wait, wait. Except for *her*. The tall girl in the blue dress.

Nice. My eyes stopped and roamed over the curvy brunette with long, glossy hair.

Sitting on a barstool with her arms crossed and a snarl on her face, she radiated banked anger—with a dash of sexy. Her lips were carmine red, full, and heart-shaped . . .

Tingles of awareness rolled over me. My cock twitched.

But she wasn't my type. I preferred them blonde, petite, and less angry. And if I ever wavered from that stereotype, inevitably I'd be punched in the heart with a sledgehammer.

Remember Remi?

I shoved thoughts of her where I put things that made me crazy—down deep in my gut.

I exhaled heavily. By now she was married to Hartford Wilcox, who also happened to be an Omega—my fraternity's biggest rivalry. *Bunch of wankers.*

I'd been president of the Tau frat at the same time he'd been president of the Omegas, and our two houses hated each other. Omegas were the preps who dressed like Ralph Lauren models and played golf. Taus were the bad boys, a mixed bunch of mongrels who did whatever the fuck they wanted. We battled for top spots in everything on campus from who won the most intramural games to who had the hottest girls as "little sisters." It wasn't unusual for fights to break out at a mixer or after a tense game of football.

Moving on, I surveyed the rest of the club, but before long my gaze went right back to the mystery girl. Roving. Checking her out. Lingering on her hair that flashed under the strobe lights. Even with her arms crossed and a belligerent expression on her face, she was, well, interesting.

My fingers itched to take her mask off.

Did I know her?

Not likely anyone from my childhood. It had been twelve years since I'd lived in London. I briefly considered it might be a student from Whitman, but that seemed highly unlikely considering Raleigh was across the Atlantic.

Spider followed my eyes. "Ah, wonder what's got her knickers in a twist?"

I shrugged, sussing her out as we moved closer to the bar area. "Guy problems?"

"Probably a real man-hater. Nice tits, though. I'd do her."

I rolled my eyes. "Perhaps she just needs a drink. I do."

"Admit it, you'd at least give her a poke," he said. "You fancy her—I can see it in your eyes. She's putting out something you like, I say. Maybe you like angry sex? There's something to be said for really going at it and tearing into each other like animals." A wistful expression crossed his face.

I laughed. Dude was a freak. "TMI, mate."

He shrugged. "Hmmm, perhaps she's looking for her rebound guy. Could be you." Nodding his head in a way that told me he'd come to a decision, he said, "Which is why I'm making a bet that you can't make that angry woman fall in love with you tonight. Annnd"—he drew the word out—"I'll sweeten the pot—at ten thousand pounds."

"What?" I sputtered. "I'm no rock star like you."

"You have money."

True. When my mum had passed, I'd inherited life insurance money, plus my father had bestowed an early graduation gift a few months back.

I shook my head. I might be a carefree kind of guy, but I wasn't delusional. I had to save every penny if I wanted to be on my own someday and not depend on Father. "I'm keeping that for a rainy day."

Which would be here in two weeks when school started.

He pursed his lips. "When did you become such a fucking boy scout?"

"I'm *not* a boy scout. I do whatever I want, when I want. I'm a party animal."

He studied me, clearly not buying what I was selling. "Okay, fine. Let's do this: ten thousand pounds if you win her heart, and if you lose, you give me the usual—one pound."

I stopped in my tracks. "What's in it for you?"

"The thrill, baby, the rush, that feeling that makes me high as the fucking sky." He grinned crookedly. "So? You in?"

"I don't know . . . one night is tough, even for a sexy guy like me." I sent him an arched eyebrow. "Give me more time. I'm rusty."

"You're such a pussy. Nope. It has to be tonight . . . you in?"

I shrugged, knowing it drove him nuts when I didn't commit to his bets.

He groaned. "You're being a big girl's blouse. Come on. Do it.

15

Do it."

"You're annoying."

"Thank you," he smirked.

"You're a dick who thinks blue hair is cool."

"It is cool or I wouldn't have it."

"And a nutter."

"Meh. Not the first time I've been called that. Admit it, you've had a good time babysitting me this summer. It's given you time to gain perspective, yes?"

Realization dawned. "You're going to miss me when I leave, aren't you? I've been making you tea all summer, screening your calls from old girlfriends, cleaning your flat, washing your Mercedes, *plus* I've been your wingman. I'm practically indispensable. What will you do without me?"

"I'll learn to knit and make you a bloody hat. Just agree to the bet already."

I laughed. "Nope."

But I was already making my way over to her.

As soon as the barstool next to her was vacated, I took it. Spider took up the other side of me, an excited look on his face as he eyed the girl in the blue dress who was trying to wave down a bartender. I thought I heard an American accent, but with one of the club's music speakers close to where we sat, I couldn't catch what she was saying.

A cackle erupted from Spider. "I'm sensing a victory already. You're gonna cock it up."

"First off, you have a serious gambling problem, and second, I have *never* been turned down."

"Shut your gob, Sex Lord. *Woo her.*"

Without her knowing, I watched her in the mirror across from the bar as she blatantly checked me out, her head tilted ever so slightly in my direction as her eyes went from the top of my head down to my Converse.

I bit back my grin and flicked a look at Spider. "She's in the palm of my hand."

"Uh-huh," he sang.

Things went sideways when a hot redhead swayed her hips over to me. She giggled. "My friends dared me to come over here and ask you to dance. You wanna?" she asked, hands lingering on my arm.

I grinned. "Sorry, love, can't." Keeping my voice low, I nudged my head at the girl in the blue dress. "I'm already spoken for."

She got the hint and stalked off while the girl in the blue dress watched it all. I smiled broadly and cocked an eyebrow at her—*hey, babe, I want YOU.*

She ignored my eye messages, seeming immune to my charm. Dammit. This mask was a hindrance.

As I watched, the bartender leaned over the bar to flirt with her, his eyes all over her chest. I stiffened, my hackles rising.

No way was he getting any of that.

This was the first girl I'd been remotely interested in all summer, and I wasn't giving her up to a lumberjack wannabe. I distracted him by snapping at him and ordering a drink.

Then fate stepped in.

The girl in the blue dress stood, weaved around, teetered in her high heels, and *whoosh!* dropped right into my arms.

Wham, bam. *Score.*

I hadn't had to do a damn thing.

CHAPTER THREE

Remi

MUSCLED ARMS CAUGHT me without hesitation, ensuring I didn't crash to the floor. *Thank God.*

"Gotcha," his husky voice said.

My free arm snaked around my rescuer's neck and held on. "Hi," I breathed as I gazed up at him. "Nice catch."

A sexy grin crossed his chiseled face. "Is your name Angel and did you fall from heaven to be with me?"

"Most likely I came from hell."

He tossed his head back and laughed.

Cool air met my lower body. Craning my neck, I saw that my dress had ridden up to my waist, giving him a crystal-clear view of my sprawled legs and blue lace garter set. Yet another pricey garment purchased for this trip. I groaned, feeling my face redden. "Oh great, now I've flashed my butt to the entire place."

"Nice knickers," he murmured, smoothing my dress down gently and not ogling me. Point for him. But then a guy as hot as him didn't have to resort to sneak peeks. He could probably have anyone he wanted.

"Is everyone staring at me?" I covered my face with my hands.

"I hate being the center of attention."

"Meh. A few. Some are laughing."

I peeked through my fingers to find him smiling down at me, flashing gorgeous white teeth.

"Come on now, it's fine. I'm teasing you. No one in this hell-hole cares," he said. "Although your shoe sailed across the room. It might have clocked someone in the head."

I sent a wish up, hoping it was the redhead.

Using my good arm, I reared myself up and rearranged myself until I was sitting up in his lap. His head still towered over me, his hands cradling my waist to make sure I stayed in place. I estimated he was at least six-five.

"Tall guys are my favorite," I murmured, and then bit my lip self-consciously. "And clearly I'm thinking out loud. Sorry."

"Good thing I'm tall then." His eyes landed on my mouth. Lingered.

I swallowed.

Now what?

You're a bomb-ass bitch with a brain the size of Texas is what! Use it!

Maybe I could mesmerize him with my random eighties trivia or tantalize him with tales of migrating bird patterns? Whatever. I didn't have to be beautiful to have rebound sex with whomever I wanted. *Yeah.*

My thoughts drifted back to that big honeymoon suite. "Um, random question here—do you like beds with rose petals scattered everywhere?"

His eyes went low and heavy. "I'd say *yes*."

My eyes skated over his broad shoulders. "Great answer."

"Hmmm, are you offering me a place to crash tonight?" His hand tightened around my waist.

I paused, thinking.

Could I go through with this?

One-night stands were not my usual. I enjoyed more cautious fun, like filling out my yearly calendar, writing life goals, and typing up spreadsheets. I had every single detail of my existence planned, right down to my future kids' names.

And the last time I'd had a spur-of-the-moment fling, it had nearly ruined—

"What's this?" Concern crossed his face as he noticed my wrist attached to my dress. I'd completely forgotten about it. "What's wrong with your arm?" A warm hand cupped my elbow, his fingers then traveling to my wrist.

"I snagged my bracelet on my dress." Another blush rose up from my neck as I recalled the spectacle I'd made. "It belonged to my grandmother—an heirloom—and was a gift from my late father for my sixteenth birthday. I'm—I'm terrified I'll break it or ruin the dress. Knowing my luck, I'd do both." I looked down at the diamond-studded bracelet and grimaced. "It will kill me to break it, but I guess I can always have it repaired."

"Here, let me see it," he said, inspecting the fabric where my hand currently dangled.

Did I notice that his face was nearly in my cleavage?

Yes, and I really didn't care.

Did I notice that his male scent made me want to rub against him like a cat?

Yes, pet me, please. Make me purr.

"Can you slide it off?" he asked.

I willed my pulse to slow down. "No, the clasp is the part that's stuck to the material and it's too tight to slide off. Trust me, I spent a while trying to get it undone." I blew out a breath. "It's been a crazy evening."

"Hmmm." His lips puckered in a cute way as he leaned in closer, and I swallowed, feeling shy all over again.

He was *so* not my type: muscled physique, a tattoo, cocky.

But tonight I wanted revenge sex.

And here he was—Mr. Beautiful—delivered on a silver platter.

It would be a travesty to not take advantage of the opportunity, right?

Absolutely, the tequila said.

He sent me a rueful grin. "This is going to sound like a cheesy pick-up line, but if you let me put my hand down the front of your dress, I'd be able to detach the bracelet without ripping the fabric. I won't grab your tit on purpose." He winked boyishly. "Wanna give it a go?"

Touch the tit! Touch the tit! I cleared my throat. "Sure, that would be nice."

With a finesse that surprised me—as if he were used to sticking his hands into ladies' clothing—he reached down the neckline of my dress, the back of his hand pressing against my lace bra. My nipple hardened—of course—and my face grew redder. Praying the darkness of the club hid my embarrassment, I avoided his eyes and studied the dragonfly on his arm. A few tense moments later, he found where the metal was snagged and gently maneuvered it through the fabric.

"Free at last," he murmured as I shook my arm out in relief. I didn't even see a hole in the dress.

"You're quite the handyman. My bracelet means the world to me, and this dress—let's just say it cost more than my car payment. Thank you. Seriously." Impulsively, I gave him a quick hug and pulled back. "Um, can I buy you a drink to show my appreciation?"

His fingers traced down my spine. "Let's start with a thank-you kiss." His voice grew husky. "I'd love to kiss a real angel."

An explosion of heat detonated in my body.

The blue-haired guy next to him snorted, probably at the total pick-up line Mr. Beautiful was dishing out. But I liked his lines. A lot.

"Ignore him," Mr. Beautiful said, indicating his friend. "He's jealous you fell in my lap and not his. Now about that kiss . . ."

"Right here in the club?"

"I like to imagine people watching us. Don't you?" he whispered in my ear.

I shivered. Maybe. The idea did sound deliciously sexy.

His lips brushed my earlobe. "Besides, doesn't a prince deserve his spoils? I caught you—you could have died right here on the floor."

"I fell from the stool. It's not like it was a building or something." But my head was already leaning toward his.

"But it could happen," he said, fingers tracing my lips, his face inches from mine.

Butterflies did somersaults in my stomach.

"I suppose there's a slight chance I could be headed to the hospital on a gurney right now."

"Indeed."

Maybe it was the tequila, maybe it was the anonymity of the mask, maybe it was the fact that he'd asked so sweetly, or damn, maybe it was just *him*, but his reasoning made perfect sense. I nodded.

His hand tilted my chin back for a better angle as his full lips fit perfectly over mine. He deepened the kiss slowly, soft as silk, with the skill of a guy who knew exactly how to stoke fires. My hands threaded through his hair as heat raced up my spine, and when he groaned his appreciation, I melted into him.

The graze of his teeth, a soft nip on my bottom lip, and I clung to him.

Hot. Slow. Mind-blowing. Kisses.

Until it ended abruptly.

He jerked back as if stung, and even though I couldn't read his expression behind the mask, I saw a deep furrow on his brow. He rubbed a quick hand across his jaw and cursed under his breath.

Had I done something wrong? Bitten his tongue?

"What happened?" I breathed, my pulse hammering. Now that I'd had a taste, I wanted more of him. I was committed to following through, and I was smart enough to know that the electricity between us wasn't the usual.

He opened his mouth as if to say something but then slammed it shut, his eyes studying me as if he were considering something serious.

"Do I suck at kissing?" I asked.

"No."

"Tequila breath?" I grimaced.

"No, no, you kiss great. Bloody incredible. That's the problem." He raked a hand through his hair, his face tightening.

He seemed like a completely different person.

What was going on?

"Are you married? Dating someone?" I asked.

"I'm the Lone Ranger."

"Why? Are you a selfish asshole who only cares about himself?"

He paused. "Yeah."

"Well, you're in luck. That suits me just fine. So shut up and kiss me."

A few beats of silence went by as his eyes bored into mine.

I stiffened. "Fine. I can take a hint. You aren't interested. Welcome to the club." I shifted in his lap as if to get up, and his hands tightened around my waist.

"Wait," he said, his demeanor softening. "I am interested. Trust me." He bit his lip in a hot way that was completely manly. "It's just—when you're angry later, will you remember that you *wanted* me to kiss you?"

"Of course. We're just having fun."

"Are you begging me to kiss you then?" His voice was husky, tinged with a note of familiarity.

My hands brushed the hair off his forehead, my nails trailing along his cheek. "Is that what you want?"

"I can't remember what I want," he murmured, and his mouth swooped down to capture mine again.

The sounds of the club faded away and all that mattered were his lips on mine, our tongues tangling. Lingering small kisses as we paused to breathe, then longer ones. His tongue licked my top lip and then he sucked it between his teeth. He owned me, and I lost myself, consumed by the fire that started in my bones and made its way through every part of my body.

He was the King of Kissing.

The Supreme Ruler.

"*Remi,*" he breathed between a kiss to my lips.

"*Yes*," I replied. He felt it too. This cosmic force bringing us together. The heavens rejoiced, the universe was understood, and all things were possible.

Magic.

I didn't care who saw—Lulu or the bartender or the blue-haired guy. Sparks spread as his mouth left mine to glide across my jaw-line to my neck, my ultimate weakness, where he sucked hard, then layered the tender spot with soothing kisses and whispers of my name—as if he knew exactly what I liked. He made his way back to my lips and ravaged them again, diving into the recesses, searching, exploring as if he were dying of thirst and I was water.

Wait.

Clarity arrived slowly, in bits and pieces, and then all at once as the threads of truth that had been lingering in the back of my mind dawned. *Fate.* She's a tricky bitch and the mere change in a foot-step, the choice to take a different path, creates a synchronism of moments that align and fall gently into place, like a butterfly that unerringly finds its way home no matter the distance.

Fate had found me and kicked me in the stomach—hell, she'd just tossed me to the wolves.

This was not a stranger.

He'd said my name.

I tore my lips from his, chest heaving. "*You* . . . but the tat-too . . . hair . . . *Dax Blay?*"

He grinned with a cockiness that now seemed all too familiar. "You can call me Dax. Or Sex Lord. Or Daddy. Whatever floats your boat."

I inhaled sharply. *How had I been so stupid?*

Hurt lodged in my throat; not that I wasn't used to his smart remarks, but when pointed directly at me, leftover anger and pain from our past came roaring back to the surface like a newly opened wound.

Don't let him under your skin.

I slapped him on the face. Not as hard as I wanted, but hard enough that my hand stung.

He gritted his teeth, gave me a hard glare, and lifted his hand to touch his cheek. "You were supposed to *not* be angry."

"Why aren't you back in Raleigh where you should be?" My fists clenched.

"Why aren't you with stuffy old Hartford?" he snapped right back. His eyes flicked to my bare ring finger and then bounced back to my face. "Aren't you supposed to be married? Why are *you* running around London kissing random men?"

"Ah! You *knew* it was me the entire time," I huffed. "Once again, you've proven I've always been a game to you."

And that thought cut so deep not even the tequila could dull it.

"Girls love my games." His insinuation made a thousand memories bombard my brain.

Me.

Him.

Us.

Seventy-two hours in a small bedroom.

Kisses. Beautiful, wonderful, endless kisses.

~~Love.~~ Lust.

And then—devastation.

Darkness.

"No snappy comeback, Remi?"

My eyes narrowed and if I could have shot flaming arrows from them, I'd have landed several in his crotch. My eyes touched there and then quickly darted away, but obviously not before he noticed.

His lip curled. "You still like what you see? Once you've had Dax, you never go back."

"As usual, your ego is so big it takes up this entire nightclub."

He grinned tightly. "Really? I seem to remember you liked how *big* I was. You couldn't get enough of my 'Mr. Argentine Duck'"— he used air quotes—"which *you* so aptly named after some rare bird with a seventeen-inch cock."

He remembered that?

Of course, he wasn't seventeen inches—but he wasn't shabby either.

My face reddened.

I changed the topic. "Nice. Just great. Do you have any idea the measures I took to make sure I avoided you at Whitman after you dumped me? Which is hard to do considering it's a small university," I said. "I've dropped two classes just so I didn't have to sit in the same room as you. I've walked out of the cafeteria if you came in. I've left the library right in the middle of a group study session. The only place we saw each other was at parties and formals. And here you are tonight . . . not going by the rules of *I never want to talk to you again*, Dax."

He grunted. "I don't know about your rules because you never told me, and I swear by all that is holy, I didn't know it was you on that barstool. Not until that first kiss. I mean, your voice was familiar and you smelled like you, sugary and sweet, sorta like a cookie—and your body"—he raked his eyes over me—"is still rocking the hot curves—"

"You're so full of yourself that . . ." I scrambled for a word. " . . . I—I can't even describe you."

He crossed his arms. "I see you still think you're better than everyone else, but you fell in my lap, and don't think I didn't see you checking me out in the mirror. You were practically shagging me with your eyes."

I cringed. "Only because I didn't know it was the irreverent self-absorbed waste-of-oxygen-who-expects-all-women-to-worship-at-his-feet that I went to Whitman with. And you're a Tau."

"And you're an Omega little sister," he retorted distastefully.

The blue-haired guy, who'd been listening intently, took a step closer to us, hands waving. "Wait, wait. So you two have a history—like before this Hartford guy?"

We both glared at him.

He chortled with glee. "This is bloody hilarious."

"No, it's not, Spider," Dax said. "All bets are off."

The guy snorted. "Never."

What bet? His name was Spider?

Spider turned to me. "I apologize for my cousin. He's had a

hard summer taking care of me. Moving on, how do you know the bastard?"

I angled my chin. "The girl he was sleeping with at the time caught us together at the frat house. She told her entire sorority *I* was the reason he broke up with her. Then these—these mean girls proceeded to egg my dorm room door, and the next day my car was covered in sticky notes with *slut* written on them, not to mention the entire campus gossiped about me for months—"

"What the hell?" Dax whipped his mask off, and I bit back a gasp at the full impact of his face. He slayed me, especially with those mercurial gray eyes with thick, black lashes longer than any girl's.

He was too gorgeous.

Too dangerous.

Too much of everything.

He was exactly what I needed to avoid.

A muscle ticked in his jaw. His fists clenched. "Eva-Maria did that to you? Why didn't you tell me?"

I'd been too destroyed to look at him, much less talk to him.

"It wouldn't have mattered," I said quietly, remembering.

Stormy eyes met mine. "I never told a bloody soul about us. And as I recall, *you* walked out on me. Maybe you should have stuck around for an explanation instead of storming out of my room."

Silence settled between us, the tension thick.

My hands shook, and I put them behind my back.

"Holy shit." Spider's eyes bounced from Dax's face to mine, obviously taking in the body language between us. "Don't stop now," he said. "I'm dying for all the juicy bits."

My mouth tightened. I sighed and looked at Spider. "The usual story: a freshman girl falls for the experienced fraternity boy who only wants a one-night stand."

"That so?" Spider asked Dax, swinging his head back to him.

"That's your version, Remi," he said, his face inscrutable, impossible to read.

My eyes swept over the sharp contours of his face, taking in the expressive eyes I'd lost myself in three years ago; the sensual lips that had owned me. Indeed, he *was* beautiful. He was soul-wrenchingly hot, the kind of guy you'd beg to love you—only I didn't beg anyone. I swallowed, forcing myself to look away from him. I focused on Spider. "The truth is, I was one in a long line of girls he *dated* that year. I lost count after number forty-two."

Spider threw his head back and laughed, his spiky blue hair glinting under the lights. "Seriously? This guy? He hasn't had a girl all summer."

"Bloody hell, you're exaggerating," Dax muttered at me, a dark expression on his face. "And how would you know how many girls I was with? You spying on me?"

"Ha. As if."

"Whatever." His arms brushed against my chest as he went to pick up his drink on the bar.

Crap! I was still in his lap.

I scrambled off his legs, but winced as my right foot hit the floor. My ankle. Of course, it started throbbing. I must have hurt it more than I'd realized. Welcome to my life.

Sucking in a sharp breath to hold in the pain, I limped over to my shoe, which thankfully some kind person had placed near the edge of the dance floor. Maneuvering carefully, I bent down and managed to snag it. I took the other one off and held both shoes with one hand.

"What's wrong with your ankle?" Dax had risen up from his seat and followed me. "Are you hurt? Why didn't you say something?"

I cut my eyes at him. "Why? Would you have been nicer?"

His lashes dropped. Opened. "I don't wish you any pain, Remi."

Why did his voice have to sound so concerned?

Why did he have to be hotter than summer at high noon?

Why, why, why had I kissed him?

I did not want to get sucked into his vortex again.

"I'm fine." I hobbled back to the bar and grabbed my clutch. Mike was nowhere to be seen, so I pulled out a handful of twenty-pound notes and left them on the bar, hoping that covered the tequila and a reasonable tip, even though the guidebook had said the bartenders in London didn't rely on tips.

I grabbed the bottle of alcohol and snuggled it close.

Dax was next to me the entire time. Watching.

"Stop hovering," I told him.

He moved to stand in front of me, resolve written on his face. And perhaps regret. "Remi, wait. Don't leave like this. You're obviously hurt from falling and upset at seeing me, and I—*dammit*—the truth is I never would have kissed you the first time if I'd known it was you. For real."

"Because I'm that awful?" Pain swirled in my chest. He'd never wanted me the way I'd wanted him.

"No. Because I wouldn't want to trick you." He sighed and held his hands out. "Look, everything else aside, I'm a gentleman, whether you believe it or not. My mum taught me to make sure a lady gets home and that she's safe. At least let me call you a cab or grab Hartford. Is he here somewhere?" He pulled out his cell.

I propped myself against the bar to take the pressure off my foot. "You really don't know, do you?"

"Know what?" His brow wrinkled.

I bit my lip and stared at the floor, feeling that familiar embarrassment I'd experienced since I'd had to explain to people that Hartford had changed his mind about getting married.

"What am I missing?" His voice had lowered. Grown intense. Narrowed eyes flicked down to my bare finger again. "Why aren't you wearing your engagement ring? Did he hurt you?" He took a step in closer, his hand tentatively reaching for mine but then dropping to rest by his side when I pulled away.

"No, it's not like that." I straightened my spine, tired of being sad about Hartford. "He—he—dumped me two weeks before the wedding. He said he needed some time to clear his head—a break." I laughed, but it wasn't real. "And we all know what a break means, right?"

His eyes widened, and maybe I saw sympathy there, but I ignored it. I didn't want his pity.

"Since the honeymoon was nonrefundable, I came here with Lulu, mostly to get away from the stares and my mom." I paused, letting it all come out. "Now I don't even have a place to live. And then there's my autistic brother, Malcolm—I help take care of him part-time, and I don't want to even think about my classes this fall or applying to graduate school. I *had* a great plan, you know—*the* plan. Marry a responsible, nice guy, get my doctorate, discover a new bird species, take care of Malcolm, have four kids, but guess what? My plan is shit. My goals are shit. Even my back-up plan sucks. It's flawed because the perfect guy decided *I'm* not the perfect choice for him." My voice cracked, but I yanked it back.

"Where's Lulu?" His voice was gentle, surprising me.

"She's having a great time—like I should be. Instead of my honeymoon, I'm in some skanky, mask-wearing club where even the walls probably have a venereal disease. I'm supposed to be taking romantic walks in Hyde Park—or at least having incredible sex."

"I'm sorry, Remi."

I cupped my cheeks, feeling the hotness. "I don't even know why I'm babbling about this to you. We don't even like each other. Please move out of my way."

"No."

"Yes," I snapped and pushed against the brick wall of his chest to get him out of my path. He didn't budge.

"I'm not bloody leaving you."

"You're freaking bossy," I bit out.

"You liked it once." A shadow crossed his face.

I had. I'd loved giving control over to someone. *I'm yours, Dax. Do what you want.*

I pivoted to go the other way, the sudden movement causing red-hot pain to ricochet around my ankle. "Ouchhhh!" I hopped on one foot and clutched the side of the bar so I wouldn't fall flat on my face.

"Christ, you can barely walk," Dax huffed in exasperation, as strong forearms went under my legs and he swept me off my feet, hefting me up.

"What are you doing?" I cried, struggling to juggle my bag, shoes, and tequila as he lifted me.

"Carrying you."

"Put me down," I said breathlessly. His closeness was wreaking havoc with my earlier anger.

He shook his head. "I'm starting to think you planned all this just so you could hang out with me."

"In your dreams."

Moments of heavy silence passed as he stared down at me.

"What?" I glared at him.

He ignored my glare, a weird expression on his face. "I've had a few dreams about you," he said.

"Nightmares?" I said smartly, but the butterflies in my stomach went crazy at the thought of him thinking about me. I shot them down one by one.

He continued. "There's one where you're wearing this mermaid costume, only you have human legs and copper-red hair. Of course, I'm riding on a kick-ass stallion as I chase you down the beach. You're screaming bloody murder—'*help me, help me*'—but you have a gleam in your eyes . . . you want me to catch you. I put you on my horse and carry you to my cave where you scream my name at least a hundred times. In ecstasy."

My mouth had fallen open during his vivid, detailed description. "You dreamed about *me* as Ariel?"

"Who?"

"*The Little Mermaid*—the Disney movie?"

"I don't watch Disney."

I blinked. "You're just messing with me, right?" Because that wouldn't make sense. Why would he even *think* about me, much less dream about me? He'd forgotten about me as soon as the next girl had hopped in his bed.

He didn't answer me, his legs moving through the crowd.

People scurried out of our way as he barreled through them, a hard look on his face. Using broad shoulders, he maneuvered his way to the stairs at the back left of the club. No one looked remotely surprised to see a man carrying a woman around the dark club. Another strike against this place.

I looked over his shoulder to see Spider following behind us, a smirk on his face. He seemed vaguely familiar, but at this point, I didn't care who he was. The most important thing in my head was the fact that Dax Blay was carting me around like a sack of potatoes. And I kinda liked it.

Straining, I squirmed to not rest against his magnificent chest, but in the end I gave in to the comfort of his hold and rested my cheek against him. My one free hand encircled his bicep to hang on, and his eyes looked down at me, a questioning look on his face. His expression softened, making my pulse skip a beat.

God. *What was it about him that made me so weak?*

The answer was simple: Dax Blay was my Achilles heel, my one vulnerability.

"Don't think that things are okay just because you're helping me."

His quicksilver eyes hardened. "I get it, Remi. You hate me. I'm a no-good irresponsible bastard."

His words sliced me open, carving into my heart and digging deep, bringing back memories better left unspoken.

I crushed those feelings down. *Hard.*

"I—I don't hate you. I could never in a million years hate you," I whispered.

His eyes flicked to mine. Searching. He exhaled and tore his away. "Yeah? Well, you got a funny way of showing it."

I bit down on my lips to keep the words in my heart from spilling out.

You can't hate the first boy you ever loved.

CHAPTER FOUR

IFE HAD JUST bitch-slapped me right across the face with the coincidence of a lifetime.

Out of all the clubs in London, why did she have to waltz into mine?

More importantly, why hadn't I realized it was *her* before we'd gotten to the kiss? Perhaps a small part of me had; the romantic side no one ever saw.

You can't have her, I reminded myself.

She's off limits.

I stomped up the stairs, club-goers pressing themselves against the railing to get out of our way. I was pissed off. No, scratch that. I was incensed, emotions clamoring all over the place, up and down and sideways, ramped up high enough to slam into anyone that got in my way.

She relaxed grudgingly as I carried her up the stairs, her reticence almost tangible, a shadow of hurt in her sapphire eyes. I didn't think that pain was from seeing me. I grunted. That thought was completely laughable.

She lowered her eyes, hiding from me, but I could see that her emotions, like mine, were all over the place. I suspected it had nothing to do with our kiss and everything to do with her missing fiancé.

Thinking of her getting shafted at the altar by Hartford made me ballistic.

But *why* was I revved up like an Indy racecar? Me—the cool guy who never looked back at the girls he'd conquered.

Because *Remi Montague*, that's why; the one girl who'd blown my mind—and scared the shit out of me—when I was just a sophomore at nineteen.

She let out a gasp.

I paused. "Your ankle? You okay?"

She nodded, that wounded gaze hitting me again, her full lips still swollen from my kisses.

I tore my eyes off her face, but it didn't stop the memories from crashing down.

We began at the start of her freshman year when she showed up for a party at the Tau house on a Friday night and, like a magnet, my eyes had been drawn to her.

She hadn't been my type at all with her prim sweater and innocent blue eyes.

Usually I went for the sorority girls who knew my game—females with plenty of daddy's money and blasé attitudes about sex. But Remi; there was something about her that sucked me in—even though she was shy, had a brain like Einstein, and dressed like she was headed to a PTA meeting.

Her lush lips told another story though, demanding to be kissed.

I told myself to leave her alone. Several times.

But like a magnet, I'd planted myself next to her. I couldn't help myself.

We talked and laughed over spiked punch. A while later, we clasped hands and laughed as they sent us upstairs in a game of Seven Minutes in Heaven. Yeah. It was silly, but we played along. We had no clue the heat it would lead to when we got in the closet and kissed . . . and kissed. She lit me up with lust and for an entire seventy-two hours together, we rolled around naked in my bed.

It had been Labor Day weekend and most of the house was empty. We'd gotten up to scrounge around for food, take showers, and chase each other around the house, but we'd dived right back in to my bed.

Fast. Slow.

Me on top. Her on top.

Sitting on a chair.

Against the wall.

She was everything I never knew I wanted in a girl—except I couldn't have her.

I didn't do relationships.

Then Eva-Maria, one of the fraternity little sisters I'd been with a few times, had shown up that Monday and ruined everything. She'd marched into my room and gone berserk, tossing books at Remi and claiming I was her boyfriend.

Remi, a girl who clearly didn't get involved with dramatics, had quickly dressed and left my room as I'd stood there naked trying to explain in a logical way that Eva-Maria wasn't really a permanent thing, just someone I slept with when I was horny.

I came back to the present when Remi tipped up the bottle of tequila in my arms to take a sip. She'd slapped me tonight. Not that I hadn't deserved it. Sure, I'd been a cocky smartass when she finally figured out who I was, but that was all a front.

I hadn't known *how* to react to her.

She had this uncanny ability of making me feel like I was a blithering arse.

I shook my head. Focus on the here and now. Get her to a booth, get her settled with an ice pack, call a cab, and get her home.

And Hartford. *Sonofabitch.* Thinking of him fanned the flames higher.

He'd dumped *her*?

In what universe did that even make sense? He'd started seeing Remi a few months after she and I had our fling, and from the looks of them around campus, they'd been crazy about each other. Not that I'd noticed.

"You putting me down anytime soon?" Her voice had a slight

slur. "This circus sideshow you're doing is giving me motion sickness."

"Trust me, I can't get you there fast enough," I retorted.

Every single booth was taken, but that didn't stop me from marching up to an occupied one in a back corner. With clenched teeth, I politely asked the three people to move. I got a few raised eyebrows and one muttering arsehole, but with Spider behind me all puffed up and ready to tango, they left.

I eased her down just as a waitress came scurrying over and asked what we needed.

"A glass of water and an ice pack," I said curtly. "She fell down near the bar. Hurry, please."

The waitress's eyes flared. "Should I get the manager for you?"

Remi waved her off with a weak smile. "Once I get some ice, it'll go down. Trust me, I've had worse."

I grabbed an extra chair from a table a few feet away and pulled it up to Remi. "Here. Elevate your foot."

She did, her eyes looking everywhere except me.

"Where's Lulu now?" I asked. She was the life of any party and a complete opposite to Remi; they were thick as thieves.

"Dancing, last I saw."

"She shouldn't leave you alone in a nightclub."

She ignored me and cuddled the bottle of tequila. "This stuff tastes better the more you drink. Want some?"

"You're sloshed, Remi," I muttered.

"Am not."

I studied her, taking in the smeared lipstick from where we'd kissed. Her eyes were glassy too, a hard glint in them, a look I'd become accustomed to over the years whenever we'd bump into each other.

I sighed and turned to Spider, describing Lulu's signature pink hair and height. He looked dubious about searching the dance floor but dashed off to find her.

After a few moments of silence, she slipped her mask off, set it on the table, and nibbled on her thumbnail, something I'd seen her do a dozen times at frat parties when she didn't know I was watching her.

Was she thinking about me?

About that fucking epic kiss?

No, you arsehole.

She's broken up over another dude. Get your head out of the sand. Plus, she's too smart for you. Even drunk, she's probably thinking about some bird in Africa and how it . . .

"Stop all your pacing," she said, eyeing me. "Will you please sit?"

I let out a breath. Part of me didn't want to leave her, even though at this point I could since Lulu would be up here soon. I rubbed my jaw, and pulled up another chair to the booth she was in. I might as well be useful. "Let's look at your ankle."

She moved her foot off the chair and settled it on my knee. A mile long and soft, her legs were hot. Remi wasn't beautiful if you looked at each individual feature: her nose was a hair too long, her cheekbones high and a bit broad, the space between her two front teeth obvious, but when you combined it together, she was one of the sexiest girls I'd ever met. Only she didn't know it.

Yeah, yeah, you love how she looks. It makes you hard. Move on.

But it was funny how I'd always spot her, even yards away on campus. Not that it had ever done me any good. As soon as she saw me, she'd be in the wind.

I traced my fingers over the swollen lump on the right side of her ankle. It was small, and from being around Declan and the gym and just from a general knowledge of playing sports, I knew she'd be okay. "I think it's a sprain, but not serious. Still hurting?"

Her shoulders had tensed as I touched her. "Not as much."

"If the swelling doesn't go down by tomorrow, you'll need to see a doctor. I can recommend one for you if you want. I've been here all summer and have a good feel for the place."

"It will be fine. I fall all the time. Can I have my leg back now?"

"Fine with me." I eased back from her ankle and scooted my

chair away from her.

The seconds ticked by as she gazed at the wall and played with her hair, which flowed down her back like a freaking waterfall. A memory stabbed at me—one where I'd wrapped my hand in her hair, tugged her face back, and hammered into her.

I shifted around on my seat.

"Why did you kiss me the second time after you knew it was me?" She doodled on the table with her index finger. Her head came up when I didn't answer right away, her eyes meeting mine. "Dax?"

I shrugged. "Because I still remember that weekend we were together . . . because—*dammit*—I don't know, okay?" I stood back up, crossing my arms. "The ice is taking too long. I'm going to see where she went—"

"Dax. Wait."

I turned back around, my eyes skating over her.

She took a deep breath, confusion on her face. "Look, I came here tonight looking for my rebound guy. I wanted to hurt Hartford by sexing it up with a hot British dude. That's why I kissed you."

"I'm not judging you, Remi."

"Then this bartender kinda hit on me, but I got T. rex arms and fell and you caught me, and I thought fate had put us together, and then that kiss . . ." She stopped and squinted. "Am I making sense? I totally am, right?"

Not even close, but I nodded.

She sighed. "Anyway, what I'm getting at is I shouldn't have slapped you. It's not like me and was a knee-jerk reaction. I'm sorry."

"I'm sorry for being an egotistical waste of oxygen." I sent her a wry grin.

Her hands twisted the bracelet on her wrist, eyes downcast. "Tell me something. You mentioned something earlier about me storming out that day . . . if I hadn't walked out on you, would we have been a real thing?"

I opened my mouth, and for half a second I didn't know what I was going to say. My eyes met hers. "Three weeks is my longest with any girl. You were amazing, Remi—but it's doubtful we would have lasted much beyond that. We were so hot for each other, I never got around to clarifying—"

She held her hand up. "Stop explaining. I figured it out pretty quick when you never called or texted—and when I saw you the next week with another girl."

The waitress showed up with water, a Ziploc bag of ice, and a towel, stopping any further discussion about the topic. After she left, I sat back down in the chair and put the towel under the ice and then on her ankle. "Sorry, this is probably going to be cold," I said gently.

"I can deal. I always do," she murmured, eyes on her foot as she took a sip of water.

"Remi?"

She looked up at me. "Yeah?"

I exhaled. "Listen. I want to make it up to you. For being an arsehole back then—and tonight."

"An ass would have left me down there fumbling around like a drunk, one-legged pirate. You didn't."

My lips kicked up. "Funny."

Her fingers plucked at the hem of her dress. "What's funny is I can't recall what I had for dinner last night, but I remember every single detail of that weekend with you. How the window was open and the wind blew the curtains. I let you . . ."

"Better watch what you say. You're not yourself," I said softly.

She laughed, the first genuine one I'd heard. "You're right. I sound like a sappy girl with a crush on the school bad boy—oh, wait, that *did* happen."

"Shall we call a truce then? Start over as friends?"

"Friends?" Her dark brows drew in.

"Yeah. You know, hang in the quad, meet at the library, go to Panera."

"Panera? Together? *Like eat at the same table?*"

I grinned. "Yeah. Or we can sit on opposite sides of the restaurant and yell back and forth."

A giggle erupted from her and soon turned into a full-blown belly laugh.

"What's so hilarious?" I asked, unable to keep the defensiveness out of my tone.

She gathered herself, wiping her eyes. "Oh, Dax Blay, you're a real comedian. I cried over you for an entire semester, I ate enough cookie dough that the cashier at the grocery store would have it waiting for me. I watched an entire season of *Orange is the New Black* in one day just to get you out of my head. I daydreamed you'd come to my door and beg me to take you back. Instead, I watched girls panting over you like hyenas on campus while you reveled in the attention. So, *no*, absolutely never, ever can we be friends. I don't want to be in the same room with you. No offense." She smiled wryly and with her index finger pointed to herself and then me. "This here—you being nice and helping me and me being drunk and chatting like we're comrades—it's a one-time thing."

Confusion set in.

She'd been depressed because of me? She'd cried an entire semester?

What. The. Hell.

Something wasn't adding up.

I'd just assumed her coolness toward me was because of Eva-Maria and she had genuinely written me off as a complete jerk. Then tonight I'd learned of Eva-Maria's bullying. *But this?*

My hands clenched. "Are you saying you were *in love* with me?"

She froze, her eyes evading mine. Seconds ticked by.

A weird panic hit and I held my breath.

Had she loved me?

No girl had ever said so.

Fuck. I hadn't wanted them to.

"Remi? Help a guy out. I can't read your mind."

She raised hesitant eyes to meet mine, a sad expression flitting across her face. "No. I don't believe in love at first sight, or falling in love in seventy-two hours—whatever. Do you?"

"No." I lifted my hands. "But I don't understand why you were so upset . . ."

Lulu marched up to the table, wearing a black skirt-thing and a shirt with rips everywhere, predictably dressed like a stylish homeless person. She set her martini glass on the table, whipped her mask off, and took in Remi's ankle, her eyes widening as she got a gander at me. A long whistle came from her mouth. "Shoot, Remi, you sure know how to party. I leave you alone for a minute and you drag up Dax Blay and company. Is this an alternate universe? Are the Omegas hanging out with the Taus?"

Spider followed behind her, his voice amused. "Found your friend twerking on the dance floor with a bunch of guys. Nice girl."

I stood up to give Lulu my seat. "Hiya, Lulu. Having fun?" My words were clipped. Pissed off.

She smirked and spoke in her usual slow Southern drawl. "Why, hello, playa, and yeah I was, until this blue-haired dude showed up and yanked me off the floor. He said Remi was hurt."

"You should have been with Remi," I told her tightly. "I'm assuming you came with her to keep her company."

Lulu scrunched her face up, put her hands on her hips, and harrumphed. "This girl? She's tough as nails. You don't know half the shit she can handle, and don't let the klutziness fool you. She survived a squirrel attack on the quad last year and only came out with a tetanus shot," she said. "And why do you care? Why are you being in charge with Remi? She doesn't even like you."

I know.

"Guys, stop," Remi said as she rose up from the table. She weaved a bit, then steadied as I reached over to help her stand. "I got this." She held me off as she propped herself against the back of the booth and gingerly tested her ankle. Placing it down on the floor, she took a couple of practice steps. "See, I'm better already. All I needed was the ice pack."

I exhaled. She did seem okay, her foot firmly on the floor as she walked.

Spider arched his brow and directed his eyes at me. "Seems like our cue to go, don't you think?"

"Yeah. Scat," Lulu said, shooing us. "I've got two guys I've been dancing with on their way up here to meet Remi, and one of them is going to be her date tonight." She turned to Remi. "Sound good?"

Remi shrugged.

Lulu nodded, practically rubbing her hands together. "They are so sweet, and one of them is in a band and the other goes to uni— isn't that a cute word? *Uni?* " She giggled.

Remi flicked her eyes at me and shrugged. "Sure, bring them on. The more the merrier."

A vein in my temple pulsed. I mean, I could actually feel it. Visions of her drunk and in a bed with a random stranger pissed me off. Didn't she know that was dangerous and stupid . . . ?

You don't own her, Dax. She belongs to Hartford—or at least her heart does.

Spider came over to stand next to me, out of earshot of the girls. He grabbed my elbow and pulled me toward the staircase.

"Bye, y'all." Lulu waved at us, a sarcastic tone in her voice.

Obviously she held a grudge as long as Remi did.

Spider turned to me as I slowed my pace, still looking back at Remi. "Dude, I know you want to stay and do your caveman protector act, but you've done all you can here. Your charms aren't working. She's a no-go. She bloody hates you," he said.

"I wasn't acting. This has nothing to do with the bet."

He clapped me on the back. "Such an optimist. I like that about you. It gives you a certain, oh, innocence that in the end only adds to your many attributes. I can honestly see why women drop at your feet, but sometimes, cousin, you just have to admit that the game is over and the chick just isn't that into you. Checkmate. I win."

"She used to be into me."

"Till you broke her heart." He grinned and ruffled my hair. "Bloody hell, it feels great to beat your arse. Let's do another wager."

As he nattered on about bets and pounds, I kept my eyes on Remi, watching as she applied red lipstick and ran quick fingers through her disheveled hair.

She'd hadn't even said goodbye, and she made it clear she

didn't want to be my friend. But as I watched her not watching me, I took in the strained lines around her eyes.

"Oi, are you listening to me?" Spider asked.

"No."

"Why the bloody hell not? I'm taking sporting bets here, and you're off in la-la land. You haven't gotten into my hash have you? Come on, let's get a drink or hit the kebab place across the street. Loser has to pay though." He smirked. "That's you."

"Yeah," I murmured, but I was only half listening.

Remi must have felt the weight of my stare because she glanced up and our eyes met and clung to each other. My pulse kicked up, and in that moment I wanted to stay with her.

You can't.

But . . .

"It's not over yet," I muttered under my breath as we walked away.

CHAPTER FIVE

D AX AND SPIDER walked away and headed toward the stairs. I watched his broad shoulders disappear until he was swallowed by the crowd.

My pounding heart finally relaxed.

God help me.

I'd kissed the boy I'd loved; the boy who'd ripped my heart out and then tossed it away like some forgotten thing. I'd inhaled his intoxicating scent and talked to him face to face. Something I'd sworn I'd never do again.

The fear on his face when he'd asked if I'd been in love with him had reiterated everything I suspected about him. His heart was locked away, enclosed in an impenetrable castle.

I had to protect myself from him.

The thing is, Dax is a temporary guy and I'm a forever girl, and the two didn't go together. Ever.

I closed my eyes, remembering the dark place he'd put me in three years ago and the secret I'd kept from him.

I opened my eyes to see Lulu watching me, her eyes soft with concern. She sat next to me in the booth and gave my shoulder a squeeze. "You feeling okay?"

I nodded. "Good."

"Uh-huh. So, question . . . how on earth did you end up with Dax and the blue-haired guy? There's got to be a good story there."

"I tripped and fell in his lap. I—I didn't know who he was."

"And?" she said.

"One thing led to another . . . we kissed." I exhaled. "It was amazing—as usual."

Her green eyes widened. "Shit."

"Yeah, mega shit," I mumbled.

"No wonder you're white as a ghost."

I nodded, filling her in on the details of him carting me upstairs.

She took a sip of her drink, eyes watchful as they raked over me. "Did I do the right thing by being a bitch and sending him away? 'Cause I gotta tell ya, you looked a bit conflicted for a moment."

I had?

She snorted. "God, I wish Hartford could have seen him kiss you though. He'd have pissed his pants. Dax Blay, the most popular Tau ever, making out with his ex-fiancée."

Hartford.

A pang struck, right in the center of my chest. Another failure. I was zero for two when it came to love.

And with that thought in mind, I checked my phone to see if Hartford had called. We hadn't had any communication since Mario's.

"Any messages?" Lulu asked.

I sighed, scrolling through my texts. "Just Mom. She wants me to come home and beg Hartford to take me back."

"And miss this fantastic country? You deserve this vacation, Remi."

I took a sip of water and set it down, carefully choosing my words. "I've been thinking. Do you think that if I loved Hartford enough, I'd give him the break he wanted and just wait for him to figure us out?"

She scrunched her nose as if she smelled something bad. "You aren't exactly the type of girl who swallows her pride and waits for a guy to make up his mind. You're strong and independent. Once they hurt you, you tend to distance yourself."

I nodded, taking that in. "But did you ever think I was, I don't know, *settling* because Hartford fit my plan: dependable, low-risk . . ."

"Girl, only you can answer that."

I leaned my head back against the seat, my eyes searching the club for Dax. "Dax certainly isn't low-risk."

Lulu's eyebrows rose. "He may be hotter than a cow brander, but he broke you, Remi." She glanced over my shoulder and clapped. "Speaking of walking orgasms, here come the guys I was telling you about."

The two Brits she'd danced with earlier came over to our booth with big smiles. Both were grunge types with dark jeans and heavy, silver jewelry. Not my type.

So. You just need to have fun, I reminded myself.

Lulu directed the taller one with a Mohawk to sit next to me while the darker-haired smaller one sat next to Lulu.

Within minutes, he and Lulu had cozied up to each other while Mohawk guy turned to me and started chatting. His name was Chad and his accent was different from Dax's. I supposed it might be because Dax had lived in the States for several years, or perhaps this guy was from a different part of the UK.

I could have asked him—but no matter how hard I tried, I just wasn't interested.

Not anymore. Not after seeing Dax.

We ordered a new round of drinks, but I declined and asked for more water, wanting to come down from my buzz. My high from before had deflated, and all I wanted to do was leave the club, lay my head on crisp hotel sheets, and sleep.

Chad tried hard to impress me, and I smiled and nodded in all the right places even though his breath smelled like stale peppermint.

We struck up a conversation about the nearby touristy things to do, but soon moved on to who designed my dress and jewelry. He toyed with my tennis bracelet, making my skin crawl.

It wasn't personal. I just wasn't in the mood.

I edged away from him and put my hands in my lap.

He slipped his arm around my shoulders in the booth and worked up to touching my hair. Soon his hand drifted across my bare shoulders and then dipped into the back of my dress to caress my skin.

Nausea saved me.

My belly had been rumbling in the background since I'd gotten upstairs, but now it seemed imminent. I needed air.

I stood up from the booth. "I need to go to the restroom."

"Don't you want your shoes?" Lulu called as I left the booth and moved toward the stairs. Concern crossed her face.

"No. I'm never wearing those heels again."

"But your feet will get dirty."

I shrugged. Normally that might bother me, but I'd had enough drinks to forget about the floor inside the club.

"Hey wait, I'll go with you," she called, catching up with me as I reached the bottom of the stairs. She hooked her arm through mine. "You didn't eat any tacos did you?"

I pushed out a smile. "You don't have to come with me, you know. Stay with the guys."

She shook her head. "Nope. Dax made me feel guilty. I'm not taking my eyes off you again." She grinned. "I told the guys to wait for us upstairs."

My ankle worked well enough to get me down a darkened hallway at the back of the club, where a blinking neon arrow indicated the ladies' restroom.

We walked inside a packed room with several drunken girls waiting in line for several stalls. Perfume and the close proximity of the women stifled me. I fanned my face with my hands. And this is why I hated clubs. I'd much rather be at home watching old movies with Malcolm.

"Once you break the seal . . ." Lulu did the pee dance. "Where you going?" she asked as I turned back to leave.

"You stay. I don't have to go. Just—don't feel well and it's too hot in here. Tequila, I guess."

"Don't go far," she called as I exited.

Once outside the room, I leaned back against the wall of the club, fighting with my roiling stomach. A bead of sweat rolled down my face and I shoved strands of hair behind my ears.

A rush of fresh air hit my face as someone walked out a back door that read EMERGENCY EXIT several feet away.

Yes! *Air!*

I turned to head that way, but a male voice stopped me. "Hiya, sweets."

I turned around to see the bartender, but he looked different, having changed from his white employee shirt to a black tee.

"I poured some shots for you earlier tonight?" A gruff laugh came out. "You probably don't even remember me."

"No, no. I'm sorry. I do actually. It's Mike, right?"

He shot me a grin. "Yeah. Last time I saw you, you were throwing shoes and turning flips."

I grimaced. "Sorry you had to witness that ridiculousness. Par for the course, I'm afraid."

He'd probably seen me sucking face with Dax too. Nice.

I edged toward the exit door a little at a time, hoping he'd take the hint, but he kept talking, mostly thanking me for leaving him the tip.

"So, I'm off work. You wanna grab a drink together or dance?" He'd stepped in closer to me, taller than I remembered, and smelling nice.

I opened my mouth to say no when I happened to glance up at one of the smaller balconies that went out over the dance floor, giving the occupants a bird's eye view of the entire club. One of the roving spotlights landed squarely on Dax's face as he leaned over the railing to gaze out.

As I watched him from afar, the slutty redhead from earlier came up to him and draped herself on his arm.

My gut clenched.

Seeing him with other girls never got any easier, although I'd learned to hide my jealousy well over the years.

As if he sensed me, he turned and our eyes connected over the heads of people thrashing on the dance floor. He had his mask back on, but his turbulent eyes were boring into mine, digging under my skin.

God, please, no matter what, I had to stay away.

"Hey?"

Shaking off his gaze, I blinked and looked back at Mike. "Sorry. I zoned out." I let out a weak laugh. "Truth is, I really want to puke right now—maybe a rain check? I'm here all week, and I'm sure my friend will want to come back." *Unfortunately.*

He took a quick step back, a wary expression on his face. "Oh. That sucks. Yeah, do what you have to do to feel better."

"Thanks. I'm going to head outside for a bit. Is it safe out there?"

"Sure. Employees use that door and there's a car park to the left and a main road to the right. You're fine." He waved a hasty goodbye and beat it out to where the action was. He grabbed a blonde by the hand and they took off to the dance floor.

Obviously, talk of vomit made guys scarce.

Once outside the exit, I saw a deserted alley, except for an old green dumpster and a scrawny cat eating from a box of takeout. The feline hissed and sent me a glare before diving back into the Styrofoam container.

A single lamppost near the street provided enough light that it was considerably brighter outside than the inside of the club. I sighed and sat down on a rickety metal chair with a myriad of cigarette butts around the legs. The employees probably took their smoke breaks out here.

After a few minutes of air, I immediately felt better.

I checked the time on my phone. Midnight in London, which meant seven at night in Raleigh.

Hartford was probably going out with his friends tonight.

I opened my camera on my phone, swiping at the selfies I'd

49

taken with Lulu around London today. After a red-eye flight the day before, we'd slept in this morning at The Tower Hotel. We'd gotten up in time to catch a pre-scheduled tour of Shakespeare's Globe and then had dinner and drinks at Swan, a hip two-story bar and restaurant with panoramic views of the Thames and St. Paul's Cathedral. The night view of the skyline had been absolutely breathtaking—just like I had carefully planned for our honeymoon. Too bad Hartford had missed it. My chest tightened.

I kept scrolling and found the last pic I'd taken of Hartford and me. It was taken three weeks ago; we'd been on a visit to UNC Chapel Hill where he was planning to attend medical school next fall. We stood side by side, wearing half-smiles, our bodies close. The air that day had been sticky and humid, as solid as breathing bricks—and I'd wanted hot Krispy Kreme donuts on the way home.

Yet . . .

What I couldn't remember was the *emotion* I felt as we posed for that picture.

Where had we gone wrong?

More importantly, why hadn't I thought of him when I was kissing Dax?

The metal door from the club clanged open, yanking me back.

Goodbye, peace and quiet.

Chad eased out the door, his narrow face turned away from me as he pulled a pack of cigarettes from his jacket and lit one, his fingers cupping the flame so it didn't blow out in the wind.

He stopped and squinted when he saw me, surprised yet satisfied. He ambled over to where I sat. "Hey, thought you went to the loo?"

In the light, his frame was more muscular than I recalled.

"Just needed some air." I stood up. "I got it."

"No need to run off," he commented wryly as I brushed past him. "I don't bite."

I felt more than saw him following me as I took long strides back to the door.

He's just weird. Keep walking.

I yanked open the door, but he slammed it shut with a forceful palm. "I'm not done talking to you."

I flinched at the stench of smoke and stale alcohol on his breath. "I want to go back in. Lulu's waiting for me."

He cupped my shoulder, turned me to face him, and trailed his finger down my arm to toy with my bracelet. "You wear some pretty things. I really like this bracelet. Are the diamonds real?"

I jerked away from him. "Keep your hands to yourself."

"Hey, it was just a question. No need to get upset. Why don't you hand it over and let me take a look at it?" His hand settled at my throat. Just a light touch, but . . .

"No! Let me go." I twisted away from him and reached for the door again.

His hand clamped tighter around my throat, squeezing on either side. My fingers clawed at his as he held me prisoner with just one hand.

"I was trying to be nice to you before, but you're a bit of a bitch," he said softly.

Panic skyrocketed.

My fingers clawed harder, jerking and hammering, but the pressure only hurt my throat.

I tried to swallow. Nothing.

I inhaled, sucking for air. Nothing.

A noise came from the street as a car came by, startling him. He switched around, put one of his arms around my waist, and dragged me behind the dumpster. My feet kicked and tried to find purchase on the ground but got nowhere. Self-defense moves my dad had taught me flashed through my head, and I tried to remember them.

He pushed me to the ground and straddled me, his legs clamping like vise-grips around my hips. "Be still," he bit out.

Okay, okay. I nodded, forcing my muscles to loosen, letting my hands fall to my sides.

His hand disappeared from my windpipe.

Fight!

My elbow connected squarely with his ribs, and he grunted and roared at me. I hit him again in the chest with a right hook as hard as I could.

I yelled for anyone who might be listening, but my voice was shit.

He slapped me, twisting my face around.

He reached for my hands to secure them. Evading, I punched him in the gut, a weak shot.

I scratched at his face, aiming for his eye, and he yelped as blood popped out and tracked down his cheek.

"Be still!" he yelled as he ripped the necklace from my throat. Sterling silver with a heart between two wings, it was a gift from Malcolm—not worth much, except for sentimental value. But then he dove for my bracelet, jerking on my wrist until I thought my arm would pop out of its socket.

I whimpered. Grief gutted me, beating the fear.

Not my bracelet!

I answered by shoving my fist at his throat—a move Malcolm had shown me—scoring a hit; he dropped back and grabbed his neck, gasping.

He pounced back, landing on my chest, and I know I should have felt some kind of pain, but the fear was too high, the need to survive overriding the circumstances. With a lightning move, he snatched the bracelet off my wrist, no doubt breaking the clasp.

No! It was all I had left of my dad!

"I've never killed anyone for a stupid piece of jewelry, but you're a different story." His face was livid with rage.

"Don't," I gasped out. "Please."

Everything I'd been consumed with for the past two weeks: my mother's disappointment, Hartford's jilting, school—all stupid, stupid, stupid.

This. This is what mattered. Life.

Savoring each moment because you don't know when it's your last one.

Being mindful and present for the small things.

The color of the sky. A daisy. Falling snow.

Don't let me die, I prayed.

I wanted to eat new kinds of donuts.

Get a tattoo.

Dance.

Fall in love.

In a blink, Chad disappeared, his body colliding with the metal dumpster like a bag of dirt.

I turned my head toward the door.

Dear God. Dax.

He rushed Chad, shoving him to the concrete where they tangled on the ground, both of them grunting and punching. Vicious sounds of skin meeting skin reached my ears. I tried to move, to get up and help. *Something!*

I hoisted myself up to my hands and knees and crawled in their direction.

Please don't let Dax get hurt.

Broader and more muscular, Dax snapped out hits, but Chad recovered, wiry and quick as his lean body scrambled away.

He flew at Dax and jumped on him, landing a sharp jab to his eye, making Dax's head snap back.

Dax roared and stumbled backward, resting against the brick wall of the neighboring building, chest heaving as they faced off. Chad leaned down, scooped up a rock from the ground, and advanced.

No!

Feebly gasping out for help to anyone who might be listening near the street or inside, I made my way to them, gravel digging into my knees and palms.

Dax inhaled and jumped at him, but Chad evaded and swung the rock, aiming for Dax's head. He missed and backed up to avoid Dax's fist.

A car drove by the street and I called out again, but my voice had vanished.

Closer. Closer. I crawled to them.

Chad's back was to me, and if I could get there . . .

Dax's eyes met mine for a second, sending me an almost imperceptible shake of his head. I ignored him. No way was he doing this by himself.

Chad, obviously giving up on hitting Dax by using the rock, threw it instead, hammering Dax in the arm.

Dax's face tightened, his fist clenching as he dashed at Chad again, only this time instead of using his hands, he sent two fast kicks to Chad's chest. *Bam! Bam!*

Chad folded in and gasped for air.

Dax advanced closer, circling him, banked rage on his face, an insane look in his eyes I'd never seen.

Abruptly, Chad hopped up, pivoted, and ran for the main road.

Dax flipped around and grabbed his shirttail, but Chad came out of it, buttons flying as he jerked away. He cursed at us both and disappeared across the street and into the darkness of the next alley.

The fading of his footsteps was the best sound I'd ever heard.

I pulled myself up to standing and leaned against the neighboring building as Dax jogged over to me. My entire body heaved in great gulps of air.

He halted within inches, eyeing me like a hawk, his face rigid with fury. His hands were clenched, his body drawn up in a tight wall of muscle. "God, Remi. You okay?"

I nodded and only then did he relax, his shoulders dropping as he bent down to lift my chin up toward the lamppost light. His teeth clenched. "Your throat is bruising."

"I'm fine," I managed, my voice rough as sandpaper.

"What the hell happened? I saw you come out, but I must have missed him following you. I got nervous that you were alone . . ." He trailed off and raked a hand through his hair. "*Dammit,* I'm sorry I didn't come out sooner."

"Not . . . your . . . fault . . ." I sucked in more air and kept my words brief. I clutched my wrist, missing my bracelet already. "Robbery. Took my jewelry."

He gently eased me in his arms and held me like I was a piece of china. "You're shaking all over, Remi. I'm so sorry, love. I'm here. You're okay. I'm okay. Everything's okay."

Warm tempered steel enveloped me, and I dissolved into the safety of his arms, my face buried in his chest. My voice wobbled. "I thought he was going to kill me—" I stopped and closed my eyes as hot tears fell, for once unable to stem the tide. "I hate crying in front of people. It's stupid."

"Shhh, let it all out. You're crashing. I got you. I promise."

Snippets of the attack rushed at me. "He—he got the bracelet my dad gave me the day he died. I—I can't imagine not having it. I need it. It keeps me centered . . ." I stopped, unable to say more without losing my shit.

He took a step back to better meet my eyes, his hands cupping my shoulders with care. "But you're alive. That's all that matters, right? If anything had happened to you . . ." His mouth thinned, and his chest heaved as he took a deep breath. "I wanted to go after the wanker, but I couldn't leave you here on the ground alone . . ."

I nodded, wiping at my face. "You scared him good, I think. You have moves I've never seen." My eyes flicked over his shoulder, part of me still paranoid.

He touched my cheek, his voice soft yet deadly. "He's not coming back, but if he does, I'll bloody kill the bastard."

I nodded, feeling just as bloodthirsty. *My beloved bracelet was gone.*

He adjusted the neckline of my dress, and I looked down. Part of the bodice and shoulder had been ripped and were barely hanging on. Sequins were dangling by threads. He took the ends of one side and tied them in a soft knot, arranging it so you couldn't see my bra.

"Perfect. Money I need down the drain." I sighed, rubbing my arms. "It would have been wrong to return it anyway after wearing it."

He paused, his eyes concerned. "Remi? Maybe this isn't the time, but if you need a loan, I can help."

My mouth parted.

He continued to surprise me. The cocky Dax I knew from Whitman had a whole different side to him.

"You're—you're sweet to say that, and I didn't mean to hint that I needed help. I'm fine."

A furrow lined his forehead. "I've been around long enough to know that when a girl says she's *fine*, she's usually lying. Why are you worried about returning a dress? I want the truth."

I shook my head. "It's just . . . I lost the deposit on my reception—money I'd been saving for months when I worked at Minnie's Diner. Lulu—she bought her own ticket, and she's offered to pay for all my entertainment, but I won't let her. When I get back to Whitman, I'll have to find somewhere to live, pay rent, pay bills . . . stuff I didn't plan for."

I nibbled on my bottom lip. "Besides, obviously there are other things to worry about—like you saved my life, thank you, and you have a monstrous black eye coming up." More details came into focus. I touched his face with gentle fingers that lingered across the scruff on his jawline. "At—at least there's no blood."

"For you, I'll wear it as a badge of honor." His eyes burned into mine.

My stomach fluttered.

What did he mean?

"Thank you," I whispered.

He leaned his forehead against mine. "Anytime. I hear bodyguard work pays well. Maybe I should go into that after I graduate?" His hands pushed my hair out of my face, trailing his fingers through the long strands.

His touch was exactly what I needed.

Without much thought except for comfort, instinctively I pressed myself against him, fitting into his arms as easy as breathing. He leaned against the brick wall of the neighboring building and wrapped me up, sensing my need to be grounded.

I felt safe. Secure. Like nothing would ever hurt me again.

I don't know how long we stood like that—maybe a minute, maybe five—but soon our breaths were in sync; the rise and fall of his chest in perfect accord with mine. One of his hands traced down my spine and then up. He outlined my shoulder blades with his fingertips. His hands drifted to my hips then caressed back up to my hair, massaging my scalp. I wanted to purr, and if it were possible, I sank even further into him. Not even a pin could have fit between us.

But what had started as an innocent hug changed. Fire licked my skin everywhere he touched. Of their own accord, my hands slid down to his waist and teased the line where his jeans rested on his hips. I went further, my fingers toying with the V at his hip until I felt him harden against me.

The chemistry had always been like that with us. Feverish. Ready in an instant.

That long weekend we'd been together, we'd never stopped touching each other. One glance from me and he'd been there on his knees, asking what I wanted, what I needed to feel good. I'd done the same, not able to get enough of him. Even when he wanted to tie me up or hold me down.

We'd been a bright burning sun, and we'd exploded at the end.

Lips brushed the top of my hair. "Remi . . . look at me," he said, his voice raspy.

If you look up, you're going to kiss him . . .

I tilted my head up and his mouth fused with mine in an instant. Insistent.

Wild.

Hot.

Yes! This is what I needed.

Desire that had been on hold since our kiss at the bar surged through my body, weaving into every atom. I groaned, and my hands rushed to his shoulders and dug in.

He was wrong—terribly wrong—for me, but it felt so right.

I felt wonderfully alive, revved up, as if I could crush a car with my bare hands, or push Dax against the wall and fuck him senseless. I recognized the feeling for what it was—an I almost-died-and-now-I-want-to-experience-life feeling.

"Wait," he breathed as I ran my hand under his shirt. "It's adrenaline. You've been through a trauma. You don't really want this—"

"Shhh." I lifted his shirt and kissed his chest, my tongue flicking over his nipple. "You taste like every good thing I've ever wanted."

His taut restraint snapped, and he swayed into me. "God, I can't tell you no."

"Then don't." My hand pushed against the hard length in his jeans. Stroked. "I remember how hot we were—how you loved to make me say your name. Don't you want that again?"

His eyes blazed. "Yes," he growled and took my mouth again, devouring me as I worked the zipper of his jeans down and slipped my hand inside. Of course he was commando.

We were frantic, our hands rushing, touching places we'd missed over the years. The press of his hands. His kisses. I wanted it all.

Finally, my body seemed to say. This. Me. Him. Fate. *Meant to be.*

His hand slipped down the neck of my dress and cupped my lace bra, teasing my nipple. I arched into him. All he'd have to do is touch me once in the right place and I'd detonate.

I cupped his shaft and stroked him from base to tip, ghosting my fingers over the tip, knowing exactly where he liked to be touched.

"Remi—you're killing me," he gasped out, laying his head back against the brick. "So many times I thought about this—"

"Remi?" A shrill voice belted out from behind us. "What the heck is going on? Our British guys ran off, and now you're out here with *Dax*? I'm confused."

Lulu.

"Yeah. What she said," Spider added in a dry tone. "Although to me it looks like you two are flossing each other's teeth."

And now everyone was here. *Just peachy.*

My body shook from denied need as I leaned my head on Dax's chest, trying to get my breathing under control as he discreetly zipped his pants up and straightened my dress.

Mortification warmed my cheeks.

One minute I was telling him I couldn't be his friend and the next I was jamming my tongue down his throat.

God, I didn't know who I was when I was with him.

Dax cupped my face, his face worried as he searched my eyes. "Adrenaline, love. Don't be sorry and don't blame yourself."

I closed my eyes.

How did he have this ability to read my mind?

I nodded and we turned to face them.

CHAPTER SIX

I RAN THROUGH the details of what had happened with Spider and Lulu, describing how I'd found Remi fighting off Chad on the ground.

I should have come out sooner.

You aren't her keeper, my brain said.

I reached for Remi's hand and laced our fingers together. She tightened her grasp, and I pulled her against me as she responded to their questions, her voice low and weak, but her composure calm—better than I'd expected from someone who'd been attacked.

But then she'd always projected *control.*

Over the years, I'd listened in on conversations about her, just to know what she was up to. The times when I'd seen her at a campus-wide frat party and we'd come face to face, you'd never have known she knew me. With a frozen smile, she'd meet my gaze—and keep walking.

Like I was a piece of fucking furniture.

Granted, I usually had a couple of girls hanging on me.

I watched her more than I should have considering she was the girlfriend of one of my rivals. It was understood that we didn't poach the Omega girls and vice versa unless we wanted to end up in a tangle on the quad. Not that I'd ever cared. If I wanted a girl, I took her, although I never went after attached ones, especially those as close as Remi and Hartford.

Plus, I'd had my chance with her, *and I hadn't wanted it.*

I came back to the present as sirens wailed in the distance.

At least someone had called the police.

Two beefy guys who I knew to be bouncers for the club flew out the metal door and scanned the area, pausing on our huddled foursome near the dumpster.

They headed toward us. "Everything okay out here?" one of them asked us.

Renewed anger hit and my fists tightened. "It is now," I said tersely, straightening to eye them. "If you have a back door, it would be a damn good idea to keep security—especially near an alley. My friend was mugged and nearly killed by one of *your* patrons."

"I'm fine," Remi said, smoothing it over. "Thanks to you."

I glanced down at her face. She smiled, albeit a weak one, and I felt a *small* bit of peace.

She was safe. She was fine.

But I couldn't completely relax.

A few minutes later, we gave statements about the incident to the officers and assured them we'd come back down the next day if we remembered anything else. Apparently, there'd been a rash of similar muggings in the area—one or two white men who hit on victims they'd met in bars and clubs. Both of the guys Lulu had picked up fit their general description. They took jewelry, money, bags, phones, even clothes. The police had told the local pawnshops to be on alert if they came in with specific stolen goods, but so far they hadn't had any hits.

Remi looked crushed when they told her they had no leads.

After the police left, Spider and Lulu went to grab us some waters at the bar while we found ourselves in the staff restroom that the manager of Masquerade had generously offered us, along with an offer of free admission and drinks for the rest of the week.

Remi had small cuts on her hands from the gravel and several fingerprint bruises on her neck that she insisted she could cover up with make-up the next day. Thankfully, the club had a small first aid kit with witch hazel and alcohol wipes. Of course, the police had checked her out and taken a few pictures, but she'd adamantly refused to go to a hospital.

She sat on a stool and I cleaned her feet off, careful to get the little bits of dirt out. It was as if we'd overcome a hurdle. We were friends. Sort of.

We hadn't actually *said* that, but I felt the connection between us.

Later, I leaned against the sink as she dabbed my swelling eye with a cold compress someone had brought us from the kitchen. One of the bartenders had also scrounged around in the employees' stock room and found her a pair of old flip-flops and an oversized, long t-shirt with the words *I LOVE NIGHTS AT MASQUERADE*. She wore her dress underneath it.

I chuckled at her shirt. "That's ironic."

Her lips quirked up. "At least I saw you here tonight." A pause. "I'm glad."

"Me too."

She nodded. "About what happened . . . with my hands down your pants . . ." A blush started at her neck and worked its way to her forehead. "I went a little nuts." She giggled. "No pun intended."

"We're good. No need to explain." I willed the bulge in my pants to go down.

"So no harm, no foul?"

"Yep, we're buddies now."

"Hmmm," she murmured softly, a smile on her face as she gazed at me, her eyes luminous with emotion. "You're definitely a hero. I owe you."

My breath hitched at the way she looked, her face truly happy for the first time tonight, and for a moment I got a glimpse of what my future might have been like if I'd allowed myself to . . .

Stop, Dax.

A few minutes went by as she checked me for other injuries, making me take my shirt off in case I had bruises. He hadn't hit me *that* hard, I insisted, but she still ran her fingers over every inch of my skin where I'd said I'd been hit. She wanted to see for herself, and I knew it wasn't a sexual thing, but true concern. A little furrow formed on her forehead as she poked at my ribs to make sure they weren't broken.

I tossed my head back and let out a belly laugh.

She jumped back. "I'd forgotten you're ticklish!"

I laughed and pushed at her hands.

She grinned, her fingers on my bicep, tracing the outline of the dragonfly wings—almost absentmindedly.

"I love this. The colors, the design, the pure emotion. This tattoo means something to you. What is it?" Her eyes flicked back up to mine. "I feel sad when I look at it. Weird, to get a feeling when you see something—as if we have a sixth sense about things." She smiled. "Whatever. I'm rambling, but I do want my own tattoo."

Her hand never left my bicep; she stroked the wings, making the same swirls and marks that were in my design. Tingles—no, sparks—were going off left and right.

This isn't about sex, Dax.

This is the real her. The real you.

Talking. Sharing. Having a moment when she's peeking into your soul.

Will you let her in?

Absolutely not.

I wasn't good enough for her, and I didn't need her in my life, jacking with my emotions and making me want something I could never have.

But her touch.

Then pull away from her, arsehole!

I swayed, leaning into her.

Hypnotic.

Mesmerizing.

So fucking perfect that I wanted to curl up with her on a soft bed, stroke her hair, and tell her everything about the meaning behind that tattoo . . .

But I couldn't.

I didn't share that.

On the surface, people saw the cocky, funny guy, but underneath was a mess of feelings—especially since the anniversary of Mum's death had just passed—and no matter how hard I wanted to explain the meaning to my dragonfly, I didn't think I could get through the ordeal without getting clogged up in my throat.

So I did what I do best. I pushed her away.

I put some space between us, letting her hand fall to her side. I changed the topic. "Dude. I want to be there when you get a tattoo."

She blinked, her face losing its glow, obviously sensing my inward retreat. "Oh. Okay. Sure. We'll have to do that." She tossed me my shirt. "I guess you need to put that back on."

I slipped it over my head. "You ready to go home?" I asked, stalking to the door and opening it for her.

Her cobalt-blue eyes met mine. "Not really. I still feel all tingly from the adrenaline. Do—do you want to go somewhere?"

"You wanna go back inside the club?" My voice was incredulous.

"God no." She nibbled on her nail, looking indecisive and incredibly lost. "I kinda want to eat something—although I'm not even sure I can swallow. At least get a soda."

"You should probably go back to your hotel and get some rest, Remi."

"To an empty hotel room? No thanks." A defiant look grew in her eyes and then just as quickly deflated. "I—I don't want to be alone, okay?"

I pushed down the bolt of need that fired through me at her words. "Alright, love. Let's go then. I have just the place."

ALL FOUR OF us walked into Tucks, a tiny kebab place across the street from the club—one of the few places in the area open after midnight. Mostly it was used for takeaway orders for people, but it had a few small tables in the back. Spider went and grabbed us one while I stood with Remi and Lulu to order.

Remi asked a ton of questions about the doner kebab, which is a huge stack of marinated meat cooked by spinning around a heat lamp. It's considered the best "drunk food" in London.

She chose the lamb inside a pita with cabbage, tomatoes, and a spicy sauce. After a few nibbles, she sat the food down with a sigh.

I bit back a curse. Her throat must be too sore to eat.

Without saying anything, I excused myself, went to the counter and ordered her a vanilla milkshake. Of course, it wasn't fancy—just a prepackaged drink, but it was cold and easy to swallow.

I set the drink in front of her, causing her to stop in midstream something she was saying to Lulu.

"What's this?" She flicked her eyes up at mine.

"You can't eat and this might help."

Her face softened. "Oh? Is that a milkshake?"

"Yeah. Ours are different from the US—less sugary and thinner. Maybe not what you're used to, but it's got some protein to fill you up if you're hungry."

Her mouth parted. "That's so sweet. Thank you for thinking of me." She opened it and sipped, her face flushing as she gazed at me.

I nodded and sat back down. Spider watched me, a questioning expression on his face as his eyes ran from me to Remi.

I ignored him.

"I can't get over Evil Chad," Lulu said later as she played with the chips she'd ordered. She'd been glum since hearing Remi and me describe what had happened.

Remi sighed. "Lulu, it's not your fault. See? I already sound much better." Her voice had improved, but I was afraid tomorrow she'd feel even worse. Declan was training for the UFC, and the few days following his fights were always the worst with soreness and bruising.

"I'm totally sick that I managed to find the only two douche-bags in London and introduce you to them. I should have known it was too good to be true," Lulu muttered. "Those accents. The hot Mohawk . . ."

"You've told us a million times already," Spider said. "You're sorry. You're a sucky friend. You deserve to be kicked in the vagina—"

He grinned at her glare. "What? I can't say that word? You need thicker skin, love."

"Oh, this is coming from Spider, the famous guitarist who hides his identity. I don't even like Vital Rejects," she snipped. "Suck on that."

I chuckled. Spider's identity was out once he'd taken his mask off. The girls had been surprised at first and, honestly, not overly impressed.

I'd laughed a lot at that on the way over.

Apparently the girls weren't into alternative indie bands.

Remi's eyes slid to me. "Are you living at the house this fall?"

I shook my head. "Currently homeless."

"Me too. Hartford got the apartment, and Lulu is in the dorms with her roommate. I'm sure at this point there's nothing left but rat-holes around campus."

I agreed. "Yeah. I'll be jumping right into apartment searching when I get home."

"Maybe if you find something—or if I find something—we can share the place?"

I froze mid-bite on my pita as three pairs of eyes looked at me expectantly. I swallowed and took a sip of water. "I don't know if that's a good idea."

Remi snorted. "You're totally right. God. Crazy, spur-of-the-moment idea. Ignore me because obviously I'm still in shock."

I grinned, picturing us living together. "We'd fight like cats and dogs, wouldn't we? You an Omega little sister and me a Tau?"

She lifted her shoulders. "Hmmm, maybe, maybe not. I don't really care about that rivalry."

"Hartford does," Lulu said. A little giggle came out of her. "He'd stroke out."

"I was mostly kidding anyway," Remi said to me. "I'm not responsible for anything I do or say tonight apparently."

I let the topic die.

After we'd finished and cleared our mess away, Lulu and Spider drifted off outside to smoke, leaving me and Remi alone. She played with her wrist, a wistful expression on her face.

"Remi, what happened to your father?" I asked softly.

Her face paled.

"It's okay if you don't want to tell me," I said.

She took a deep breath. "No, no it's fine. It's just I didn't expect you to ask. We never got too deep with each other that weekend we were together."

True.

"I know how it feels to lose someone," I murmured. "I've been there."

Her eyes studied my face, and then as if she'd come to a decision, she nodded. "It—it was a car wreck on my sixteenth birthday. His SUV hit a patch of ice, crossed the median, and slammed into a tractor-trailer . . . Instant death is what the coroner told us. He—he was on his way to pick me up from my piano lesson. We were supposed to go out to dinner that night and eat at this hibachi place that was my favorite."

Her hands clenched on the table. "Anyway, I waited around for him for a while then caught a ride home with a friend. Police officers were at my house. He'd given me the bracelet that morning. He'd been so excited because it had belonged to his mom." She bit her lip. "Life never was the same after that."

A sharp emotion pricked at me, digging at my chest, shifting around and flailing about like a restless animal. She'd been through hell. *Like me.*

I reached across the table and unfurled her fist, finger by finger, until her palm was exposed. I pressed mine on top of hers and let our hands touch.

"I've never talked about this to anyone except Declan, but my mum passed away when I was ten—stage four lung cancer. She was dead in two months. I barely knew my father, but Declan and I had to leave behind everyone we knew and move to Raleigh to live with him. Life never was the same after that," I added softly.

Understanding lit her face. "How—how did you deal with it?"

"I was a kid, so I cried. A lot. Sometimes a smell would trigger it, someone's laugh that sounded like hers, a favorite food. I walked around with a piece of concrete in my gut for a year. I daydreamed I was the victim of a horrible joke, and she'd suddenly come back to life and run into my arms outside the school. TV crews would film it and then we'd catch a plane back to London and everything would go back to normal—only this time, I'd be a better kid. I'd pick up my dirty clothes. I'd tell her I loved her more."

Her lips trembled. "I used to think the same thing—that my dad would walk in the door, give me a hug, and then we'd all sit down to dinner. He told terrible jokes, but I miss them."

We sat in silence, each of us studying the other one, processing each other's grief.

A glint of understanding crossed her face. "Is—is your mom's death the reason you push girls away?"

I froze. "Why would you say that?"

"It would make sense. Loving hurts, but losing someone . . . devastates you. Changes you."

The air became charged with something I'd never felt with a girl.

The thing is people you love *do* disappear—like Father when I was a baby and Mum when she died.

I never wanted to revisit that pain again.

I refused to give someone that kind of power over me again.

But she was staring into my broken heart, and I was *letting* her.

I sucked in a breath. "Yes."

"And control is how you cope," I added a few beats later, coming to my own realization.

She lifted clear blue eyes to mine. Earnest. Beautiful. She nodded. "Yes. Plans make me feel safe."

And those few words were all we needed to understand each

other perfectly.

Why we were broken the way we were.

A few moments went by, and eventually it became odd that our hands were touching yet we weren't actually holding hands. She pulled hers away, her fingers once again tracing over her wrist.

I let out a heavy sigh. "Don't be sad about your bracelet. I can't stand it."

She flicked questioning eyes at me. "Why do you care so much?"

Fuck, I don't know!

I shrugged, playing it off. "Just glad you're okay."

"I know how lucky I am," she said, "and I'm going to be more careful, but I'm also going to savor every moment of this vacation. I could be dead tomorrow." She smiled. "I'm getting a tattoo and asking Lulu to show me how to dance."

I nodded. "Since you're into making changes, my offer of friendship still stands—only if you're willing to eat at Panera with me."

"Okay," she said after a moment, leaning across the table with a gleam in her eyes. "But we'll have to have some guidelines. A plan."

I snorted at her obvious enthusiasm. "Why am I not surprised?"

She grabbed a pen from her purse, pulled out a clean napkin, and began scribbling, her deep blue eyes glancing up at mine from time to time as she wrote.

"I'm almost scared to ask what you're doing," I commented, trying to read her handwriting upside down.

"I'm making rules, or really just one because there's only one rule for friendship with Dax Blay."

I chuckled. "And what's that?"

Her eyes lingered on my lips. "*No kissing.* Ever. Not on the mouth or anywhere that may cause lady parts to tingle. The End." She sat her pen down and considered me, a little grin on her lips. "It would help if you didn't have the most perfect ass in the whole world, but I guess you can't change that."

I arched a brow. "Too hot for you to handle?"

She rolled her eyes. "Shut up, Romeo."

I grinned. "You're priceless."

"You think I'm goofy."

"No, absolutely not. Sounds like a very good plan. I'm totally on board." I kept my face straight.

"Are you sure you can do the no kissing thing?"

"I seem to recall just a bit ago your hands were down my jeans . . ."

"Okay, no need to elaborate, Sex Lord."

"Uh-huh."

She pushed the napkin over to me. "Can you sign your name?"

"You're such a nerd. Should we pinky swear, too?" But I took the napkin and looked down at what she'd written out.

"Thank you for the compliment. Now shut up and sign on the line and date it, there and there," she said, pointing at the hastily drawn lines. "I already did."

I shook my head. If this is what it took to be friends with a girl who'd managed to get under my skin three years ago and stay there, then yeah, I was intrigued.

I signed it and pushed it back to her.

She pushed it back. "No, that's your copy." She got another napkin and redid the entire thing, putting her copy in her purse.

This was serious to her. I grinned.

After all copies were put away, she lifted her milkshake up in the air. "A toast to friendship with a guy I once had a three-night stand with."

I smiled. "May the odds be ever in our favor."

She giggled, and we clinked drinks.

My eyes landed on her full lips as she wrapped them around her straw.

What had I gotten myself into?

CHAPTER SEVEN

Remi

FTER DAX AND Spider had seen us off in a cab, Lulu and I
headed to The Tower Hotel. A few blocks from our destination
we saw the majestic Tower of London all lit up, and because I
was still wired, we stopped and hopped out to walk the rest of the
way back to the hotel. It felt safe since a few people were still mill-
ing around the street, taking in the illuminating glow of the historic
building. My foot throbbed slightly, but I knew from experience it
wasn't bad. I powered through the ache with determination.

Half an hour later, we walked in the lobby around three in the
morning. Thankfully most of the guests were sleeping. My bruises
had continued to darken as the night progressed, and I could only
imagine what they'd think if they saw me with a giant t-shirt and
flip-flops. *Wild American girls.*

Lulu dragged along beside me as we hopped in the elevator and
headed to her room on the twelfth floor. I was on the fifteenth in the
honeymoon suite. It sucked we were so far apart, but the hotel had
had limited rooms to choose from considering we'd made her res-
ervations at the last minute. She'd been the one that had insisted on
separate rooms, mostly because she wanted me to get lucky. And she

had plenty of money since her parents were big in the country music scene in Nashville.

She leaned against the wall of the elevator, obviously exhausted as she gazed at her phone, checking social media. Her mouth was uncharacteristically turned down. She suddenly straightened. "What the heck?"

"What?" I craned my neck to see what she was looking at, but she swiped the photo away on Instagram. "Was that Hartford?" I asked, a sinking feeling growing in my stomach.

"Shit. Yes."

"Is he with someone?"

She shook her head. "I don't know. You know how hard it is to interpret social media. It's fake and filtered. You can't believe half of it."

I scowled. "Show me the pic or I'll just bring it up on my own phone."

Sighing, she scooted over next to me and swiped her phone back to the photo. It was Hartford at Cadillac's, one of the local college bars at Whitman. Next to him—right on top of him—wearing an overly brightly smile was a perky blonde with super white teeth.

"That's Katrina Somebody. She's in most of his pre-med classes," I said, clicking on the picture, taking in every single pixel, looking for large pores or a flaw on her perfect face.

Was she prettier than me? Smarter? Funnier?

Bottles of beer littered the table and several people photo-bombed in the background. *Were they* together, *together?*

I searched Hartford's smile, his eyes, looking for a clue. His sandy-blond hair had recently been trimmed and his jaw was shaven. Wearing a plaid button-down shirt I'd never seen before, he radiated confidence; no sign of the conflicted guy who'd told me he needed to think about us before he made a final commitment.

Lulu shrugged. "He captioned it #studybuddy #goodtimes."

I flattened my lips, studying how Katrina's hand curled around his arm, how his head tilted in her direction.

I looked at the date of the posting. Our wedding night.

Emotion poured in, making my chest freeze. I took deep breaths and braced myself against the cold wall of the elevator.

It's okay. It's okay. It's just the guy you spent two and a half years on out with someone else.

I wanted to throw up.

"Remi, I'm sorry," Lulu said, a pained expression on her face. "I'm just messing up your entire night, aren't I?"

"I'm fine." I breathed out, handing the phone back to her.

At least I wasn't tossing out expletives, beating my fists on the walls, or crying. Definitely progress.

"You're too calm. It's kinda freaking me out." She gave my shoulder a squeeze. "You're trying to figure it out and put meaning to it, but more than likely, it's just a random pic."

"He looks happy. She looks happy. I think they're *together.* Maybe I wasn't the one for him and he saw it." I bit my lip hard. Blinked.

Her face reddened in anger. "If that asshat cheated on you, I'll freaking kill him when I see him. . . . *dammit* . . . he's such a gargantuan ass! He probably goes to some kind of asshat convention each year in, I don't know, Asshat, Texas."

"Tell me how you really feel." I sent her a weak smile.

She nudged her head at the pic. "He's black and white and you're digital color, babe. You can do better."

"Like who?"

"I may have had more than my fair share of martinis tonight, but I definitely noticed sparks between you and Dax. It's weird. He's starting to grow on me. It's just—tonight at the diner, the way you looked at him and the way he looked at you. I want a guy to look at *me* like that."

"It's lust. That's all Dax has to offer anyone. He only wants to have fun."

She stewed on that as the door swished open at her floor. "I can walk you to your room and we can talk for a while if you're still wide awake?" she offered.

"No. Get some sleep. Don't worry about me."

She grudgingly left. I waited until she got in her room, and then I popped back in the elevator and pulled out my phone, which had been turned off. I turned it back on, but instead of getting on Instagram and stalking Hartford, I pulled up my phone contacts and gazed at the cell number Dax had added before we'd left the diner. I snorted when I saw he'd added his name as Sex Lord—but with a question mark. Was this Dax's version of humility?

My finger hovered over the call button.

What would I say?

The elevator pinged for my floor and I got off. With a deep exhalation, I tucked my phone back in my clutch while at the same time digging for my key card.

"Where is it?" I muttered, riffling through the zipped side pockets.

Awareness that I wasn't alone in the narrow hallway seeped in, and my eyes swept the area. No one was going to or leaving their room, but at my door I saw a male figure reclining on the floor, his head dipping into his chest as if he were asleep.

What was he doing here?

I walked over to him and bent down.

"Dax, wake up." I shook his shoulder gently. "Hello?"

Heavy eyes fluttered, squinting open. "Remi?"

"Who else would it be?" I plopped down on the carpeted floor next to him. "The question is, what are you doing outside my hotel room?"

Bloodshot, tired eyes roved over my face and landed on my lips. "After you left, I got this weird feeling. Paranoid that Chad knew where your hotel was or that he'd gotten your full name. I called you but you didn't pick up, so I came over to make sure you were okay. I tipped the porter to give me your room number."

"My phone was on silent since we talked to the police. I just now turned it on. Sorry."

"Where've you been?" he asked, coming more awake and scratching at his unshaven jaw.

"We walked from the Tower of London. Guess I was too hyped

up from everything."

His eyes narrowed. "You should have come straight back."

I arched a brow. Smiled. "Since when do you keep tabs on me?"

He let out an exasperated sigh, stood, and put out a hand to heave me up. "Maybe I've decided you need a bodyguard 24/7 just to keep you safe."

"You applying?" We faced each other inches apart.

"You don't want me to fill that position. We both know it." He blew out a breath. "Come on, get your key out and let's get you inside."

I found my key, slid it through the slot and opened the door. Dax stepped inside in front of me and held the door open as I came through.

"Thanks," I said.

"Give me a sec," he said. "I want to check the room."

What? I was fine.

No one was in my room but him, and he was the one I didn't need to be alone with.

He stalked around the space, checking the bathroom, under the bed, inside the closet, and even outside the window to the small iron balcony.

"Only a ninja can scale that," I said, watching him in bemusement.

"Looks clear," he said, stumbling over his feet as he walked toward me.

"Dax. You're exhausted. Please, sit down." I pointed at a chair. "Why don't I get some coffee sent up for you before you head back?"

"No, that's okay. I didn't drive. I took a cab right after you."

"Well, I'm pooped." I set my clutch down, kicked my shoes off, plodded over to the bed and fell backward right in the center of the plush duvet. Rose petals the maid had placed there flew in the air.

I lifted my arms above my head and stretched. My eyes closed. "I never thought I'd say this, but I'm glad to be in this big bed to-night even if it is without getting laid. Although the night is still young." I giggled, opening my eyes and winking at him.

I meant it as a joke, of course, but his face darkened and I immediately stiffened.

The room stilled, filling with tension.

I sat up and pulled my shirt down.

His eyes landed on my lips. Bounced away. Came back.

He raked his hand through his hair and it fell back into a perfect tousled mess. "Um, I need to head home."

He turned to go.

"Wait."

What are you doing, Remi?

I stood up, suddenly breathless, and met his intense gaze. He was beautiful—even tired. My eyes went over him, taking in the steely eyes, the tension in his broad shoulders, the way his hands were clenched at his side—the obvious bulge in his jeans. *Oh.*

I swallowed and nudged at the comfy chair and ottoman in the corner of the room next to the window. "Do—do you want to sleep here?"

"No."

My arms crossed and I forced out a laugh. "Don't be silly. Stay, I insist. We can have coffee in the morning and talk. Here, let me grab some extra blankets and a pillow from the closet. I saw them earlier when I was unpacking." I brushed past him, but he grabbed my hand, causing me to come to a halt.

"No, Remi."

"*Yes, Dax.* It's what friends do. We help each other out."

"It's not a good idea." His voice had grown husky and he hadn't let go of my hand.

"Why not?" My thumb was stroking his palm as if directed by a part of my brain I had no control over.

"Because if I stay in this room with you, it's going to be in that bed, and we aren't sleeping." His eyes searched my face, lingering on my mouth.

"Why—why do you always stare at my lips?"

His eyes darkened.

"Dax?"

He sent me a hooded look. "Because I want them on my mouth, kissing me. On my skin, sucking me. Everywhere." His thumb brushed across my bottom lip, gently tugging it down.

I shuddered, quivering from the picture he painted.

He dropped his hand and exhaled deeply. "We agreed to be friends, but when you stand this close, all I can think about is stripping you out of that shirt, pushing you down on that bed, and screwing you until you moan my name a hundred times before noon."

"Only a hundred?" I said.

Stop it, Remi!

His lashes dropped. "You're in dangerous territory, Remi. Tread carefully . . ."

"Just . . . let me touch you. That's all." I reached my hand out and rested it on his heart, feeling the rise and fall of his chest.

We stared at each other, and a million *what ifs* raced through my head.

What if we had sex? Would it ruin our fragile friendship?

What if he immediately moved on to some sorority girl this fall? Would I fall into that pit of despair I'd been in three years ago?

What if I let go of the past and just did what my body was screaming for?

You'd have one hell of an orgasm tonight.

His eyes narrowed, a muscle jerking in his cheek. "I can't handle this. I'm barely hanging on here."

"Me too."

He lowered his head until his mouth was an inch from mine. "Forget friendship. I want to fuck you."

His words banged around in my head.

My tongue darted out to wet my lips. "Hartford . . ." I stopped abruptly at the anger flaring in his eyes. God. I hadn't meant to say his name. He hadn't even been on my mind.

"Exactly." He let go of my hand, a pulse beating at his temple. "Goodnight, *friend*." He sent me a final look and turned and walked out the door.

CHAPTER EIGHT

I WOKE UP at one in the afternoon to the smell of bacon frying and the sound of Spider yapping on the phone. Rubbing my face, I crawled out of bed and sat on the edge, snippets of last night in Remi's hotel room coming back to me. I groaned. I'd really cocked it up with her last night, and I hadn't even been drunk.

Clearly I'd been thinking with my dick, especially when she'd been flashing those legs, prancing around the room and offering to let me sleep in the same room as her. No doubt—us in a hotel room was a recipe for disaster.

I got angry again, remembering her saying *his* name and not mine. *Sonofabitch.*

Moving on from thoughts of her, I looked around the room. I'd be leaving next week, I thought as I took in the cream and white color scheme Spider had gone with. Roomy and furnished in mostly chrome and leather, it was a nice flat, and he was quite proud of it. He'd hired a designer and had a hand in picking out all the rugs and accessories. He took it seriously because it was his, and even though I could be a messy bastard, I'd picked up after myself.

My phone pinged with a text. *Declan.* He and Elizabeth were the two people I missed the most this summer. They'd fallen hard for each other last fall—two of the luckiest people I knew. Just watching them together made me envious, and part of me wanted the magic they had, but I was too scared.

I picked up the phone. I'd called him yesterday to see if he could find me a place to rent around campus and put a deposit on it until I got back into town.

There's nothing to rent close to Whitman, but I found you an older house: 3 bedrooms, 2 baths, 2500 square feet. Even has a little patio out back. Seventy thousand and it's all yours. Steal of a deal.

What the hell?

I didn't want to buy a place. I wanted a place to crash until I graduated.

I FaceTimed him since it was free.

"Hiya, bro, what's up?" I said as soon as he answered. His hair was wet as if he'd come fresh from a shower. It was eight in the morning there.

"Hey, man, what's up with the black eye?" Rustling sounds as he moved into his kitchen.

I touched my face, seeing the ugly gray bruise under my eye on the screen. "You know me, always into something."

He squinted at me. "Be careful. I still haven't taught you all my moves yet." A grin popped up on his face. "Not that you'd ever be as good as me anyway. I'm the best."

"I'm the best at everything else." I chuckled.

"Whatever, tosser. Just tell me how you've been."

"Trust me, you'd be impressed. I run ten miles a day, work out and, sit down for this one, I actually read some books this summer. I'm just starting one you might be familiar with. *Pride and Prejudice*. It's a little slow and there's no sex. I pretty much hate it."

He laughed.

I saw Elizabeth in the background, her blonde hair tied up in a messy bun. She waved enthusiastically.

I blew her a kiss. "Hey, love. I miss you."

She blew me one back and called from across the room. "Miss you more. Come home soon, please. I need a shopping buddy. Declan refuses to help me pick out purses like you do."

In my viewer, I watched Declan smile as he took in Elizabeth pouring a cup of coffee. He chuckled and turned back to face me. "I guess you got my text?"

"Yeah, but I don't want to buy a house. Or I could move my arse in with you guys, and then Elizabeth will fall for me . . ." I laughed.

"Dude. We barely have room for our shit."

"Yeah." I was mostly kidding anyway.

He continued, "I checked with the housing department for open dorm rooms, but got nothing. That number will change once classes get started, but that would put you living with Dad until they had an opening."

Ugh. Dorms.

Even worse, though, was Father.

I groaned, picturing my father's three-story mansion with fancy furniture, housekeepers, and my five-year-old stepsister. "No way."

Declan grinned. "You could do it. Save some money. Hang out with the horses. Swim in the pool. Have family dinners."

"And never have sex again."

"True." He laughed.

"You sound happy. Things going good with the gym?"

"Thanks to Dad," he said, "and Elizabeth."

He sent a grin to Elizabeth, who'd popped up to kiss his cheek. "Anyway, maybe you'd like to invest in an older home, live there, and maybe do some work on it, and then resell it. Or rent to college students. The real estate market is on fire, and you'd be good at it."

I smirked. "Me?"

"Why not? You're a smooth talker and handsome, so why not capitalize on those traits? I'll help out with the business side if you need it, although I think you'll be just fine."

Hmmm. "Are you saying you don't think I'm smart enough to graduate, and this is my fallback?"

"No, wanker, I'm saying this house is a steal for the money and you have that and more in the bank. Even if you don't sell it, maybe it would be nice for you to put down some roots. That's all." He sent me a brotherly scowl through the phone.

Interesting. "Ah."

We moved on to other conversation, mostly about the upcoming trial of Elizabeth's attacker who'd broken into her apartment and attempted to kill her back in November. In the fray, he'd sliced the artery in Declan's leg, and it had been touch and go for a while until we'd known he'd make it through surgery.

"He didn't make bail, thank God, so he's sitting it out in jail until the trial in January," he told me.

"Any chance he'll get off?" I asked. His father was a senator of North Carolina, but our father had deep political connections as well.

"I don't know. Time will tell."

That didn't sound good, and I could tell he didn't want to delve into the explanations with Elizabeth there, so we talked for a few more minutes until he had to leave for the gym, and then Elizabeth got on. We chatted for half an hour until she finally had to go take a shower.

Falling back on my bed, I stared up at the ceiling. Mulling. Brooding.

This summer I'd turned a corner; perhaps the day I'd driven out to the Hampstead Rehab Center to bring Spider home. He'd come out the front doors a withered version of himself, face gaunt, lines feathering out from his mouth. Drugs and being on the road had worn him down to a skinny whip of a guy. Even with the guiding compass of his bandmates, he hadn't held his shit together.

And the thing that struck me the most—*he was alone.*

No groupies. No girlfriends. No parents that wanted him.

I knew the pain of being alone, when greedy people want something from you because you're the son of a rich man or because you're popular.

Remi had never been like that. She hadn't kissed my ass when I'd treated her indifferently. Hell no—she'd strutted out of my room like she owned the place, sweater and all. Most girls would have gone along with whatever I said just to be near me, but not her.

She'd wanted a version of me that I couldn't be at nineteen.

She'd wanted love although she'd never said it out loud.

I slipped on some jeans and walked into the large bathroom attached to my room. I washed my face and arranged my hair with my fingers, my brain running in all directions, mostly about what I'd do after I graduate. There's not much out there with a degree in psychology if you didn't go to graduate school.

What did that leave?

Bartend? Maybe. I did have four years' experience of drinking at the Tau house and knew a lot about mixing alcohol. Billy, the owner of Cadillac's, had offered more than once. He claimed I brought people in the door.

Work at Declan's gym? I'd spent all last spring working out with him at his gym, and had really gotten into the fitness groove, but working for Declan? Mixing family with job responsibility is tricky.

Invest in the housing market? Hmmm. I didn't know shit about houses.

You could learn. Maybe. The idea grew on me.

As if by instinct, my feet found themselves at my closet, and I reached up to the top shelf and pulled down a letter. It had been written from Mum before she passed away, and I carried it everywhere. Father had given one to each of us when we were thirteen years old: one for me and a different letter for Declan.

Letter in hand, I sat down on the bed.

Dear Dax,

This letter is goodbye, but please know I'm writing it with smiles not tears. I'm rejoicing because someday, when the time is right, you will read this, and there will be a connection, a gossamer thread that binds us together—you on earth and me in heaven. Perhaps a star will twinkle extra bright or a comet will race across the sky. Perhaps a dragonfly will land on your shoulder or a rainbow will be in your backyard. It's me, becoming part of our infinite universe as I watch you grow.

I'm dying with cancer. There's a slight chance I might live a few months longer with medication but it would make me very sick and tired. I don't want to waste away in front of you. I want you to remember me as the fun mum, and with the time I have left, I want to spend every second with you playing Monopoly, making bangers and mash, singing "Hey, Jude" and "Here Comes the Sun."

Am I scared as the hour of my death closes in? Yes. My heart breaks to know I won't be here to carry you through the pain of losing me, the tumult of your upcoming teenage years, see you fall in and out of love, or experience the feeling of holding your own children.

But what I can leave you with is advice. You are young now, but someday I hope it gives you comfort to know that I too have been where you are, and I was far from perfect.

I got pregnant with you unexpectedly and married a man I'd fallen madly in love with but barely knew. You were both born, and soon he realized he'd never loved me. He wanted to go back to his home in the United States. It was not his fault. Please know this. Have compassion for him even though you barely know him. You can't make someone love you and you can't make them stay with you. But look at the blessings I received. YOU. If I could go back and change a thing about meeting your father and what happened, I wouldn't, knowing you and Declan were waiting for me at the end.

I recall the moment you first saw the beach on holiday in Italy. You took my hand and we walked out as far as we could. You played for hours, and when the sun finally set on the horizon, you reached for my hand. "It's like a painting, Mum," you whispered, and I knew then your heart was special. You saw that we are but particles of dust on this earth and there are things bigger than us.

As a baby, you rarely cried and I often worried why, but as you grew into a headstrong yet kind lad, I realized God had sent me a child much like myself. Impulsive and fun. Full of joy. He knew I needed you. Your mischievous nature and giggles get me through my weepy days—even though you may not realize it.

"Your wings already exist . . . all you have to do is soar."

My little darling, I didn't write that quote, but I've said it to you since you were in my tummy. It's our mantra, and every time you say it back to me, I have the assurance of knowing that, if anything, I will leave you with hope and a belief that you can be and do anything you want.

I Love You.

Margaret (Mum)

Emotion rode me like it always did when I read her words.

She believed I could do anything.

I was like her, she'd said.

I swallowed. God, I wanted to be good for her. I wanted to succeed at *something.*

A glass shattered from the kitchen. *What the hell?*

I bolted from the room. Spider might be all cocky smiles, but underneath I sensed the darkness he harbored. He'd never shown any signs of hurting himself, but I was a worrier, and dammit I'd gotten used to the bloke.

Wearing a pair of Union Jack boxers and nothing else, his lean frame was bent over with a dustpan sweeping up broken glass.

"What's going on?"

"Ah, so the princess has risen," he said, standing to face me. He nudged his head toward the stove. "I made bacon. Eggs should be done in a minute." He indicated the bowl of yellow liquid he had sitting by the stove. "Doesn't that sound like a jolly time?"

As long as I'd lived here, he'd never turned on the stove.

"Uh, yeah." I paused, scratching my jaw as I assessed him. "You doing okay today? Feeling any cravings?"

"Bite me." His eyes veered toward me then bounced back to the pan he stirred. "Just got the shakes. Too much vodka last night."

I ruffled his crazy sticking-up-everywhere blue hair. "Alright then, Chef Spider. I'll make the coffee."

He busied himself scrambling the eggs while I finished the coffee and scrounged around in the fridge until I found orange juice, jam, and butter.

"Want some toast?" I asked, eyeing the bread I'd picked up at the bakery a few days ago.

"Sure." He shrugged, his shoulders still thin but more filled out than when I'd first picked him up three months ago. He'd also gained some muscle, about twenty pounds of it. It was a hell of a good start, and helping him figure out which sets and reps to do for the optimal results had been good for both of us. Of course, at first, he'd dragged his feet and said he would never be a gym rat, but I'd laid down an ultimatum: if he wanted to continue wagering with me, he had to show some incentive in taking care of his body.

A few minutes later, we sat down to eat. His eggs were a little over-scrambled, the bacon greasy, and the toast barely warm, but we wolfed it down.

"Spider?"

"Yes, princess?"

"I've been thinking . . ." I said, trailing off, trying to wrap my head around exactly what was in my gut.

"Uh-oh, your face is pale. Should I pour us a drink first?"

"No," I smirked. "What do you think about me buying a house?"

Bacon fell out of his mouth. He blinked. "You're asking *me* for advice?"

"Why not? You're a homeowner. Why wouldn't I ask you?"

"I'm flattered. Here? You mean I'd have some family in London?"

"No, man. Back home where I have to finish school."

A shadow crossed his face and I sensed disappointment, but he grinned, albeit a crooked one. "Oh. Yeah. That makes sense. I mean, you do have a life, and you don't need to be taking care of me all the time."

"Dude. You've been clean of the heavy stuff for three months, and it doesn't have anything to do with me being here. You'll be fine once I'm gone and you get back on tour."

He nodded, wiping his mouth with a napkin. "I know. I know. It's just, Mum is who-knows-where with some Italian playboy and Dad's in New York—shit, you and Declan are the only family I see."

"You can always pop in and see me in Raleigh."

"Yeah." His fork poked at his eggs.

"You know I have to leave soon, right?" I said the words casually, but watched his reaction carefully.

He shrugged.

I changed the direction of the convo. "Look, you're older than me. I'd love your advice. Do you think buying a house is a good investment?"

He rubbed his hand across the black widow on his neck. "I listen to my gut when I can't decide the big stuff. What does yours say?"

I exhaled. "I'd honestly never thought about it until Declan brought it up this morning. I suck in the classroom, but I love working with my hands—and the idea of taking care of my own place, like you do here, gives me a rush."

"Sounds like you've already made up your mind."

"Yeah." Maybe I should call Declan back. "So what's on the agenda today?"

He took a sip of coffee. "Lulu called."

"Oh?" I guess they'd exchanged digits. Spider might be a smartarse, but women loved that on him. "You interested in that?"

He shook his head. "No."

"Then why bring her up?"

He shrugged. "She happened to mention they're headed out to see some sights today, and I thought we might want to tag along—you know, as tour guides."

"I need a break from Remi."

"If you're just friends, then what's wrong with hanging out?"

My lips tightened. "Nothing. Just need some space."

"You like her. A lot." A knowing grin worked his face.

"No more than I like any other girl."

"Uh-huh. Okay, that's fine. I'll text her and say we're busy."

I stood to put my plate in the dishwasher. "Good."

"By the way, don't you think you're forgetting something this morning?"

I shrugged. "No. Why?"

He chortled in glee as he held out his palm. "Oh how easily he forgets . . . pay up, mate. You officially lost a bet last night, and I want my money."

"Wanker. Whatever." I rolled my eyes, dug around in my jean pockets, found a quid and slapped it on the table.

He picked it up. Inspected it like it was a Spanish gold coin. "Fucking best day ever."

I gave him the middle finger behind my back as I wandered back to my bedroom to hop in the shower.

CHAPTER NINE

I WOKE UP around lunchtime feeling like crap. My head throbbed, my throat ached, and it looked like a family of mice had taken up in my hair. I cranked up Sia on my phone, popped a couple of Aleve that I'd packed, and showered for half an hour.

Today was about me.

And I wanted to take in London—even if I felt like death warmed over.

Because I was still breathing and that meant *something.*

After a breakfast of pastries and jam, I felt much better. Months ago, I'd set up a guided walking tour for Hartford and me, so Lulu and I kept the reservation. With other tourists, we started our pilgrimage at the iconic Big Ben and the Houses of Parliament. I gazed up at the clock I'd only seen in pictures and inhaled the warm August air. It was a beautiful day, and I felt wonderfully overwhelmed by the history around me.

Eventually we made our way past quaint shops to Westminster Abbey, the place of coronations, burials, and royal marriages, containing over seven hundred years of British history. We spent two hours there, exploring the Royal Tombs, the Nave, and the Poets'

Corner. Although Shakespeare was buried at Stratford-on-Avon, the Abbey had a statue memorial for him, and I made sure Lulu snapped a pic of me in front of it, which I promptly sent to Malcolm, who loved the Bard.

After the tour ended, we took the tube to the London Eye for a ride in one of their luxury capsules—another activity I'd arranged. We munched on chocolates and sipped wine as we circled the skyline in luxury, taking in the breathtaking views over the city. Lulu and I giggled a lot, and I wouldn't realize it until later, but I didn't think of Hartford once. But Dax—he was always in the back of my mind.

Later we stopped at a pub called Hops, a cozy place with paneling and heavy wooden booths. The air smelled like ale, cider, and fried food. Perfection. We found a table and gorged on fish, chips, and local beer in a frosty mug. My throat still ached, but the drink was heaven—cold and wet as it went down. Feeling relaxed and happy, we sat there for an hour chatting about our successful day of sightseeing.

My phone buzzed after we left the tavern.

I saw the caller and let out a long exhale. I showed the number to Lulu and she rolled her eyes and mouthed, *"Sorry."*

"Hi, Mom," I said into the receiver.

She'd called three times already.

"Darling! I've been trying for hours. How are you?" I heard the underlying anxiousness in her voice.

"Good actually."

"Oh." A pause. "Have you heard from Hartford?"

My chest squeezed. "No."

"Why don't you reach out to him, Remi? You're the one that left town."

My hand clutched the phone. *Breathe, Remi.* "How's Malcolm doing?"

She sighed. "He's fine. Look, I know you're upset, but you really should take care of this thing with Hart—"

"Sorry. I have to go. Tell Malcolm I'll see him soon."

I ended the call with her voice still in my ear.

Lulu tossed an arm around me, her eyes soft. She knew exactly how infuriating my mother could be. "What's next?"

My eyes got caught on a ritzy hair salon across the street, and I mentally calculated how much money I had. "I'm going to chop off my hair."

She grinned. "Meh. It's better than your head."

TWO AND A half hours later, my hair was minus eight inches and cut into a sharp, angled bob that barely covered my nape in the back but was longer in the front. A line of bangs covered my forehead just above my dark eyebrows.

Gone was the brown, and in its place was a rich color between copper and red.

Needless to say, it was dramatic.

I fingered one of the tresses. "I look like the magenta-throated woodstar."

Lulu arched a brow. "I have no clue what that is."

"It's a gutsy little bird from Costa Rica."

"Forget birds, girl. You look—oh my God—crazy hot, like a stripper, but classier. Like Uma Thurman in Pulp Fiction but with red hair."

I swung my head around, loving the sassy feel.

"Your mom is going to poop her pants," Lulu mused.

I grinned. "No talk of anyone from Raleigh. Come on, let's get out of here, get ready, and head to a club. I still have one more dress to ruin before this vacation is over."

She grinned, a mischievous expression on her face. "Masquerade? Dax and Spider are going after I mentioned we might go, of course."

I raised my eyebrows. *Seriously?*

She raised a finger. "I know that look, but the poor girl in you will appreciate the fact we have free drinks and admission there. Score. That's a hundred bucks easy. And I know you were attacked there and you hate the atmosphere, but at least you know the bad guys definitely won't be back. And now that you and Dax have signed a *friend contract* there shouldn't be an issue. Right?"

I sighed. "Right."

Three hours later, we walked into Masquerade after going back to the hotel to get ready. Lulu went with a silver halter dress with spiked heels that she'd worn to a frat formal last year, and I put on a cream-colored silk number with itsy bitsy spaghetti straps. The skirt was cut into thin strips that swished when I moved. Rhinestones weighted them down, and a nude-colored silk lining kept everything hidden from view. Barely. It was the shortest and sexiest dress I'd ever worn. I went braless since the bodice was thick enough to keep me covered if I got chilly. On my feet, I'd slipped on a pair of white Converse even though Lulu begged and even threatened to cry. I was adamant. There'd be no more tripping over myself.

I applied my make-up with a heavy hand, using black eyeliner, dramatic gray eye shadow, and tons of mascara. I also had carefully defined brows that Lulu had insisted on doing for me. The final touch was a pale buttercream lip-gloss that left all the attention on my hair.

Our names were actually on a list at the ticket counter. Lulu clapped excitedly at this, and even more when the guy at the front door allowed us to pick out free masks from the selection under the glass counter at the entrance. Of course, we chose the most expensive ones—velvet-soft and dramatic with feathers and sparkly jewels around the eyes. We slipped them on and giggled at each other. Lulu snapped a few selfies of us before we elbowed our way to the bar area and found two stools next to each other.

She ordered top shelf vodka martinis while I checked out the crowd, searching for Dax's broad shoulders or Spider's telltale blue hair.

"Do you see them?" I asked.

She sipped from her drink, scanning the room. "No, but Spider said they had some phone calls and errands today. I'm sure Dax is tired after getting home late last night." She turned her gaze on me, giving me a knowing look. "He's probably still pissed at you. What's your plan, girlie?"

I sighed heavily. At breakfast, I'd told her about Dax's late-night visit, the tangible sexual tension between us, and that I'd accidentally said Hartford's name at the wrong time.

"I don't know. I'm just winging it." And I was scared to death. I didn't know how to define all the feelings I had for him.

"Do you think you'll ever tell him what happened, Remi?"

I flinched. "Why would I?"

She ran her finger along the rim of her glass. "Maybe because it would make you feel better—"

"No." My voice sliced through the air.

She sighed. "He's changed. Or maybe he hasn't and he's always been nice, but we never saw it. He's cocky and thinks he's hot shit—which he is—but underneath that pretty exterior, he's a great guy."

My mouth turned down, remembering the past. The darkness.

She took my drink, sat it down with hers, and dragged me out to the dance floor. "Come on, let's stop talking. You said after the Chad thing, you wanted to dance, and I want to see it."

I groaned. Today I was feeling less *you only live once* and more *don't make a fool of yourself.*

"Just get in the middle where no one can see us," I called out over the rock-techno-classical-music mix as I followed her through a crowd of people dancing.

"All you need is some confidence. See? *He* likes it." She nudged her head at a guy next to us, whose eyes were glued to me as we passed by.

I laughed, gaining some confidence. I could do this, right? It's just wiggling around to a beat.

We found a small open area and she motioned at me to move. I nodded, slid my feet from side to side, and snapped my fingers.

"Swing your arms a little. Don't be such a robot," Lulu said, demonstrating.

Okay, okay.

Find your rhythm, Remi.

I lifted my arms and drew circles in the air with my elbows and shook my hips, something I'd seen Malcolm do when he was excited after beating me on the Xbox.

She grimaced. "No. I don't know what that was. Here try this . . . Use your hands and pretend like you're washing your hair in the shower, but in a sexy way. Move your hips slow and easy like a snake trying to hypnotize someone."

I rolled my eyes. "I am *not* doing that."

"No, watch." She dropped her shoulders and swayed, her hand caressing the sides of her scalp.

Dammit. Anything looked good on Lulu.

Fine. I moved my hips and massaged my hair with my fingertips. *Sway. Shampoo. Repeat.*

Lulu giggled.

I stopped, hands dropping. "What? Do I look stupid?"

"No, silly!" She grabbed my hands and twirled me around the dance floor like we were kids. "You're sexy as heck . . . even I'm getting turned on. It's the perfect move for you."

"Really?"

She nodded.

We danced to several songs, and soon I let loose and bounced around doing whatever. Besides, no one other than me seemed to care I was a bad dancer.

Lulu called out over the music that she was thirsty and wanted to grab some water. "Iris" by The Goo Goo Dolls came on—one of my favorites and a surprisingly slow selection by the DJ—so I waved her to go on without me.

Closing my eyes, I reached above my head and moved my arms to the beat, easing my hands down my neck and chest, touching my curves.

I imagined it was a slow and sexy striptease . . .

From behind me, steel hands settled on my hips as a male body pressed against mine and settled into sync with me.

I froze.

"Don't stop now," he whispered in my ear. "You're bloody beautiful, and I want to dance with you."

A heartbeat later, I lifted my arms again and swayed, and his fingers followed, tracing the length of my hand, my arms. Leaning my head back against his shoulder, I took note of the hard chest. His intoxicating scent.

His nose grazed my bare shoulder, and I reached behind me, my hand threading through his hair and tugging. He groaned.

The song ended, a faster one taking its place, but we ignored the beat, swaying softly against each other.

He lifted my hair and his lips touched my nape, his tongue licking the sweat from my skin.

Desire rippled over me and I shivered.

"Are you hot for me?" he asked, his voice low and intimate. As if we'd done this a million times.

"Yes," I moaned as his teeth lightly nipped at my shoulder.

His right hand left my hip so he could run his hand down my back.

He unzipped my dress inch by inch.

The music was suddenly louder, harmonizing with my thudding heartbeat.

A part of me was yelling for him to stop, while the other side was remembering how good it felt to have a man touch me. I went with it, ignoring the other voice in my head.

From behind me, he slipped one hand inside my bodice and palmed my breast, massaging, fingers plucking at my nipple.

I groaned at the heat throbbing in my body.

"Hold your dress up so it doesn't fall. Dance for me," he ordered, and I did what he said, rotating my body against his as I held on to the dress. He slipped the other hand inside my dress, both hands caressing me.

Everywhere around us people danced, caught up in the loud music. Strobe lights highlighted random faces and then jumped away. No one even glanced at us. They didn't notice us, and I felt alone with him even though I clearly wasn't. It was surreal.

It was *him*.

"You want more?" a dark voice asked. Raspy. Thick with lust.

My breath hitched. "Yes."

His hand slipped lower and teased the band on my underwear, dipping in to graze my center. Once. Twice. Then moving away. I felt the loss like a pang.

"More," I begged. "Touch me."

He cupped me firmly then, the possessiveness of his hand seeming to claim ownership. A finger slipped inside me as his voice whispered in my ear. "Do you like this?"

"Yes." I whispered, my voice shaky.

He groaned, his lips against my neck as he teased me. "Would you let me fuck you here?"

I paused, my hips freezing against him.

"Don't hesitate," he said, a dangerous edge in his voice.

I shivered, wanting more of his fingers. More of his mouth. More everything. "Yes, yes."

Then everything stopped.

He zipped my dress and twirled me around to face him.

Anger rode his face, confusing me, but I couldn't stop my eyes from taking him all in: the taut jawline like a movie star, broad shoulders big enough for me to lean on, biceps that would protect me, and that fascinating dragonfly tattoo I wanted to lick.

I sighed.

Hello, Mr. Beautiful.

Acting on pure instinct and clearly not common sense, I traced my free hand down his chest to the V at his hips. I ran my hand over his hard crotch. "Hi there, Sex Lord."

He stared at me, his eyes dark with some unreadable emotion. "Stop."

"You started this." I snaked my arms around him and sucked his neck the way he'd done my shoulder. He tasted of sweat and man, and I wanted to inhale all of him. I was flirting with danger, and this time I couldn't blame it on tequila or adrenaline or exhaustion.

I wanted to climb him like a tree.

His jaw clenched as he pulled away from me. "First off, I came out here because . . . dammit . . . you and that short-as-fuck dress, and second—*I could have been anyone behind you.* Even Chad. What were you thinking?"

"That I was going to get lucky?"

My answer didn't make him happy. He laced his fingers with mine and pulled, forcing me to follow him as he barreled his way through the throng of people on the dance floor. Well, if he'd come out here to *protect* me, then that had certainly taken a left turn.

Obviously he was ticked about something, but he'd never hurt me. Even as he pulled me through the crowd, he kept glancing back to make sure I wasn't getting dragged down.

He stopped briefly at the bar where Spider and Lulu sat deep in conversation. They glanced up when we stopped, their eyes big as Dax didn't speak to either of them but grabbed what I assumed was his Newcastle with his free hand and then headed to the back of the club.

"Just so you know, I'm only letting you yank on me like a caveman because I'm curious about what's got you in such a tizzy. Where are we going?"

"You'll see," he growled.

Okay then.

He headed down the hall toward the restrooms.

Crap. Not the stifling room with all the drunken girls.

I slowed down. "Thank you, but my bladder is fine. Plus, it's hot in there and the last time I went in, I really wanted to puke . . ."

He burst through the ladies' room door.

Three women swiveled to face us, their eyes lighting up appreciatively as they took in the handsome male at the door. He straightened athletic shoulders and grinned charmingly—although I could see it was forced.

"Ladies, sorry to bust up in here, but if you'd excuse us, I'd like to have a few moments alone with . . ." He sent me a narrowed look." . . . this girl."

They blinked. Looked around at each other.

"Uh, this is the ladies'. Why don't you take it outside?" one of them snarked as she leaned over the sink to apply more lipstick.

Dax cleared his throat. Smiled. Again. "The lead guitarist for Vital Rejects is at the bar. He has blue hair and I've told him to buy you as many drinks as you want."

"For real?" squealed Lipstick Girl. Her hands fluttered around her blonde hair. "Oh my God. I love him. He's so hot when he plays and when he got in that fight in Vegas—"

"Yes, he's the ultimate bad boy. We all know." Dax added, "By the way, that free alcohol offer ends in five seconds. Five, four, three, two . . ."

They sent us one final look and all three scurried out of the room.

As soon as the door was shut, he let my hand go, threw the deadbolt, and paced around the small room, his demeanor a little possessive and a whole lot sexy. He was like an angry lion, ready to tear into someone. I watched him, frankly fascinated by his emotional response. Why was he upset? What was going on with him?

He came to a stop, as if he'd made a decision, and stalked toward me. I backed up until I was pressed against the sinks that lined the concrete wall. Glittering eyes raked over me, and quivers of heat danced up my spine at the lingering desire I read on his face.

God. I wanted him and his domineering attitude. But it was crazy. Insane. *Hadn't I learned my lesson with him already?*

He slapped his palm against the wall, his face leaning down to mine. "Tell me you knew it was me out there."

I exhaled. So *that's* what this was about.

"As soon as you put your hands on me, I knew it was you." *Only you.* "I'd never do that with a random person, Dax. That's not me, and you should know it."

He'd been the only crazy thing I'd ever done.

Relief flickered over his face and he let out a pent-up breath.

I scowled. "You're acting like you're some kind of—I don't know—pissed-off alpha male who's marking his territory. You don't own me. We're friends—"

"Who got to second base in front of the whole damn club," he snapped.

"I was willing to give you a homerun." I bit my lip. *What about your contract, Remi? Oh, how fast you broke.*

He inhaled sharply, his eyes landing on the bodice of my dress then darting away. He took a step back from me and crossed his arms.

"What? You—you don't like my dress? Look," I said, holding up one of my feet to show him my shoes. "I wore sensible shoes so I wouldn't fall."

"Your dress is too short."

"I happen to have really long legs."

"*I know.* They've been wrapped around me several times."

Oh, he went there. I crossed my arms. Two could play at this game. "What do you want me to wear? A nun's habit?"

Something—a memory—passed over his face, and his gaze softened. "I don't know—just dress like you do at Whitman."

I gaped. "Since when do you pay attention to what I wear?"

He raked his eyes over me. "More than I should. Those tight pants you wear that hug your arse, the little white sweater you like when it's cool outside . . . and your pearls. I've thought about those pearls . . . what I'd like to do with them."

My stomach fluttered. *My pearls?* "And my hair? You don't like it either?"

He closed his eyes briefly. Swallowed. "I love your wild hair, but now I can't . . . *dammit* . . . this is all wrong. It's—it's been a totally weird day. As soon as Spider cooked breakfast, I should have known it was wonky. Hell, as soon as I saw you here that night, I should have known fate was screwing with me." He raked a hand through his hair, frustration evident.

"What else happened today?" I put my hand on his shoulder, leftover anger vanishing.

He leaned into me.

"It's a long story, but Declan mentioned a house for sale in Raleigh. I thought about it and spent most of the day on the phone talking with Father and Declan to work out details. I may buy it. It's impulsive as hell, but it's such a good deal that I'm afraid to wait until I get home, plus school will have started by then."

"I hope it works out for you." I squeezed his bicep.

He flicked his eyes over me. "Then, Spider told me you guys were coming here tonight, and all I could think about was Chad, and what if *he* was here too. I had to come. Shit." He exhaled. "Every guy out there was eye-fucking you, and I was just as bad. Dammit, I didn't mean to go that far when we were dancing . . ."

Our dancing had gone too far. As soon as he'd touched me, I'd been ready to throw caution to the wind.

I sighed. "It takes two to tango. It's my fault too. Let's blame the sexy dancing on the dress or the music or martinis or whatever." I sucked in a breath. "But we *can* be friends. We have our contract. I want to be close to you like that."

He lifted his face, soft gray eyes searching mine. "Christ, me too."

I smiled tentatively, and he cupped my face and ran his thumb across my bottom lip.

"Friends," I said with a slight shake in my voice.

He nodded and let his hand fall to his side.

CHAPTER TEN

AFTER THE DANCE-FLOOR fiasco, the four of us spent the rest of our time at Masquerade upstairs in the booths. The air had been cleared between Remi and me, and I felt okay about it. *Somewhat.*

I felt much better when Spider handed over his leather jacket and she wrapped it around her waist. Good thing the rocker wore leather in the summer.

She and Lulu sat across from us, giggling and telling stories about Remi's propensity for accidents and Lulu growing up in the music industry in Nashville. I asked questions, storing away nuggets of information about Remi. Spider sat back and watched, more interested in slinging back vodka than chatting. Knowing him, he was concocting some sort of bet in his head.

"When I first met Remi in the dorm room, she tripped over a stack of books and landed face first in the trashcan," Lulu said, laughing.

Remi grinned and rolled her eyes. "Please. I've been accident-free for at least a day."

I smiled, studying her over the top of my beer bottle. My hand curled in my seat, imagining wrapping my fingers around that copper hair, tugging her hair back, and kissing her until she begged me to . . .

Whoa. Slow your roll there, Romeo.

You just re-committed to being friends. Make it last this time, arsehole.

I caught her glancing at me too, an easiness in her eyes that said she trusted me.

Trusted. Me.

I sighed. I had to keep my thoughts and my hands to myself.

Around midnight, we walked outside together and found a cab for the girls. Spider and I headed back to the flat, and Remi called me when she got to her hotel room. I made her walk through the entire place as I listened.

Was I overly paranoid about her attacker?

Maybe.

My fists clenched every time I pictured her under that arsehole. Her bruises may have been covered with make-up, but I fucking *knew* they were there, and it drove me crazy.

We talked on the phone for two hours. We both put the speaker on as we changed for bed, brushed our teeth and flossed. Later, we crawled in our beds and talked about everything. Movies. Books. Life.

I lay spread-eagle on top of my white duvet as she opened up and told me about her brother Malcolm, who was autistic. And then later, I told her about the letter my mum had written me.

"Is the dragonfly for your mom?" she asked.

"Yes."

"What does it mean?"

I exhaled. I was diving into deep waters. "A dragonfly showed up the day of her funeral and followed our car when we left. I was leaving my home, my friends, everything. Declan and I—we felt like it was her that day, and that was before we'd even read her letter. She'd always had a fascination for them, tons of charms and notepads and necklaces. My brother has a smaller tattoo of a dragonfly on his neck. I never realized I wanted one until this summer."

"A lot of things have changed this summer. Hartford and I are over. You and I are friends." She sighed. "Who would have thought that?"

Yeah.

A bit later, I was in the middle of telling her a story from my childhood, when I heard her snore.

"Remi?"

Silence.

"*Hello?* Wake up, sleepyhead."

All I got was heavy breathing.

I grinned. And I don't even know why the sound of her sleeping made me happy, but it did.

"Goodnight, love," I whispered and ended the call.

The next day, I FaceTimed Declan to talk more about the house. With me on the phone, he drove over to the place and walked through it room by room. It was an older craftsman-style home; the kitchen needed renovating, but the hardwood flooring was intact and only needed a good buffing. I took a big breath and decided to go for it. I called Father, who was thrilled, and he offered to help speed up the buying process with his lawyers. I accepted.

Because the house had been on the market for a while, we were able to get the seller to agree to a meeting in three days—which meant I'd need to leave London in two.

I got online, reserved my ticket, and wham, bam, I was jumping right into being a real adult.

"YOUR TATTOO SHOP used to be an old medieval church?" Remi asked as we entered the vestibule of the Friar's Church Tattoo Shop. She took in the stained-glass windows and arching buttresses. "The architecture is amazing."

I was leaving London the day after tomorrow, and I wanted to spend my last full day with Spider, Remi, and Lulu. So after handling the house details with Declan, I'd called the girls and offered to take

Remi to see a few sights, and then to get the tattoo she'd mentioned a few times during our phone conversation the night before.

I smiled at her enthusiasm. "It's been completely rebuilt except for a few of the original stones on the foundation. Friar Laurence replicated every single detail that he could find about the original building, down to the lion and lamb stained-glass windows . . . and now it's the best place in London to get ink. I wouldn't go anywhere else. Besides, you have to see the sanctuary." I motioned toward the heavy, wooden double doors.

Remi came to a halt, giving me a quizzical look. "You love this place?"

"Yeah, why?"

"What is it? The building itself or the fact that it's a tattoo shop?"

I thought about it. "Both appeal to me."

"What if you had your own Friar's Church in Raleigh?"

"You think *I* could open one in Raleigh? Me?" I laughed.

She smiled. "Dude, you're going to be a homeowner. Paid in full. You can do *anything* you want." She paused, her hand on my arm. "You're an amazing person, Dax. Don't let anyone ever tell you otherwise."

"Wait, did I hear you say 'Friar'?" Lulu said, her face scrunched up.

I nodded. "The owner and employees dress like monks, so don't get frisky with the help, Lulu."

She rolled her eyes. "I don't go for men in dresses."

We walked into the sanctuary where all the action was. On one side stood several artists at their individual stations, wearing floor-length brown robes tied with a piece of rope. On the other was a large seating area, a library of books with art designs, and a small bar.

Remi's eyes were wide, taking it all in, from the gold chandeliers and candelabras that lined the wall to the brown stone floor. "I feel like I'm in a play. Or lost in time."

Dressed in his robe, the reception friar greeted us and led us over to a circular seating area with heavy wooden chairs and musty bookshelves. The shop also had a small bar in the back, and that's where Spider headed. Remi and Lulu busied themselves getting comfy and browsing through the tattoo books.

Friar Laurence, a rotund balding man in his forties, came over a few minutes later and seemed glad that Spider and I had come back and brought new customers. After the introductions were made, we told him that Remi would be getting her first tattoo.

He nodded, a pleasant smile on his face. "Sure. We've got a few stations opening in the next hour or so."

Remi nodded, a torn expression on her face.

"Hey. You scared?" I asked.

"No, I can handle the pain—I was thinking about what Hartford would think . . ." Her voice trailed off.

"Who gives a shit what he thinks? He doesn't deserve you," I snapped.

Startled blue eyes studied my face. "That sounds like more than just a frat rivalry. You really don't like him, do you?"

My lips tightened, but I reined my anger in. "He's tolerable."

Hated that fucker for what he did to Remi.

"Oh, for God's sake, will you two just screw already? This back and forth is giving me a headache," Lulu said as she walked over to join us from her seat, obviously having overheard our conversation.

She snorted. "God, just joking, guys. You can both close your mouths now." A sigh came from her. "Anyway, my head is seriously pounding, so I'm going to head back to the hotel."

"I'll go with you. We can take the tube and leave you guys the car," Spider chimed in, coming back to join us carrying a drink in his hand. He tipped it up. "You good with that?"

Me and Remi alone?

Keep it in your pants, Sex Lord.

Of course, we tried to talk them into staying, but it had been a long day of showing them the sights in London, and neither of them wanted a tattoo.

After they left, we grabbed the rest of Remi's tequila from

Spider's Mercedes in the car park and headed back to the tattoo shop. Along the way, the rumbling of thunder reached our ears. I looked up at the darkening sky and grinned at Remi. "You ready for a surprise London shower?"

She nodded.

Rain fell softly at first, just a drop here and there, but in seconds it was pouring.

"Hop on," I said, bending down so she could reach my shoulders.

Giggling as she clutched the tequila, she climbed on piggyback style. I hiked her up further, hooking her thighs up with my hands and holding on.

"I hope you know what you're doing!" she called over the downpour.

I took off at a fast walking pace toward the church, dodging sudden puddles and a few cars as I weaved through traffic.

We reached the building and entered the vestibule, where I sat her down on the marble tile to dry out before we went inside the sanctuary.

"That was incredible, the best thing I've done in London," she said, pushing wet hair off her face. "I thought you might drop me though. I'm no lightweight."

My eyes roved over her, lingering on her full breasts, skating down to the curves of her hips. Perfection. My gaze ended on her wet lips.

Stop it, Dax.

"Wait a minute . . ." She did a complete circle in the small area. "It just dawned on me that the owner's name is *Friar Laurence*." She giggled. "Holy Shakespeare, it's like *Romeo and Juliet.*"

"Not following," I said, brushing water off my forearms.

"Don't you see? Romeo and Juliet fell in love at a masquerade party and were married the next day in secret by a *Friar Laurence*—in an old church. Of course it was set in Verona, but still . . . weird, right?"

An idea struck and I ran with it. Grinning, I hooked my arm

through hers. "Let's get married here then. Right now. You get your wedding fix, and I get to tell Spider we got hitched and watch him piss his pants."

"What?" Her face whitened.

"As a joke, Remi."

"Oh." She blinked. "Yeah, of course. Sure."

"Dammit. We need rings though," I said, thinking, my eyes going around the vestibule entry. There was nothing here to use. I pulled out my wallet and fingered a fiver. "I can fold a couple of these and make them?"

Her lips twitched. "I have a couple of hair ties in my bag. Let's use those."

She pulled out a wad of colored rubber bands, and between us we selected our "rings." I picked out the brown one and she picked a blue one, wrapping them around our respective index fingers to make them smaller.

I bent down on one knee and held up the "sapphire ring."

"Remi, will you be my good lady wife?"

A slow blush started at her neck and covered her face. She bit her lip.

"Don't you fancy me, love?" I clutched my heart, using all the dramatic acting skill I possessed, which wasn't much. "Am I not enough for you?"

She barked out a laugh and then sobered. "Since the moment we met," she said softly, her eyes darker than usual, an indigo-blue.

I rolled my eyes. "Good one." She smiled. "Will you marry me?"

"Yes," she murmured.

I slid the band on her finger and stood. She stared down at it, her brows drawn in and lines around her eyes.

My shoulders slumped. "Remi? Shit, I'm sorry. We can stop if this isn't fun—"

She swallowed. "No, no. Just give me a minute."

"Are you thinking about Hartford?" I asked. "I'm being insensitive. Of course—"

"No, I'm not actually." She looked from the ring to me, a thoughtful expression on her face. Our eyes locked, and she smiled tentatively, seeming to come to a decision. "Come on, my new fiancé, we just got engaged. Let's go talk to the friar."

I grabbed the tequila from the floor where I'd set it when we came inside, and we headed back inside the sanctuary.

CHAPTER ELEVEN

Remi

MY HEART CLENCHED when Dax got on one knee and for half a second, it had felt *real.*

But it wasn't.

Girls were a game to Dax, and I had to keep that front and center.

We went inside the sanctuary and found Friar Laurence. He grinned as Dax explained what we wanted, and he was more than happy to fake-wed us. Apparently it wasn't the strangest thing he'd been asked to do inside the shop.

We gathered next to one of the tattoo stations, and with the sounds of machines running and a girl screaming over getting her nipple pierced, we prepared to exchange vows.

Not exactly the First United Methodist Church of Raleigh.

I slipped the "topaz" band on Dax's finger. My eyes met his.

"I need some vows to really get into this," he said with a wicked grin. "You go first."

I laughed, surprisingly willing to go along with his carefree attitude. Dax had always had the uncanny ability to make me feel easy about almost anything—except breaking my heart.

"Fine. I take you, Dax, my friend, as my pretend-husband. I promise to drink tequila with you forever, but if you need me, I will write goals for you, make spreadsheets, flowcharts, and contracts." I grinned. "If you insist, I will also eat with you at Panera."

He considered me, his eyes the color of morning mist.

"Well?"

He cleared his throat, a suddenly serious expression on his face as he slid the blue band on my finger. "Dearest Remi, I take you as my pretend-wife. I promise to be your protector and never leave the toilet seat up. I'll kill all the spiders, and I'll attempt to not freak out when you compare my body parts to birds or make me sign contracts." He sent me a heated look. "I promise to cherish you until my last breath."

My mouth parted. I exhaled.

Give that boy an Academy Award.

"I now pronounce you man and wife," Friar Laurence said with a solemnity that made me nervous.

"Wait. This isn't real is it?" I asked the monk.

He chuckled and shrugged. "I *am* an ordained minister."

"He's teasing," Dax said, pulling my attention back to him.

Oh.

"Now what?" I asked, looking from the Friar and back to Dax. "Don't we kiss or something?"

The Friar smiled, eyeing us both dubiously. "Do whatever you want. I've done my job here, and I have a client waiting." He pointed to another station where a lanky guy was busy tattooing a customer. "That's Zack. He'll be doing your art today in about an hour. Just go on over when you're ready."

He walked away, and we turned back toward each other.

Dax took my hand and laced our fingers together.

Were we going to kiss?

My eyes went to his mouth, taking in the plump curve of his sculpted lower lip, the indentation.

"You're looking at me like you want to kiss me," he said with a naughty chuckle.

"Maybe. It *is* the final step in a marriage ceremony."

"Just don't fall back in love with me," he teased.

"*Pffft*—who said I ever did? Plus, I'll think of England the entire time."

"You'll think only about me because I kiss that good."

"You're a cocky bastard," I said, smiling.

Another chuckle. "True. Do we need to tear up our contract?"

I thought about it. Shrugged. "No. This is pretend."

A knowing gleam lit his eyes. "Admit it, I'm irresistible."

"You're something."

But the back and forth banter stopped when he tilted my chin up, his eyes low as they landed on my mouth. Air, textured and heavy, settled over us.

"I'm going all in, Remi."

What?

I yanked my chin away. "What does that even mean? This is supposed to be a *pretend* kiss, but you just said *you're all in*, and the Dax I know is never all in. He's casually indifferent to women, a player who goes through women like . . . like a bird goes through worms. You're a man-slut."

"You mean man-whore?"

"I like you too much to use that word."

"Indeed," he murmured, biting his lip. "I like you too, angel."

My heart ached, and I dipped my eyes so he couldn't see how devastated I was by his nonchalant endearment. He didn't mean it. Not really. He called lots of girls *angel*. I'd heard him.

All the old feelings and darkness I'd struggled with for three years came roaring to the forefront of my mind, and I took a step back.

"I—I can't kiss you," I breathed, my hands fisting.

"It's easy. You pucker up and it's done. I don't see the problem. We've done it a thousand times," he added, pulling me back against him. "Kiss me, Remi."

I shivered, feeling our undeniable pull. "You make me so crazy, I want to scream."

"Hallelujah?"

I shook my head. "No. I'm—I'm scared."

Scared he would bury my heart alive and walk away. Again.

"Kiss me. Please."

My breath caught at the way he begged me. "We can just tell them we did."

A long exhale came out. "*Goddammit*, Remi, just kiss me." His voice was hoarse, his need apparent.

My mouth parted and his crashed down, fusing with mine. Our tongues met and I attempted to keep it light, but he didn't allow it, his hands digging into my scalp as he groaned and deepened the pressure. Heat licked up my spine.

God. I pulled back.

"Let go, Remi," he whispered. "Feel what's between us. Just one kiss. I promise."

But . . .

It wouldn't be just one.

The smell of him, like summer rain and sunshine, hit me, and my arms curled around his hips, my fingers slipping under his shirt and digging into the muscles of his back.

He kissed me, owning my lips with lust and passion, and slowly, ever so softly, I went down the rabbit hole with him, where the entire world whispered *yes, him.*

He pulled back too soon, and my lips chased after his; I whimpered until he kissed me again, shorter ones, slowing us down. His hands bunched in my hair and he tugged, making me gasp.

"This is crazy," he breathed. "I—I don't want to hurt you, but I can't stop myself . . ."

My heart fluttered like moth wings, papery and breathless as if I might disintegrate. "Dax." I swallowed. "This feels . . ."

"Good?"

"Yes."

"Is it the best kiss you ever had?" His tongue licked my upper lip. Lightning bolts of heat struck my body.

A reluctant moan came from me. "Yes . . ."

"I won't let him have you," he murmured.

I didn't have to ask who *him* was.

His lips captured mine again. Demanding. Pillaging.

My entire body thundered with need. I wanted him more than donuts and birds—more than I'd wanted Hartford. I wanted him to take me hard and fast, then slow and soft. I wanted to tell him the burden I carried, the horrible thing I'd kept from him.

He. Will. Destroy. You.

I snapped away from his hold and rubbed my arms, trying to make them warm at the sudden chill.

He watched me as I snatched the bottle of tequila, twisted open the cap, and took a giant swig. I passed it over to him with numb fingers. "Drink."

He grabbed the bottle and took a swig, wiping his face with his hand. "If that's what you want—but it's not. You want *me*."

Stop!

"Don't—don't make this hard for me," I said.

He cracked his neck. Exhaled. Emotion spread over his face, but to define it would have been impossible. Where his eyes had once been soft with heat, they were hard. "Fine. What do you want to do?"

"Right now? I want a tattoo. What comes after that is still up in the air."

He took another sip. "Alright, let's bloody well do this then," he muttered and led the way to the right side of the church where the tattoo stations were.

BLARING SUNLIGHT FROM between the blinds of my hotel window was the first thing I noticed as I cracked my eyes open.

The second was the jackhammer going to town inside my head. *No more tequila. Ever,* I swore to myself.

I groaned, flipped over to my other side away from the sun, and closed my eyes. It was too early to get up.

But . . .

A niggling started in my brain.

My eyes popped open, and I warily studied the hotel nightstand, the pile of clothes on the floor, my shoes. All seemed well—until a muscled forearm curved around my waist and hugged my hip.

Holy British Shenanigans. What had happened last night?

First fact: I was naked.

Second fact: So was the person behind me.

Third fact: My eyes went back to the nightstand. *No condoms.* My entire body froze.

A loud snore came from the other pillow. With a quick turn of my head, I peeked over my shoulder and made out dark hair against white hotel sheets.

Of course it was Dax. He was the last person I remember seeing.

And then it dawned. *Dax Blay was naked in my bed!*

My hands shook. Okay, okay, I can handle this. Just work through the night. Figure out where you went ape-shit and had sex with the one person you said you'd never sleep with again.

Tequila. Check.

Running through the rain. Check.

Some talk about Romeo and Juliet. A pretend wedding at the church. Check, check.

Okay, so far so good . . .

Tattoo-time. We looked at some designs and drank. Yes, I sat down in the chair to get my ink and . . . the memories blurred together.

More tequila.

Holding hands with Dax.

Giggling at my tattoo.

Cab ride back to the hotel, clothes falling off me then him . . .

Nothing.

With tentative fingers, I propped myself up on my pillow and slowly peeled back the white gauze bandage on my chest. I gasped. A heart-shaped red, white, and blue Union Jack flag about the size of a half-a-dollar coin sat above my breast. *DAX* was written in black ink across the middle. I must have read it wrong—*why on earth would I get Dax's name on my body?*

I read it again. Shit. Maybe it was one of those rub-on deals?

I scratched at the tender skin around the area. "Ouch," I whimpered as my fingers grazed the reddened skin.

My mouth dried. This wasn't a dream.

I'd been branded.

I inhaled a great gulp of air and turned to the sleeping head next to me. "Dax!"

"What—what is it?" Dax said sleepily, both eyes opening, his long black lashes fluttering. And that got me riled up too. Why were his lashes prettier and more extravagant than mine? Ugh. He stirred around on the bed and gazed at me, hair falling around his handsome face. I noticed a small crease on his cheek from the pillow, and I forced my hands to stay clenched and not reach out to trace it. Carnal lips tilted up in a knowing smile; a smile that screamed *we just had sex.* "Morning, love. Sleep well?"

I slapped his leg with my pillow. "First off, you have no right to look this good in the morning, and second *why did you let me get a Union Jack on my boob?*"

"I didn't *let* you do anything." He rubbed his temples and winced. "Damn. It's too early for a pillow fight. I need water and a hot shower first." His eyes traced the crest of my boobs under the sheet. "Wanna join me, *wifey?*"

"Don't call me that," I said, covering myself better. "We need to talk about the sex we had that I don't remember."

"You don't remember?" He sucked his bottom lip between his teeth. "Now that is a bloody shame." He crossed his arms behind his head and considered me, amusement on his face. "You weren't this much of a grouch in the mornings the last time we slept together."

I scowled. "That was three years ago. Things change. Just tell me what happened."

He smirked and took his sweet time, sitting up slowly, fluffing his pillow and propping himself against the headboard.

He was torturing me. *On purpose.*

Finally, he found a good spot and his eyes found mine, but they weren't happy. "Would you be upset if we shagged?"

"*Yes.*"

His face tightened, a shadow in his eyes. "Fine. We didn't."

Oh. I felt deflated, as if all the energy had fled from the room.

"Besides, don't you think you'd remember a night with me?"

"So you slept next to me all night without trying to have sex? While we were both naked?"

His lips flattened. "I'm not like that, Remi. And you took off my clothes, not the other way around."

What?

"Yes. You insisted we sleep skin-to-skin."

My face flamed. What had gotten into me?

Come on, Remi. You can't be too *surprised.* He's your drug of choice. Always.

I shoved those thoughts away.

"You do that often?" I sputtered. "Sleep with a girl and not have sex?"

"Never," he said curtly. "You're the first. You should feel special."

"I don't," I snapped. "I feel confused." And disappointed?

Scooting over to his side of the bed, he stood, the pristine sheets sliding away from his tan skin revealing hard muscles in his back and an ass so magnificent that someone should definitely write a sonnet for it. "Ode to Dax's Butt" would work.

He walked around the foot of the bed, and my eyes flitted over his chest, down to the six-pack and the deep V at his hips—which led my eyes to his . . . his shaft as it grew right in front of me.

"I see you noticed Mr. Argentine Duck is awake."

I flicked my eyes up to his and held them there. *Don't look down.* "He appears quite happy."

He shrugged. "Morning wood. Happens to everyone. Don't take it personally."

"Thanks," I snipped back. "I don't need reminders that you get hard for all girls."

"No problem." A muscle clenched in his jaw.

Why was *he* so ticked?

For the first time, I noticed the patch of white on his chest. "Your tattoo. Let me see what you got." It was much bigger than mine.

He peeled back the gauze until the hand-sized design above his chest was clearly visible.

"What's that?" I squinted.

He stared down at his chest. "Looks like an American flag and an eagle with your name on it. Since you don't recall, we got matching tattoos—or *friendship ink* as you called it. It was your idea, and judging by the horror on your face, you regret it."

My mouth opened. "I haven't had time to process it!" I groaned and flopped back against the pillows. "I mean how am I going to explain your name on my body to people?"

He looked at his nails, completely unconcerned about my distress. "I don't see the problem, love. Most girls would love to have my name on their body."

I trembled with banked anger. "The problem is you're Dax and I'm me! We don't go together."

His face darkened, and I almost thought I saw hurt there. No, that couldn't be right.

His chest swelled as he took a breath. "Fine. Tell them you were drunk and it was an impulse. That'd be the truth, right?" He pivoted away from me, strode over to the window, and pulled the blinds open. I blinked as he dropped down and started doing push-ups, his clipped voice counting out a fast one hundred.

Of course, I watched. Because I'm clearly still drunk. Not really, but I felt woozy just being naked and this close to him.

With his sculpted muscles executing an effortless athleticism, he rose up and down from the floor, the tendons in his arms and shoulders bulging.

I tore my eyes away.

I should be mad at him for acting so surly—but I wasn't. Maybe it was because his one-eyed monster was rock hard and seemed to be looking right at *me*.

He stood back up, and then as if he'd had enough of me, he stalked into the bathroom and shut the door.

Well.

His moodiness was worse than a teenage girl on her period, but right now I couldn't worry about him.

I needed clothes!

Jumping out of bed, I ran to the closet and pulled out a white peasant top with lace at the hem and a pair of cropped red pencil pants. Because of the tattoo, I went braless.

Next stop was the mirror. I let out a gasp. Holy morning of shame, my hair was a bush on one side and flat on the other. Globs of leftover mascara and black eyeliner smudged the skin under my eyes. Groaning, I pulled a brush out of my make-up bag and went to work on the tangles.

Crap!

I should have never drunk tequila!

I should have never gotten a tattoo!

But at least you didn't have unprotected sex!

I snorted.

My phone rang. Rummaging through the mess I'd dumped out on the bed from my bag, I snatched it up and answered.

"What?" I bit out.

"Remington?" A familiar male voice came through the speaker.

The room spun. Only one person used my God-given name.

"Hartford?" My hand clutched the phone like a lifeline.

A beat of silence. "Yeah," his deep voice said, and I heard flapping in the background as if he were outside and it was windy. I imagined him in Raleigh, finishing up his morning run and walking back to the apartment.

Leftover anger bubbled to the surface, but I kept my voice even. "What do you want?"

"To see you." A long sigh. "Look . . . I'm sorry."

Elation surged. My eyes closed in relief.

He wanted to see me. He was sorry.

I bit my lip to keep a shrill laugh from escaping.

"Remington? Are you there?"

"Yes, I'm here." I paused. "What—what are you sorry for?"

"I don't know. Everything, I guess."

He didn't know?

My free hand gripped the edge of the nightstand.

"Remington? Are you there?"

I inhaled a deep breath. "I'm here. Are—are you sorry for the wedding dress I'll never wear? For the gifts I returned? The emails and phone calls I had to make? *For hurting me?*"

"Remington—"

"You know what? Stay on your break. Tell your *study buddy* I said hello, and *fuck off*." I hit the end button.

Tears threatened my eyes and I pushed them down. *Don't cry. Don't cry.*

"Remi?" Dax had come out of the bathroom, a towel wrapped around his middle. His hair was wet from a shower and rivulets of water traced down his chest to his hips. His forehead furrowed as he raked his eyes over me. There must have been something telling in my expression because in three quick strides he stood in front of me. "Who was on the phone?"

I rubbed my face. "Hartford," I croaked, trying not to break.

He exhaled, sat down on the bed next to me, and gave me a gentle shoulder hug. "Shit. I'm sorry. Are you okay? Do you want to talk about it? I know I joke around a lot, but people tell me I'm good to talk to."

I looked at the phone and then back at him. I did want to talk, and somehow I knew Dax would keep whatever I said between us. "Our relationship was so easy, you know? He never cheated or even glanced at another girl, and I'm sure he could have. He wanted *me*, and I thought he wanted me forever, but . . ." I twisted my wrist, aching for my bracelet. "It's just . . . after my dad died, I wanted someone like him. I even had a list. I wanted someone kind. Responsible. Smart. Someone who'd help me take care of Malcolm someday and wouldn't mind that he was part of the package. But sometimes . . . I think I miss the idea of Hartford more than *him*."

He brushed a strand of hair out of my eyes. "Do you love Hartford?"

I closed my eyes. "I do, but we were so perfect, and maybe this is weird, but part of me wonders if maybe true love or soul-mate love isn't perfect or easy at all, but dirty and hard and crazy." I sucked in air. "I don't know. I'm confused and angry—yet I want to see him."

He tilted my chin up, his eyes meeting mine. Compassion mixed with something else I couldn't define—sadness?—crossed his face. "I'm here for you, whatever you need. I—I've never been in love, but I can see you're hurting, and it makes me . . ." He stopped.

"What?" I asked.

He exhaled, his face tight. "I just don't like seeing you upset. If he were here right now, I'd beat the bloody shit out him."

I studied him, taking in the banked anger he was obviously keeping on a leash for my benefit. I pushed out a smile. "I believe you, and thank you for the sentiment, but he's a battle I need to fight on my own."

He reached over and touched the hair tie that was still on my finger. "You're the kind of girl who will never be alone for long. You're too beautiful and the best kisser I know."

"I'm not beautiful."

"Indeed, you are." His voice rang with sincerity. "I thought so the moment you walked into my Tau party with your sweater all buttoned up. There's something about you I don't see in other girls."

My mouth parted. "Like what?"

"Balls. You lost your dad, and somehow, it made you stronger."

Something inside me cracked—or shifted. I looked into his stormy gray eyes and saw understanding staring back at me. And desire.

Maybe it was finally talking to Hartford after weeks of silence, maybe it was the fact I had another man's name on my heart, or maybe it was simply the fact that he *got* me.

But suddenly I wanted to forget about Hartford, and the only way to do that was to have throw-down hard sex with the one guy I'd never been able to get out of my head.

CHAPTER TWELVE

I STOOD FROM the bed and faced him, causing him to start at my abrupt movement. "You have too many clothes on," I said and pulled the towel off from around his hips.

He inhaled as I stared down at him, his erect cock like a lead pipe as it rested on his thigh. Hard. Thick.

I lifted my eyes to meet his molten gaze. His chest rose. Up. Down. Lust shot through me. "You've been hard for me all morning."

"Remi?" he breathed, biting his lip. "Don't—"

I put my hands over his mouth and went to my knees in front of him. "Shhh. I—I just want to . . ." I swallowed, struggling to find the words. "I—I want you to rip me apart then stitch me back together."

He sucked in a shuddering breath. "Think hard about this, Remi, because I can't tell you no."

"I have. A million times."

I traced my hand down his chest slowly, easing over his defined pecs and abs. His body was perfection, tan and smooth.

He groaned at my touch, his head going back, his entire body tightening in anticipation of what he could clearly read in my eyes. I wanted him. I wanted him fiercely, with the kind of passion I believed few people ever experienced.

I bent over, took him in my mouth and sucked, sliding my tongue over his long shaft from base to tip. My hand snaked around his hardness and tugged as I devoured him.

"*Fucckkk.*" His hands went to my hair and clutched.

I pumped his velvet skin as I took as much of him as I could.

He breathed my name and maneuvered my head, silently telling me what he wanted.

But I already knew. I'd never forgotten.

My mouth explored him, tasted him, finding places I remembered, mapping out new ones.

He tried to pull me up. "Remi," he said hoarsely.

I raised my face to him. "You want me to stop?"

His chest rose. "No. I—I can't breathe. I—what are you doing to me?"

"What I've wanted since the night I kissed you at Masquerade."

He slid his thumb across my lips. "This will change things. I don't know how it will end. I can't promise you anything. This is all I can give you."

I nodded.

I wanted the forbidden fruit, even if it was for just one time.

He pulled me to my feet, cupped my face. "But I don't want you on your knees for me—not this time. *I want you.*"

Getting his meaning, I stood up, unzipped my pants and let them fall to the floor. With shaky hands, I lifted my blouse over my head. My panties were next as I slipped them past my ankles and tossed them on the floor. With his eyes burning into my skin, I walked over to the wardrobe and pulled out my strand of pearls and looped them around my neck. Long and creamy, they hung past the V between my breasts.

"You like?" I asked softly, turning to face him as I threaded them through my fingers.

He came toward me, a majestic male, his heated gaze never leaving mine. "I do."

"Want me to put one of my little cardigans on?" I smiled

impishly.

His eyes went low and heavy. "No. I want you just like that."

"Wait," I said.

He halted, teeth snapping together. "Don't tease me."

"I'm not. It's just . . . the contract. Let's say no kissing on the mouth—and we can still be friends, right?" I paused, nibbling on my bottom lip. "Your friendship is important to me, Dax."

He'd reached me by then, and his hand curled around my neck, careful of the bruises there. "You could say anything right now and I'd agree to it." Grazing his nose up my neck to my ear, he whispered, "And you better hang on the first time."

My body clenched at *first time*.

He eased between my legs and hoisted me up by my bottom to straddle him, biceps bulging as his hands palmed my ass. My limbs wrapped around his hips as he pivoted us around and eased me down on the edge of the bed.

He pushed my arms out to their sides and pinned them there gently but with the touch of a warrior. My chest rose. Waiting. Anticipating him.

"You like control?" I whispered, angling my chin up at him, spurring him on with a defiant look, knowing he liked the resistance.

"You complaining?" His eyes caressed my lips and I bit down with my top teeth, knowing his fascination with them.

"Never."

As he lowered his head toward mine, I thought he was going to kiss me, but he veered down, capturing my nipple with his mouth.

One touch and I yelled out, my body arching up to him. *Yes!*

His tongue toyed with my breasts, moving from one to the other, even as his hands kept mine imprisoned. In the back of my mind, I told myself that this had always been inevitable since the moment we'd kissed at the club. This was fate, weaving her tapestry, making us part of her intricate plan.

Being careful of my tattoo, he swept his jaw across my chest to my hipbone, his nose running over every inch. Just when I thought he'd forgotten my breasts, he came back and licked. Bit. Nibbled.

Teased.

I groaned, muttering. This was torture.

I wanted it fast. *Hard.* And then I wanted it again. And again.

"Say my name," he said, his mouth on my shoulder, kissing down my arm, sending heated tingles everywhere.

"Dax, Dax, Dax."

He grunted, his lips on my wrist, kissing the place where my bracelet had been. Turning my head, I watched him kiss my palm softly.

No, wait.

I struggled to get out of his grasp, and his eyes found mine.

"Don't be . . . don't be sweet," I said.

He closed his eyes, as if to shield something. Nodded. "Right."

He let my arms go and they clawed at him, pulling him down and crushing our bodies together. Nails raked down his back. I massaged the muscles that had grown since I'd last touched him like this.

He went to his knees, placed my legs over his shoulder, and kissed down my chest. As sunlight streamed in the room, he laved my skin with his tongue, eyes watching my face.

He tongued my hip, outlining my birthmark and kissing it. I screamed when he finally put his mouth on my core, my body bucking. Wet kisses and long licks. Soft touches. Pulsing over my skin. I moaned loudly, embarrassing myself. I stifled my voice with my fist.

Warmth built in my spine, sending electricity through every atom. Goosebumps rose. The hair on the back of my neck vibrated as I rushed to the edge of something wonderful.

"Say my name when you hit it." His voice was dark, almost tortured, and I sensed the control he was keeping.

His finger slipped inside, sliding, curling over the bundle of nerves in my G-spot. He sucked my clit, leaving no part of me untouched, and I rose up to watch him, my heart in my throat, as his hand grabbed my hip to get me closer.

Closer. Closer.

His eyes locked with mine and . . .

Boom. Sparks flew in a million directions when I came, gasping his name, my body clamping around his fingers.

Out of nowhere, unshed tears burned in my throat, regret and lust fighting in my head.

Why had he never wanted me the way I'd wanted him? When we had *this?*

It wasn't just sex between us. I knew it, and I suspected he did too.

But it wasn't enough for him to pick *me.*

Pushing those intruding thoughts away, I lay back, my body spent and legs quivering.

He stood, broad shoulders heaving, his expression off. A pulse throbbed at his temple. He looked dangerous. Bitter. And hot as hell.

Together we were a fucking mess of feelings.

He stalked over to his jeans on the floor, picked out his wallet, and pulled out a square package. Snapping it open with his teeth, he got the condom out and slid it on his straining length.

I groaned, desire roaring back. Flooding me.

He strode back to me. Silent.

Yet saying everything with his hungry eyes.

"I want you more than I've ever wanted any girl in my entire life," he said harshly, looking down at me on the bed.

"You sound angry about it," I said as I rose up to my knees and touched his shoulder, tracing down his chest, passing my name over his heart.

He shuddered, his entire body vibrating. "Remi. It's been so long . . ."

Since he'd had sex? Or since he'd had me?

I kissed his nipple and sucked hard, my hand moving to his shaft. He grunted and tossed his head back, maneuvering to give me a better grasp. I stroked him, pumping. I loved seeing him like this. He was a total Tau, a conqueror, but I could make him weak at my touch. Ready to break at any moment.

Need clawed at me, scratching to get out. "I want to see you come undone for me," I said.

His eyes zoomed in on me. "Tell me something, do I make you

come harder than Hartford?"

I didn't answer, but stroked my nose up his neck. I whispered in his ear, "Get behind me."

Without uttering a word, he pushed me down on the bed, flipped me over like a ragdoll and raised my hips up.

Standing at the foot of the bed, his hands traced down my back. Soft.

His length teased my entrance, dipping in the wetness—until he was gone.

"No," he growled and flipped me back over, positioning himself between my legs. "I want to see your face."

Yes. My heart hammered in my chest. Anything he wanted. *Anything.*

He nudged inside me a few inches then slid back out. "Remi," he gasped. His thumb caressed my lips, and I bit his finger then kissed it gently.

He bent over me, a dark and pained look on his face as he slid out and then back, going deeper each time, getting me used to his thickness. I squirmed, my body adjusting to the tight fit. Working up to a slow pace, he finally hit all the way home, and I moaned.

There. Yes!

"More," I begged, rotating my hips toward him, but he ignored me, using that torturous slow pace. He picked up the pearls, wrapped them around his hand, and tugged, forcing me to raise my chest to his so they didn't break. He buried his face in my neck as my hands dug into his back.

"I want to be so deep inside you that nothing will ever tear us apart," he said.

I grabbed his ass and pushed him further inside me.

"Remi, please, I'm going to break soon," he called, his voice torn to pieces.

"Me too."

A warm tongue ran up my neck as he pumped me hard and sure, yet with a carefulness I didn't understand. He twisted his hips for a new position to go deeper, grinding, and I writhed underneath him, feeling the summit ahead.

I was close, so close.

His fingers strummed my nub, rubbing the wetness around. Teasing me. He wore me out, sweat dripping from his face to mine and he owned my body, making it do whatever he wanted. He was a drug; his body the antidote to all the sadness I'd suffered.

He stared down at me, his eyes dark as he opened his mouth to say something, but then didn't.

Fire built once again, and I vibrated, grabbing the sheets and riding out the orgasm as my muscles spasmed around him. *Yes!*

He froze, watching me undulate around him. My throat clogged at the torment on his face. So much emotion—from both of us—yet I couldn't say a damn word.

Then, as if he'd flipped a switch and was done being gentle, he bent my knees to my chest and pushed my legs together. My body tightened, ready for what came next. He wanted to put his stamp on me—own me. He slammed into me, pounding, sliding all the way out and then ramming home. We scooted to the headboard. The clock fell off the nightstand. The lamp teetered as he worked me to the corner, his body pushing me higher and higher.

I begged for more. Always more.

He delivered with one palm on the wall and one pressing on my legs. Arching his back, he crested, roaring his release into the room, his cock tightening and expanding.

Collapsing next to me, he kissed my cheek and pulled me up to the pillows. He settled me in front of him, my back to his chest. "Remi . . ." He stopped, his voice thick. Strained.

I just nodded, unable to look at him. I couldn't. I wanted to cry.

What we'd just experienced had been too great. Too incredible.

It broke my heart.

He kissed my shoulders as fingers traced the lines of my back, drawing delicate swirls on my skin, a mere nuance of touch that held me in its thrall.

Was he writing my name? His?

He was incredibly sweet and gentle in the afterglow, just as I remembered.

I never wanted his hands to leave my body.

But they would.

He'd forget about me and trace lines on some other girl's back. And then another. All the while, I'd have to pretend like my heart wasn't forced to jump off a skyscraper, screaming the entire way down.

What did you expect, Remi? Flowers and a profession of love from him?

My belly grumbled and his hand stilled. In a hushed voice he said, "Hey. You must be hungry. Why don't I run out and get us some coffee and breakfast?"

I nodded. Feeling awkward.

What should I say?

Thank you?

Oops?

Was this a one-time deal?

"Donuts?" I managed to say.

He nodded and slipped away from me gently, his hand trailing along my skin as he stood up from the bed. Abruptly, he leaned down and kissed my wrist where my bracelet used to lie, his eyes soft.

I watched as he dressed, slipping on his jeans. His gray t-shirt was next, sliding over his chest and abs as he slipped it over his neck. He raked a hand through his nearly dry hair and it fell in the usual perfectly tousled mess. He grinned at me, catching my gaze, and my breath hitched at how much I wanted him to stay in this room and never leave.

Something was off, a sixth sense as if this was the absolute last time I'd be with him.

I almost asked him to stay and we'd order room service and go for round two.

I should have, considering what would happen next—but I didn't.

Instead, he tied his Converse, sent me a lingering look, and walked out the door.

TEN MINUTES LATER, I was drying off from a quick shower when I heard Dax knocking at the door. I should have given him a key. Wrapping a towel around my head turban-style and slipping on the fluffy white hotel robe, I plodded out of the steamy bathroom on wet feet and flung open the door.

This is it, Remi. Tell him how you feel . . .

I put a smile on my face to cover my nervousness. "Hey you. I hope you got chocolate—"

Warm hazel eyes with golden flecks met mine. Familiar sturdy shoulders leaned against the wall next to the door. He ran his gaze over me, a careful expression on his face. He exhaled and straightened. "Hello, Remington."

CHAPTER THIRTEEN

AZED, I COULDN'T have told you a damn thing leaving the hotel. Even worse, I wandered around for a good ten minutes like a lost puppy until I got some sense and checked my phone for local bakeries. Finding one a few blocks over, I headed that way, walking at a brisk pace. Once inside, I checked out the menu and ordered two large lattes and an assortment of pastries. My mouth opened and I talked, but I couldn't tell you what I ordered.

I was numb, reeling from Remi, my brain as spent as my body.

I touched her name under my shirt. I didn't regret it.

But something wasn't right. I was left with a vast uneasiness, as if something had irrevocably changed and I'd never be the same.

As if something horrible was about to happen.

Maybe I should have stayed and kissed her on those lips and told her to forget her stupid contract.

But I didn't.

Because I was fucking scared of the power she held over me. She made me vulnerable.

The cashier sent me a quizzical look and handed over what I'd ordered. I shoved money at her and peeked inside to see donuts, biscuits, and muffins.

Good. At least I'd been coherent.

The entire way back, I considered and tossed away different things to say to her when I got back.

I was going to tell her—*fuck, what was I going to say?*

That we are impossible? That I wasn't worth the time? That she'd get tired of my shenanigans? I mean, I didn't even know how to be a real boyfriend. Hell, I didn't even know what I was going to do after college.

A few minutes later, I still hadn't decided, but I knew something had changed between us and we had to sit down and address it. And then make love again.

I entered the hotel, hopped on the elevator, and punched the button for her floor. The door pinged opened, and I nodded at a passing guest as I headed down Remi's hall.

I halted, my skin prickling. Her door was open. *Chad?* I turned my walk into a full-on run, juggling the bag and drinks in the carrier.

But I froze at her door.

Air got sucked out of me and a brick hit me square on the chest. *What the—*

Hartford stood with his back to me, wearing a Whitman shirt, his arms wrapped around Remi's waist as they kissed. Her hair was wet and hid her face. But her hands—her hands were around Hartford's shoulders. Holding him.

I inhaled, my body itching to rip him off her and pound him into the wall.

She was mine. She'd never be his.

"Remington, babe, I need you," Hartford murmured, his hands slipping under the robe she wore.

She said his fucking name, and pain sliced into me like an axe to the heart.

I flipped around and bolted down the hall until I came to the stairwell, slamming it open and tearing down the stairs two at a time. Out of breath and sweating by the time I got to the bottom, I found a trash container at one of the floors and chucked everything from the bakery.

For half a second, I'd let myself believe—*fuck it*. I was done with her.

"SOD IT ALL, you're rat-arsed," Spider muttered as he tried to steer me into his flat. I weaved and fell into the foyer wall, knocking over the umbrella stand and a picture of Spider with his band. I cursed as it clattered across the marble tile. The sound of glass shattering hit my ears.

"I'll replace that," I slurred. "I'll buy you a hundred of them."

He exhaled, holding onto my shoulder. "No need for that kind of extravagance, cousin. Just put one foot in front of the other until we make it to the den."

He managed to get me to the couch where I crashed down, the entire room spinning like a top. I squinted at the rustic-style light fixture above me, the twinkling lights running together in one big blob. I blinked, trying to clear my vision.

Probably shouldn't have had that last vodka.

He'd found me at Knights, one of the bars in the West End we went to on a regular basis, which had a VIP room for clients who preferred to be away from the regular crowd. They also provided any extra entertainment if you desired. I had.

The club was intimately lit with dark paneling and full of ritzy clients. I'd waltzed in with one objective: to erase Remi from my brain. I'd tossed Spider's name around like a football and because the owner remembered me, I'd ended up in private room with two expensively dressed call girls. Maybe. They might have been cheap strippers from the bar across the street. I really don't know.

The three of us had had a party in a private room with loud music, red leather couches, and a whole lot of vodka. At some point, Spider had shown up and proceeded to wrangle me in his car. Guess the owner had called him. I hadn't cared at that point.

"What you doing?" I muttered at him, raising my head up from the arm of the couch.

"Taking your ugly-arse shoes off." He sounded annoyed as he untied the laces.

I laughed. "This is bloody rich. You're taking care of *me*."

He shot me a dark look—I guess. It was hard to judge a person's emotions when you've been throwing back drinks for the past three hours.

He tossed my shoes over his shoulder, and a few minutes later I felt him stuff a pillow under my head. "You think you'll be sick?"

"Hell no. Bring on the Grey Goose from the cabinet." I slung my head back toward the kitchen, and immediately got nauseous.

"Uh-huh, I think you've had enough for one night."

"Said Spider never." I laughed.

He disappeared and came back with a small stainless-steel trashcan. "Just in case. Don't want you to ruin my hardwood." He smirked, his face softening as he stared down at me. "Remi's called me a dozen times looking for you and every message she leaves for you gets a bit shittier. You better have a damn good explanation for me being your bloody secretary."

"Remi—she's—we're over."

"I didn't know you'd *begun*."

Neither had I.

"Did you pop your London cherry tonight?" he asked.

I peered up at him. "What?"

"Did you get laid at the bar? You had two girls all over you when I walked in," he said, enunciating his words slowly.

"Couldn't . . ."

"Ah." He left again, and came back with a bottle of Gatorade and two Aleve. "Come on, let's take your medicine or you'll feel like shite tomorrow on your way home."

Sitting up, I guzzled the liquid and swallowed the pills. As I stretched back on the couch, he grabbed a blanket from the hall closet and draped it over me. Once he was satisfied, he sat down on the heavy, metal coffee table and contemplated me.

"What?" I growled.

He arched a sardonic brow. "I've never seen you as a moody

drunk is all. Not sure I take to it well. I like fun Dax better—not this rock-bottom dude."

I grunted. "I'm not rock bottom." A pause. "Thanks for the ride home, man."

"Yep."

I nodded. Carefully, since the room still spun.

He rose up to leave.

"What—what did Remi say?"

He opened his mouth and I held a hand up. "No. Don't tell me. It doesn't matter. I saw everything I needed to see."

His hands on her naked skin. Her arms around him.

"Just—just make sure I make my flight tomorrow. I need to get back to Whitman."

"You got it. Sleep tight, princess." He turned down the lights and walked out of the room.

I closed my eyes and drifted into a dark oblivion.

CHAPTER FOURTEEN

I PLOPPED DOWN on the plaid couch Elizabeth had picked out for me at a second-hand store in Raleigh yesterday and gazed around at my house.

My house. All twenty-five hundred square feet of it. I wanted to shout it from the rooftop. Hell, maybe I'd climb up there later and drink a beer. Because it was mine and paid for.

"What are you grinning at?" Declan said as he stalked in the front door carrying a box of dishes.

"Just can't wrap my head around this place." I stood and took the box from him, although it was clear he didn't need the help. I wasn't the only one who'd bulked up even more over the summer.

"You put a lot of work into it these past few days," he said, glancing around. "Feels good, huh?"

I nodded.

Elizabeth called down from the upstairs railing. "All done cleaning the bathroom and extra bedrooms. It's ready for your new tenant—if you get one." She grinned broadly and bounced down the stairs, her hair in a ponytail and a smudge of dirt on her cheek. She was a sweet girl with dramatic dark eyebrows and white-blonde hair;

I wasn't surprised Declan had fallen fast and hard.

I grinned. "Someone's gonna bite. I posted the ad on Craigslist, the local paper, and put it up on the Whitman website."

Declan snorted. "You're gonna wind up with a psycho, mate."

"It's not like I could get one of my frat brothers to move in," I replied. "Judging by the Tau house, they wouldn't pick up after themselves, and I don't want a bunch of parties going on. They might mess up the new paint job we did yesterday." With Declan and Elizabeth's help, I'd managed to paint the entire interior a nice cream color—or Vanilla Bean as Elizabeth called it.

Declan chuckled. "Those are words I never imagined you saying."

Elizabeth arrived at the bottom of the stairs and Declan turned toward her, their eyes meeting and clinging to each other as she went straight into his arms. He bent down and kissed her—for no apparent reason other than he couldn't keep his hands off her. Her hands wrapped around his shoulders as she kissed him back soundly.

I'd gag, but I was used to their PDA.

"Feel free to christen the spare bedrooms," I said, turning away from their display and making my way to the kitchen. "Just leave mine alone."

I busied myself by carting boxes into the kitchen, finding a cabinet, and stashing the plates and bowls. My thoughts invariably ran to Remi. She'd been on my mind on and off since I'd left London over a week ago, but I'd had the house to keep me occupied.

She sent me several texts after I'd walked out of her hotel, but I'd never responded. Obviously, she'd had no clue I'd seen her and Hartford together.

I pulled my phone out and scrolled through the messages sent over the span of four days.

Remi, Day 1:

What happened to you? Why didn't you come back? I've tried to call you at least ten times, and now Spider says you're passed out. Hartford is here, and I don't know what to do. I need you, Dax. You said you'd be here for me. Please.

Remi, Day 2:
Spider says you left for Raleigh this morning. I know you're reading this. I thought our friendship meant something to you. Guess I was wrong.

Remi, Day 3:
I can't believe I let myself get sucked into sleeping with you. If that was all you wanted, why didn't you just say so instead of going to all that trouble of pretending to be my friend! You're a douchecanoe and I hate you.

Remi, Day 4:
I don't hate you, but I hope your dick falls off.

That had been the final message.

I sighed. In the end, it was good that Hartford had shown up.

Because girls like Remi weren't meant for me, and it's better to nip it before it festered.

Love hurts, Dax.

Nope. It wasn't love. It was LUST. And now that I'd nailed her, I could move on.

Another box was on the kitchen table and when I opened it, I saw it was the new glasses Father and my stepmother, Clara, had given me as a housewarming gift. They still had the store stickers on the bottom, so I filled up the sink with soap and hot water to wash them, making a mental note to consider investing in a dishwasher. On a whim, I grabbed the red and white apron off the hook by the back door that said *Mr. Goodlookin' Is Cookin'*—a gift from Declan.

I didn't know how much actual cooking I'd be doing, but the sentiment had made me laugh.

A bit later, the doorbell rang.

"I'll get it," Elizabeth called from the living room.

"'K," I answered back, my hand in sudsy water. "It's probably

Axel. He wanted to bring over pizza on moving day." Axel was one of my frat brothers and a football player; I was closer to him than any of the other guys.

A few minutes later, I sensed more than heard movement behind me, and I paused, my skin prickling. I couldn't tell you why except that it had to have been a sixth sense or a gut feeling. *Fuck.*

"Hey, you have someone here about the house," Elizabeth said.

"Dax?" a hesitant voice asked.

Shit, shit, shit.

That voice. Remi.

And when she said my name like that, as if the word actually hurt, my chest constricted.

Schooling my features into a mask, I turned around. My eyes ran over her, taking in the fiery hair and the bruised look in her eyes. I smirked and smiled cockily. "Hey there, angel."

A slow blush stole up from her neck to her face, and she looked down, refusing to meet my intense gaze—that was fine because my eyes were on the arsehole beside her.

CHAPTER FIFTEEN

I RANG THE doorbell and a blonde girl answered, wearing cut-off shorts and a gray tank top that read *Front Street Gym*. She looked vaguely familiar, but I was too unfocused to pin it down.

Since arriving back from London, I'd spent the last few days scouring every apartment building, duplex, trailer, and rental within a few miles of Whitman. Everything was rented already or in a shitty neighborhood. If I could get this house, I'd win the freaking lottery. I crossed my fingers, hoping the roommate was just as nice as the house.

If this didn't work out, I'd be forced to live with my mother and drive sixty miles' round trip each day to class. Not to mention listening to my mom berate me about my weight, what I wore, what time I got up, how late I stayed up, and who I hung out with.

Clutching the advertisement from the Whitman website I'd printed off, I let out a breath, feeling the urge to vomit.

"Can I help you?" the pretty girl standing at the door asked.

"Um, you asked for a roommate and I'm applying. I even have the first month's rent and a deposit ready today—that is if you haven't found anyone yet." I sent her a hopeful look.

Classes did start in two days.

She blinked, her eyes raking over my two companions, Malcolm and Hartford, then landing back on me, taking in the blunt cut hair, denim sundress and yellow flats.

I smiled, indicating the guys with me. "This is Hartford, a student at Whitman, and my brother, Malcolm. They tagged along with me to check it out."

Wearing a light blue polo shirt and khaki shorts, Hartford nodded and smiled. "Hi, I think we've had a class or two together."

Yep. There he was. My missing fiancé who'd arrived at my hotel six days earlier and tossed me into an emotional tailspin.

He'd knocked on my door, gone to his knees, and pleaded with me to take him back. Tears had been shed.

"You'll always be the girl for me," he promised, and the only reason he'd gotten cold feet was because he was afraid we were too young to make such a big commitment.

And the pretty blonde girl on Instagram? She'd happened to be at Cadillac's while he was there and nothing had happened between them.

Basically, by the time I'd disappeared to London, the perfect guy had decided he couldn't live without me.

Everything I'd wanted was back within my grasp.

"Everyone deserves a second chance," my mom kept telling me.

Of course, we weren't getting married anytime soon, but I couldn't toss away our relationship either. We'd spent more than two years together and had a lot of memories. Good ones.

I got pulled back to the present when I noticed Malcolm snapping his fingers, one of the repetitive movements he used to alleviate stress. Meeting new people made him jittery, although most times it was the other person who got intimidated. At sixteen, he was already six-one with lean muscles and prone to say whatever popped in his head. His blue eyes bounced from me to Hartford and then back to the blonde.

He nodded, curly brown hair bouncing. "I'm Malcolm, and I

want to see where Remi will live."

"*Maybe* I'll live here," I told him gently. "We have to take a look first and see if it works out. Someone may have beat me to it."

The girl smiled, making her even prettier. "No, it hasn't been filled. Come in, please. I'm not the one who lives here, but I'll introduce you to the person who owns the place. We've been moving in for the past couple of days, so it may be a bit messy." She took a step back to let us enter. "I'm Elizabeth, by the way."

"Remi," I said with a nod, realizing I'd been so scattered I hadn't even told her my name.

We all filed inside the small ceramic-tiled foyer that opened into a spacious area with an old brick fireplace, freshly waxed hardwood floors, and a pretty bay window with the panes cut into small diamond shapes. A faded couch, a navy leather recliner, and a gray media center with a huge television took up most of the den. Except for the couch, most of the furnishings looked new. The house smelled of tart lemons, perhaps from cleaning, and fresh paint. Whoever owned it took pride in it.

So far, so good, Remi.

A tall, heavily muscled man wearing a black baseball hat was on a ladder in the center of the den hanging a ceiling fan, but came down as we entered the room. He greeted us warmly, but that wasn't what caught my eye. Nope. My eyes got tangled up on the small dragonfly tattoo on his neck.

And the chiseled jawline, straight nose, and piercing gray eyes.

Dread pooled in my stomach.

"Hiya," he said and put his hand out to me. "I'm Declan."

His familiar British accent sent goosebumps over my skin, and I gripped the straps of my purse as if it were a lifeline. *God help me.*

Stuffing down the urge to make a dash for the car, I stuck my hand out and shook his firm grip. "I'm—I'm Remi Montague. I'm here about the ad for a roommate." I waved the printout, noticing my hand was shaking.

Hartford sent me a quizzical glance. I tried to smile.

Hartford and Declan shook hands. Everyone on campus knew

Declan—and Dax.

"This house yours?" Hartford asked with a slight frown, no doubt because while Declan hadn't been a Tau, everyone knew his brother was the poster boy for the fraternity.

"Nah," Declan said but didn't elaborate, careful eyes on Hartford. Apparently the rivalry extended to family too.

The blonde girl put her hand lightly on my shoulder, and I realized she'd said my name a few times. " . . . want to follow me?"

Feeling numb yet oddly excited, I nodded, and she led us down a small hall, turned a corner, and we entered the kitchen.

With faded oak cabinets that had seen better days, a round table with orange vinyl-covered metal chairs, and a brand new stainless steel refrigerator, it was a mix of old and new.

But the only thing in the room that held my attention was Dax, standing with his back to us, legs slightly parted as he washed dishes at the sink. Wearing low-slung jeans, his ass flexed as he moved, his shoulders broader than I remembered.

My body felt thin as if I might float away, and my heart pounded so loud I was sure he heard it. The last time I'd seen him, he'd been between my legs, sweat dripping as he pinned me down to the bed.

"You have someone here about the house," Elizabeth said.

"Dax?" I pushed out.

Without turning, he dried his hands off and leaned over to turn down the low beat of rap music coming from his phone. He pivoted to face us, and everything I'd been battling with since he'd left London came roaring back to the surface. Anger and heartbreak reared up, all the memories from London flashing through my head. I bit the inside of my cheeks to keep it all in.

He'd screwed me in London, literally, and I'd fallen for his games. *When would I learn?*

Cold-stone eyes flicked over Hartford, Malcolm, and then landed on me, sweeping me from head to foot. "Hey there, angel."

At the sound of his voice, I wanted to sink into the floor, a barrage of emotions hitting me. I hadn't been prepared to see him. Not so soon.

Dismissing me, he gazed back at Hartford, and they glared at each other warily, two different specimens: one built and dark, the other lean and blond. The tension stretched like a rubber band, and if they'd had swords, they might have pulled them out.

Thank God Hartford had never known about Dax and me freshman year.

It was Hartford who broke the ice, his face expressionless. "Had no idea this was your house, Blay . . ."

"Or you wouldn't have come?" Dax smirked.

"Yeah," Hartford replied with an unapologetic shrug.

I touched Hartford's arm. "Dax rescued me from the guy who mugged me in London. Remember?"

"Of course," he said to me gently and touched my face. Looking back at Dax, he sent him a nod. "Remington took me by the club where it happened. Glad you were there to help out." He wrapped an arm around my shoulders and squeezed. "I'm still blaming myself for letting her leave town, and if anything had happened to her, I don't know if I could have stood it." His hazel eyes came back and found mine. I smiled tentatively.

"Yeah, I took care of her. Isn't that right, *Remington*?" Dax replied tightly, his eyes searching my face. A muscle jerked in his cheek when our eyes met, his body rigid as a piece of steel. His hands curled, and he looked as if he wanted to smash something.

I was confused. *What had I done?*

I bit my lip, hoping Hartford wouldn't notice. Because this— this wasn't just a fraternity thing.

Malcolm's wide-eyed gaze bounced from me to Dax, a questioning look on his face. I sent him my *it's okay* smile. Social cues were his weakness, but when it came to me, he didn't miss much.

But then it was as if Dax threw a switch because his entire demeanor changed. With careful movements, he removed his apron, hung it on a hook, and leaned back against the counter as if he didn't have a care in the world. He let out a long sigh and crossed his legs.

"So you're here about the apartment?" he murmured, flicking

his eyes at the paper I had in my hand.

"She can't live with you," Hartford said, his tone cool.

Dax tossed back his head and laughed. "Dude, chill out. I saved your girl's arse. Plus, I was asking *her*, not you." His head swiveled to me. "Remi?"

"I was, but obviously, we aren't a good match . . ."

His lashes dropped then opened. "Why not? Aren't we *friends*?"

I shifted on my feet. "I—I'm afraid we might not mesh."

Hartford said, "She doesn't want to live with a guy, Blay, that's all." *Especially a Tau* went unsaid. "We're grateful for London but were hoping for a female roommate."

Dax harrumphed. "School starts in two days. Good luck. But I get where you're coming from. You're worried I'll be making a pass at your girl, but *attached* females aren't my thing. Plus, I'll be studying a lot—gotta graduate this year, ya know—and helping my brother at his gym. Who knows? I'll probably end up sleeping most nights at the Tau house."

"I'm sure there'll be plenty there to keep you entertained," I replied smartly.

Hartford didn't seem to notice my slip-up or perhaps he chalked it up to typical rivalry talk, but I'd never been one to get in on the boys' disputes.

"No doubt," Dax agreed softly.

Elizabeth, who'd been steadily drying the dishes since we started talking, turned around. "If you need a reference for Dax, I'd be happy to vouch for him. You couldn't find a sweeter roommate." Smiling, she dropped her dishtowel over the sink. "If you guys will excuse me, I think I hear Declan calling for me from the den."

As she walked out, it gave Hartford the chance to pull me to the side. He kept his voice low. "Just live with me, Remi—at least until you find a decent place."

We'd had this conversation a hundred times. Yes, we were working things out, but jumping right back into the same place we'd been would be a disaster.

"That's not a good idea," I said as quietly as I could, but it was clear Dax listened intently, his head cocked to the side.

"You can't live with . . . Dax," Hartford said after a long exhale. "I'd rather you stayed with your mom. I'd definitely worry less."

I shook my head. "My mom's house is too far from campus to drive each day. I'd be exhausted. Plus, she drives me crazy."

Hartford sighed, his eyebrows pulled low. "Then let's keep looking. Something will come up."

"We've looked for days," I groaned. "There's nothing, except that place over the drycleaners—"

Dax straightened up from the counter. "Sorry to interrupt, but in all honesty, I have someone else coming over tomorrow to check the house out, so if you want the room, we'd need to get this settled tonight. Otherwise"—he waved his hands around the kitchen that was in disarray—"I need to get back to work."

He was trying to get rid of me.

And that thought speared my heart.

I exhaled, rubbing my eyes. My legs felt like rubber and my body was bone-weary as if I had the flu. Since the moment I realized Dax had deserted me, I'd been listless. Lost. My thoughts were scattered so much I couldn't seem to make a decision about anything. My brain was shit.

But . . .

What *was* I going to do? I couldn't live here or with Hartford or my mom. Perhaps I could get a cheap hotel room for a few days until something came up . . .

"Remi?" Malcolm asked me, and I blinked up at him, realizing I had leaned my shoulder against him.

"You okay?" Hartford asked me, a look of concern on his face. He touched my shoulder.

I nodded and straightened. "Sorry. Long day."

"Before you decide, let's have a seat and I'll tell you more about the house," Dax said out of the blue, indicating the four chairs at the table.

I glanced up to find his eyes on my face. They'd softened. "I'll grab us some sodas. What would you like, Remi?"

144

I found myself sitting down in one of the chairs and asking for a Coke. Hartford hesitated, but plopped down with a resigned expression on his face. He declined Dax's offer of a drink. Malcolm looked pleased and took the Coke Dax handed him.

Dax took the seat to my right, and because it was a round table, his chair was close enough to mine that the heat from his skin was a tangible thing. His masculine scent slammed into me, bringing back memories of the hotel room. I stuck my hands under the table and kept them clasped together. Tight. Malcolm sat on the other side while Hartford sat across from me.

I felt dazed as Dax gave us the details about the rent—a four-hundred flat fee due the first of each month while he covered all the utilities. Generous—much less than I'd expected.

But you can't live here!

He ran through the deposit fee (a hundred dollars) and a small list of rules he'd typed out along with a lease agreement. I'd be responsible for my own food and would get the smaller bedroom upstairs, which came with an attached bath and a small office where I could put a desk or anything else. I paused. Perfect for Malcolm when he stayed over sometimes.

"Basically, you'd have the run of the upstairs while I get the downstairs. We can share the kitchen, den, and patio outside." He tapped a pen on the table, his bicep flexing and calling attention to his tattoo. *Tap. Tap.* Mr. Beautiful was antsy.

I also noticed he hadn't shaved in several days and there were bags around his eyes, as if he too had had some restless nights.

Stop staring at him!

Malcolm must have been watching him too. He squinted. "You're what girls call a hottie. I bet you have a lot of sex."

"You can't talk about sex in front of people you just met, Malcolm," I said, grimacing. "At least give them a few days."

"Thanks, I suppose?" Dax laughed and put his hand out. "Sorry, I didn't say hi before. Guess I was distracted. You're Remi's brother, Malcolm, right? She told me about you."

Hartford stiffened at that.

Malcolm shook his hand. "Yes, and to clarify, if this arrangement works out, I'll be staying over sometimes. My mom works nights as a manager at a potato chip factory. Pringles. It makes her smell funny, but she had to go to work after my dad died. We used to have money but now we don't as much. Remi likes to watch me because I wander off. Not too far. Just to the store and back but it drives her crazy. I also like to eat pickles and drink lemonade. I like your house. It's bigger than the rat-hole apartment we found above the dry cleaner on 5th Avenue. It had roaches and people were doing drugs out by the dumpster. Hartford said we couldn't stay there. He and Remi were going to get married, but he dumped her and now he wants her back. She's sad. I talk. A lot. Does it bother you that I'm autistic?" Language development had never been Malcolm's weakness. If it's true that autistic people have a special gift, his was gab.

Dax grinned, the first genuine one I'd seen. "Not at all. It'd be nice to have another guy around. Do you like to play Xbox?"

"I will kick your ass at Halo."

"Language," I said but no one seemed to notice.

"You can try," Dax snarked. "And, by the way, I love pickles too. There's a whole jar of dills in there right now that my step-mum, Clara, brought me. She canned them herself."

Malcolm took that in. He adjusted his wire spectacles and focused on me. "He's cool. You should totally live here."

"Yeah. What he said." Dax gazed at me, his tongue dipping out to dab at his lower lip. He bit it, and I tore my eyes off him. Jesus. *What was he doing?*

As if directed by a part of my brain I had no control over, my right hand toyed with the small strand of pearls I'd put on with my sundress.

Dax inhaled sharply, dropping the papers he'd been holding on the floor between us. Bending down from his chair, he reached to snatch them, his eyes snaking over my legs. I crossed them and he flinched, a flush rising in his cheeks as he sat up and put the paper on the table.

I dropped the pearls and twisted my wrist. *What was wrong*

with me? Why was I baiting him?

I glanced back at him to see that his face had whitened. I followed his eyes, realizing he'd seen the engagement ring on my finger.

I stared at the rock that symbolized everything I wanted. Hartford had asked me to wear it again, and I'd finally agreed the day we landed back in Raleigh. Part of me had wanted to make my mom happy and keep Malcolm from worrying about me. The rest of me was ambivalent as hell.

Hartford's impatient voice brought me back. "We're losing daylight here on the search for an apartment, Remington."

Instead of answering, I focused on Dax. His eyes caught mine, and bit-by-bit, everyone else in the room disappeared.

"I'm going to live here," I said, turning my gaze back to Hartford.

His face reddened. "You can't mean that—"

"I do. The rent is right, there's a place for Malcolm, and it's minutes from campus. It's everything I want."

"Except it's a guy you're considering living with," he said, his voice sharp.

"I have nowhere else, Hartford."

And you're the reason I'm in this predicament, my eyes said.

Had he so easily forgotten?

"I'm choosing where I live. No one else," I added firmly.

He flicked his eyes to Dax and then considered me, a look of distaste on his face as if he smelled something rotten.

Dax cleared his throat. "Uh, I can give you a few moments alone . . ."

"No, that's not necessary. I want the room. Right, Hartford?" My lips tightened. If he didn't agree with this. . . .

A few tense moments ticked by until finally he exhaled, leaned over, and put his hand over mine. "I'm sorry to be a pain, babe. I just want what's best for you, and this isn't it. With that said, I'll support whatever decision you make." He shot a dark look at Dax. "Anyway, I'm just down the road, and you can always stay over with me anytime."

"Sure," I said with obvious relief, glad he was getting on board.

Dax pushed the papers over for me to sign.

I stared down at them.

Him. Me. In a house alone.

What could possibly go wrong?

CHAPTER SIXTEEN

AFTER REMI AND company walked out the door with a promise they'd be back with some bedroom furniture and the rest of her things at seven, I strode back into the den and collapsed down on the recliner.

Fuck, I was certifiably insane.

In what universe could I live with Remi in the same house?

How was I going to keep my hands off her?

You will because she's wearing his ring and he's what she wants. He's on her list, remember?

While Elizabeth popped outside to talk on the phone with her friend Shelley, Declan grabbed two beers from the kitchen and handed me one. "So, a new roomie? That means income. Not bad, little bro."

I gulped a swig down, my fingers toying with the label on the bottle. "Apparently."

"She's got a big-arse diamond on her finger." Declan didn't miss much. "Hartford's fiancée?"

I nodded.

"You think it's wise to live with her?" His eyes studied me.

"I can keep my dick in my pants."

He tipped his beer up. Wiped his mouth with the back of his hand. "Uh-huh."

I scoffed. "What? *Her?* You know she's the Queen of Plans and Getting Shit Done? Trust me, I'm not up to her standards." I spread my hands apart. "Plus, she's with an Omega."

"Yep."

"She's a klutz too. Falls over everything. She slipped in this club and fell right in my lap. You should have seen it."

"Really."

I sucked down a swig. "She's into birds—big time. Like she's planning on getting a doctorate—weird, right?"

"Maybe."

"And that hair. It was long and she went and chopped it all off. I mean, the red is cool, don't get me wrong, but it's not long enough to wrap around my hand . . ." I stopped.

"I hadn't noticed," Declan said dryly.

"We got matching tattoos at the Friar's Church."

"Okaaay." He'd been standing but sat down across from me on the couch, and even though I wasn't looking him in the face, I felt the weight of his stare.

"Anything else you want to tell me about her?"

I exhaled. "Her dad died a few years ago. She—she knows what it's like to lose someone. I told her about Mum—and the dragonfly. She got it."

"Hmmm."

"We got fake-married."

Declan sputtered. "Not sure what that means, but you have my full attention. Care to explain?"

"No." I stood and paced around the room, checking the window at the front to see if they'd left yet. They had. But she'd be back. Soon. I checked my phone. In about three hours. Great. I rubbed at the half-beard on my jaw. I needed a goddamn shower, and I hadn't shaved since London.

"You've fucked her before, haven't you?" Declan's voice came from behind me.

I sighed, still staring out the window. "Yep."

"And London?"

I turned to face him. "I didn't fuck her in London—wasn't like that. *She fucked me.*"

Surprise crossed his face, then a slow understanding. "And now she's with him?"

I exhaled. "They were on a break."

He sighed, his gaze evaluating me. "Ah, dude. I bet there's a story there. Do you want to talk about it?"

I grimaced, shoving that shit way down. "No. I want to forget it ever happened."

He stood up from the couch and patted me on the back. "Yeah, bro, I think we're gonna need some more beer."

AT SIX, AXEL came over with a bottle of Patrón, several pizzas, and a couple of the fraternity little sisters. Even though classes didn't start until Monday, sorority rush had been going on and, as usual, several of the girls had been hanging around the Tau house.

I'd dropped by a few times to check in on how rush was going, but since I wasn't president this time around I didn't have any pressing duties. I'd walked through the entire house, feeling a little detached. It was odd. I mean, I'd spent four years living and partying at that house. With my charm and penchant for a good time, I'd brought the girls and pledges in by the droves. I liked everyone, and ninety-nine percent of the time, it meant nothing, just a way to pass the time. I may have sucked at my GPA, but my friend list was extensive.

Yet . . .

Something in my gut said I'd moved on from the Tau shenanigans over the summer while helping Spider, or maybe it had begun sooner. After Declan met Elizabeth, I'd witnessed firsthand what they had—love and unicorns and rainbow crap.

Part of me longed for that too. My forever girl.

Axel, the two girls, Declan, Elizabeth, and I finished eating piz-za as the doorbell rang. I glanced at the clock. Seven on the dot. Of course–Remi was punctual as shit.

Declan arched a brow at me. "She's here."

"This is going to be interesting you living with a girl," Elizabeth murmured. "Want me to get it?"

"I got it." I wiped my mouth with a napkin and stood, taking my beer with me. Time to deal with reality.

When I opened the door, Remi and Hartford stood there with several boxes at their feet. The sun had already set and it was nearly dark, but I saw they'd come in a Toyota truck filled with furniture. Hartford's silver Lexus SUV was parked behind it with several box-es inside.

"Hey," she said, following my eyes. "I borrowed Lulu's truck."

"And she would be the only girl I know who drives one," I said, forcing a smile.

Her lips twitched. "Yeah, she's a country girl underneath all that craziness."

I nodded. *Okay.* See, we could be civil. I sucked in a breath and willed myself to relax. Best way to do that was to not look at her, so I directed my attention to Hartford. "Let me grab Axel and Declan and we'll help you out."

"You don't have to," she said.

"I want to."

She paused. Looked at the ground then back at me. "Okay."

Hartford's brow wrinkled as his eyes went from me to her.

After calling for Axel and Declan, we went out to the truck with Hartford and carried in her iron bed, nightstand, dresser, and boxes of clothes. Even with going up the stairs, it only took an hour to get things situated where she could start unpacking.

Hartford went down to grab the last box from the truck while Axel and Declan put her bed together. I carted the box labeled *Bath* and put it on the floor in her loo. I riffled through it. Curious. I pulled out some hair thingies, a round brush, a small bag of make-up, and generic shampoo. Compared to my extensive list of styling products, hers was seriously low maintenance. I opened her deodorant and sniffed, looking for her scent. Nope. Rummaging to the bottom, I pulled out a small bottle of perfume, but it didn't smell like her either. *Dammit.* I was jonesing.

The door opened. I flipped around, tossing the bottle back in the box.

"What are you doing?" Remi asked.

"Nothing. Helping."

"By sniffing my perfume?"

"No, that's stupid," I snapped.

"You were going through my things." She shut the door and leaned against it, and it was the first time I'd looked at her in the light since she'd arrived. Her eyes looked red.

I scowled. "Have you been crying?"

A pause. "No. I'm just tired."

I didn't care. I put my shoulder against the wall, letting my gaze move over her and eat her up.

"You never came back to the hotel," she said quietly.

My jaw clenched, and I felt my face redden.

A wrinkle grew on her forehead, a confused expression on her face. "Wait. Are—are you angry with *me?*"

"Have you fucked him?"

Her face paled. "Don't ask me that."

"You did." I gritted my teeth, rage simmering.

"Your question makes no sense . . ." She stopped, her lips compressing. "I don't have to explain anything to you. Not like this. You're acting weird when you're the one who *never* showed up. You got what you wanted and left. It was a total redo of my freshman year, only this time, you were the one walking away . . ." Her voice hitched. "As far as I know, you planned the entire thing. Did you?" Luminous blue eyes searched mine.

"You don't think much of me, do you?" I shook my head.

"I did."

I glanced at her left hand. "You're wearing his ring."

"He wants to work things out—"

"Can't you make up your own mind?" I sneered.

"Don't . . ."

"Don't what?" I took a step toward her. "Am I supposed to wipe you from my memory now?"

Fuck. I wanted to.

"Why do you care?" she asked, her voice rising. "I'm just like all the rest. Easy come, easy go. Right?"

I glared at her.

She gripped the doorknob, her knuckles white. "I—this is a mistake. You obviously have a problem with me, and we won't be able to get along—"

"Too bad you already signed the lease agreement." No way was I letting her walk out my door.

Her eyes glittered as she angled her chin at me. "Sue me."

Flattening my hand against the door behind her, I leaned down to her neck, my nose sliding up her throat. She smelled like that fucking scent I'd been dying for. *Sugar.* I wanted to lick her from head to foot. Instead I sucked in a shuddering breath, steeling myself against her.

"You don't intimidate me," she whispered.

"Oh yeah? You're shaking, Remi," I breathed into her ear. "Are you thinking about us in that hotel room? Are you thinking about how much better I am than Hartford?"

She pressed herself even further against the door, her chest rising rapidly. "What . . ."

"I am, aren't I?"

She gnawed on her lip.

I wanted to kiss it.

She covered her face. "Stop—"

"You know how I know I'm better? Because any guy who'd leave you at the altar—any guy who'd let you *live with me*—isn't a fucking man. He's a goddamn pussy."

Her throat worked as she swallowed. "Please . . ."

My mouth kicked up in a wicked grin. "Better yet, let's have a repeat of the hotel room. Why don't you get down on your knees right now and wrap those tight, wet lips around my—"

She slapped me, and I stumbled backward, my arse landing square on the toilet. God, I deserved it, but I couldn't stop.

I smirked. "Damn. If you wanted me to sit down, all you had to do was ask, angel."

"Don't call me that," she snapped. "You call everyone that and I hate it."

Shaking it off, I shrugged and stood back up and faced the mirror, checking my appearance as her eyes spit fire at me. I pretended to be bored as my fingers fixed my hair. My hand trembled and I dropped it to my side.

My reflection looked like shit.

I had bags and shadows under my eyes.

My head hurt.

I needed a fucking lobotomy.

My gut was all twisted.

Confused.

Angry.

"I don't even know you anymore," she mumbled, shaking her head.

Welcome to my world. I didn't know who I was since London either.

She made to open the door, and the voice of sanity permeated my thick skull. "Remi . . ." I grabbed her arm, but immediately dropped it at the scathing look she sent me.

"What?" She crossed her arms.

I rubbed my forehead. Exhaled. "Stay—please. I know you need a place for you and Malcolm. I promise, I'll barely be here. I'll spend a few nights at the Tau house and maybe Declan's. Classes start Monday, and I want this settled. I know you do too. If—if it doesn't work out, I'll refund your rent and you can find somewhere else."

"Don't you have someone else coming to look at it tomorrow?"

I closed my eyes. "I lied."

"Why?"

"You know why," I said.

A knock came at the door, Hartford's voice behind it. "Remington? Everything okay?"

CHAPTER SEVENTEEN

Remi

DAX WALKED OUT ahead of me, his voice blasé. "Had to put some things on the high shelf in the closet for *Remington*."

He paused and glanced from me to Hartford. "I'm headed downstairs for a drink. Either of you want anything?"

Hartford sent me a questioning look, and I shook my head.

"No, I'm going to finish up my bedroom now," I said. It was decided. I was staying.

"Whatever." Dax sent us a backwards wave and bounded down the stairs two at a time. Axel had already gone downstairs since we'd been in the bathroom, and over the railing, I watched them fist-bump as two giggling girls came down the hall from the kitchen. I recognized them as Tau little sisters although I didn't know their names. Dax threw an arm around each of their shoulders.

And so it begins . . . Dax and other girls.

God.

How on earth would I be able to handle seeing him with someone?

You have to. You've done it before.

But, but . . . it was different this time. We were different.

No. You still have Hartford, my head reminded me.

"Is there tension between you and Dax?" He'd followed my eyes.

"No, just school starting. You know how anxious I get." I smiled. "I haven't even gotten my planner filled out yet."

He nodded, looking uncertain. "Okay, but let me know if anything changes . . ."

"He said he wouldn't be here much. I'm fine." My voice sharpened at the end, and I immediately felt guilty.

Pivoting around so I didn't have to watch Dax, I went into my bedroom. Hartford followed. Declan and Axel had finished getting the slats and the mattress on the bed, my dresser was against the window, and someone had even put my clock out on my nightstand.

Hartford came up behind me and wrapped solid arms around me, and I leaned back into him, needing comfort from my confrontation with Dax.

We stood that way for a while, each of us silent, until he said, "I'm not happy about you living here, but I'll do whatever it takes to get you back on my side. This is just a bump in the road. We'll get married as soon as you want to. Maybe after graduation?"

I turned to face him. "Maybe."

He tucked a strand of hair behind my ear. "Want me to stay the night?"

"Soon." I smiled.

His head came down, his lips taking mine gently, and I kissed him back, opening up to him. He slid an arm around me, pulling me down on him as he fell back on the bed. His hand cupped my bottom. "God, I've missed you, babe."

"Me too."

He kissed me harder, sliding his hand up my back and unsnapping my bra under my shirt. Deepening his mouth over mine, his hand caressed my breast and I stiffened.

He pulled back and stared at me, letting out an exasperated sigh as his arms dropped to his side. "What's wrong with you? You haven't let me near you since we broke up."

"Rome wasn't built in a day, Hartford." I rose up to sit on the edge of the bed. I fixed my bra. "And there's a lot going on today." Truth. We'd driven Malcolm back home to my mom's before loading all the furniture. All I wanted to do right now was curl up in my bed and go to sleep. I rubbed my eyes.

He sent me a disappointed gaze but stood. Bending down, he brushed my forehead with warm lips. "I'll head out so you can get some sleep."

I nodded.

We walked out the door and down the stairs to an empty den. Wandering into the kitchen, we saw Dax and friends out on the covered patio outside.

"Let's see what they're doing," he said, taking my hand.

I stiffened. "Why? I mean, you don't even like them."

His eyes narrowed. "If you're going to live here, it's a good idea if I'm on friendly terms with your landlord."

I didn't buy that for a minute, but I followed him.

We walked out the back door onto the patio. I didn't see Elizabeth and Declan anywhere, and I assumed they'd already taken off, but Axel, Dax, and the two girls were there, sitting on a wicker sectional with blue cushions. A coffee table was in the middle with a bottle of Patrón on it. As we approached, I watched Dax pour a shot-glassful and toss it back.

The brunette sat next to Axel, also a Tau, while the blonde sat between Dax's legs, a smile of satisfaction on her face. She looked like all the girls Dax went for—blonde, petite, slutty.

We said hi to everyone. Axel introduced the girls to me; the brunette was Bettina and the blonde was Alexandria.

"Did Hartford get you all situated?" Axel said with a smile. He was a popular football player; I didn't know him well, but the general consensus on campus was he was nice to everyone.

I smiled back. "Yes, and thank you for helping."

Dax never glanced at me, his eyes on the tequila label he currently peeled. His other hand rested on Alexandria's inner thigh.

I tore my eyes from them.

"I still have some unpacking, but it's a huge relief to have the hard stuff done," I announced, even though it seemed the only ones listening were Axel and the girls. "This house is great. I love the craftsman style and the big porch. My favorite is the stone chimney . . ." I stopped. Sighed. I was rambling.

"Yeah, it's cool," Axel said, eyeing Dax with an unsure look on his face. "Um, do you guys want to join us for a drink? We've been toasting the house."

"Several times," added Bettina, giving Axel a big kiss on his cheek.

"No, but thank you, *Axel*," I said, shooting daggers at Dax. How could he completely ignore us? If this was any indication of how he was going to treat me, I wouldn't last a week.

"I thought you liked tequila," Dax said, his voice low but still not looking at me.

I startled. "I—yes."

At Hartford's questioning glance, I said. "At the club in London, I was upset about everything that had happened here . . ." I paused. No need to announce that Hartford had dumped me. "Dax, um, saw me drinking tequila."

"Ah," he said, his hand holding mine tighter. "I'm sorry," he said softly.

I smiled.

Axel glanced at my ring. "Did you guys set a date?"

I groaned inwardly. He probably had no idea that we'd had a date but canceled it. He was just making conversation.

"Soon," Hartford said, his eyes on Dax's bent head. "Remington's the love of my life."

Dax's hands tightened on the bottle of Patrón. I might have missed it, but I couldn't seem to keep my eyes off him. I tore them away.

Axel grinned good-naturedly, completely clueless. "Damn, man, that's cool." He glanced at Dax. "Dude, maybe we need to find us a girl like Remi and settle down, huh?"

The girl next to Axel popped him on the arm. "Hello. Right

here."

He laughed and kissed her on the nose, making her giggle.

Dax's face rose, his eyes piercing me. "Meh. I prefer my life the way it is. *Easy peasy.*"

My heart squeezed. *I know,* it said.

"Drinking and partying never gets old, does it?" Axel agreed with a laugh.

"Indeed, it doesn't." Dax said, taking another shot.

I needed to put some space between us.

I cleared my throat. "Okay, I guess we'll go. Hartford's heading out and I'm going to crash. This day has been—hard."

"That's what she said," Dax chimed in with a sly grin at the girls and they giggled. He flashed his eyes at Hartford. "I figured you'd be sleeping over, mate . . ."

Hartford frowned. "I'll take a rain check on that. I've got family coming in from out of town tomorrow for my sister's eighteenth birthday dinner. We're having a big to-do at the house."

"How sweet," Dax murmured and flicked a glance at me. "You going?"

I blinked at the question. "Uh, no. I—I have plans that I can't change."

Hartford sighed, giving me a disappointed glance.

I squirmed. Hartford had invited me to his family get-together, but I'd passed since I was taking care of Malcolm tomorrow. I didn't miss those days for anything. Since my dad had died, I had tried my hardest to fill his shoes the best I could.

Alexandria, who'd been listening to our conversation but saying nothing, turned and pulled Dax's face to hers. "You're ignoring me. I need some attention. All this talk is making me sleepy."

"We can't have that." He grinned and she leaned in and kissed him, pressing her mouth against his, her hand on his cheek. It was a deeply passionate kiss that went on way too long, but I forced myself to watch.

See, Remi. He treats every girl the same. Kisses them all. Fucks them all.

Hartford said his goodbyes, and we used the glow of the floodlights to walk around the house and make our way over to his Lexus at the curb.

He reclined against the passenger-side door and pulled me to his chest. His sandy hair blew in the wind, and I ran my fingers through it. With the streetlight hitting his face, his eyes were more golden than I'd ever seen them. Warmth came from his gaze.

He gathered me close. "God, I'm so glad you're back in Raleigh."

"Yeah . . ." I trailed off.

His lips tightened ever so slightly.

"What?" I asked.

A long exhale came out. "I don't know. Something just feels off with us." His eyes went back toward the house. "And Dax is sending off weird vibes."

"You can't expect to snap your fingers and things go back to the way they were for us, and I can't explain Dax except that you guys aren't exactly buddies."

"Just—tell me something."

"What?"

He cupped my face, his gaze earnest. "Tell me you love me. You haven't since we broke up."

I hadn't been ready to. But, what was I waiting for?

I let out a breath. "I do love you. I'm not going anywhere and neither are you."

He pressed his forehead against mine, a torn expression on his face. "We should be married right now and living at my place. I want you back—all the way and in my bed. Don't you want that?"

My fingers played with the diamond on my finger, twisting it around, my heart heavy.

He kissed me on the nose. "Am I putting too much pressure on you?"

I nodded.

Seeming satisfied with this, he pressed his lips to mine one more time, told me he'd text me later, got in his car, and drove away.

Once his taillights were gone, I came back in, and since they were all outside, I did a quick tour of the downstairs. There were two more bedrooms, a bathroom, the kitchen, and a tiny laundry room closet in the hall. Dax's bedroom was just off the den, a big room with a king-sized bed with a white down duvet—unmade of course, the covers kicked down to the foot. A cluttered nightstand sat next to the bed with papers, schoolbooks, and a photograph I couldn't make out no matter how long I squinted. Knowing it was wrong but not caring, I tiptoed inside his room.

Drawn to his bed, I trailed my fingers along the velvet soft duvet. The sheets were white and soft as silk. I smiled. Leave it to Dax to have the best bedding imaginable.

I zoomed in on the picture on the nightstand. It was of Dax and Declan as young boys, maybe around nine or ten. Between them was a tall lady with dark hair and a bright smile on her face. Had to be his mom because the resemblance was uncanny. They sat under a tree and Dax's head leaned into her shoulder, as if he wanted to be even closer. A mischievous smile played across his face.

Pain cut through me at the way her hands clutched around each of them as if she'd known she was dying. It was obvious she'd adored them—yet death comes for us all, no matter the sweet life we have.

And you never get used to them being gone.

Dax hadn't. I hadn't.

We just dealt with it in different ways; I wanted security, while he wanted a guarded heart.

With a sigh, I set the frame back down and stepped over a mound of video games and movies to peek inside his closet. It was wide open, and I saw that his clothes were neatly organized, his extensive collection of jeans hanging on the bottom while the shirts were hung by color.

Looks like I wasn't the only one who had an issue with OCD.

A door from somewhere in the house opened and shut.

I froze. *Eeeek.* Tip-toeing around the spots of clutter, I dashed into the hallway and did a quickstep into the kitchen.

Dax had his back to me at the refrigerator as he held the door open and peered inside.

A few seconds ticked by and he remained motionless, his legs slightly apart as he stood there.

Should I say something?

He exhaled as his free hand rubbed his forehead.

Five more seconds went by. Then ten. At twenty, he said *"Fuck this,"* slammed the door shut, and strode out the back door without even noticing I was there.

THE NEXT MORNING, I woke to the sound of a sparrow outside my window, singing a loud stuttering song.

This birdie sounded annoyed. I knew exactly how it felt.

I crawled out of bed and plodded over to the window. Peeking through the blinds, I saw Dax's black Range Rover was gone from the small driveway to the right of the house. He'd driven a Beamer for the past few years, but had traded it in last semester. Parked on the street by the curb was my older model Toyota Highlander.

My phone buzzed. Glancing down, I saw a pic of Malcolm eating a pickle spear along with a bowl of Captain Crunch.

I giggled. Every other Saturday was our day—and sometimes Sundays, depending on how much my mom needed to get done. With her working now, she spent her weekends doing housework, laundry, or just running to the grocery.

Ready for you to pick me up, he texted.

Be there in an hour, I replied.

Where are we going?

Where do you want to go?

I want to hang at your house. I like Dax. He's cool.

He's something, I said.

Yeah? What?

I laughed out loud. God, I loved him, especially when he didn't get my jokes.

I showered quickly, threw on a pair of shorts, a Whitman tee, and flip-flops. My hair was too short for a high ponytail, so I spent time blowing it dry and then straightening it so it swung around my neck.

I popped in the kitchen to scrounge for a breakfast bar I'd stashed in the cabinet the night before, but came to a halt. To my surprise, on the table rested an envelope, a bag with the top folded down, and a drink carrier with two large Starbucks cups with lids.

I gingerly picked up the envelope, flipped it over, and saw my name had been scrawled in lopsided handwriting. My hands tore it open.

Remi,
I'm bloody sorry for last night. You're right. I'm a douche. Please forgive me. What I said was wrong, and you didn't deserve any of it. I swear it will never happen again. I don't have a coffee pot yet, and I didn't know what you liked, so I picked up a regular coffee and a latte. They may be cold by the time you see this. There's cream and sugar in the bag along with some breakfast.
Dax

P.S. A key to the front and back door is under the mat out front. FYI: I'll be home late tonight.

I plopped down in the nearest chair, staring at the paper, my fingers running over his signature. Like him, it was expressive with a big swoop on the end of the x.

I considered writing him a reply on the back, but in the end I didn't.

I didn't know what I'd say.

Opening the bag, I saw three chocolate donuts and a giant sugar cookie. My mouth watered, and I realized I'd never eaten dinner. After warming up the latte in the microwave, I stuffed a donut in my mouth, grabbed my keys, and headed out to see my mom and Malcolm.

I'd worry about Dax later.

CHAPTER EIGHTEEN

T HE MORNING AFTER Remi moved in, I got up around seven to meet Declan at the gym. He was training hard for an upcoming MMA exhibition in Charlotte, and he'd picked me as his training partner. *More like punching bag,* I smirked as I cranked my Range Rover and left the house. I stopped at Starbucks, grabbed some items, and ran them back to the house for Remi. Then I sat down and wrote her a note.

Last night after Remi had gone upstairs and gone to bed and Axel and the girls had left, I'd found myself standing outside Remi's door. Dying to talk to her and I had no freaking explanation for it. With my hand on her door, I'd stood there for an agonizing ten minutes, debating on whether or not to knock.

My hands had touched her doorknob, my fingers itching to turn the handle and walk inside. I needed to apologize, to beg her to forgive me for my stupid comments in the bathroom.

But . . .

I had no right to even consider going into her private room when she was asleep. In fact, I was being a stalker by even standing outside her door because she was nothing to me. Not even a friend anymore.

Just a bloody roommate.

She was the only girl I'd ever talked to about Mum, the only girl I'd ever fake-married, the only girl I'd ever made love to . . .

I walked away, tearing myself away from the door that stood between us.

Hartford stood between us too.

The best thing to do was to move on—be the usual goodtime Dax and forget about us in London.

I gritted my teeth and forced thoughts of her away.

Thank God I was going to the gym because I needed to punch something.

I walked into Front Street Gym. The older lady at the front desk—Maria—gave me a quick wave and a smile. Declan had hired her in May when he'd had the grand opening.

"Hey! How's the house?" she asked.

I grinned. "Got a fresh coat of paint on it and a roommate. It's all good."

She cocked her head. "Hmmm, Declan said you might be open to selling."

"Absolutely. You buying a house soon?" I'd been headed to-ward Declan who was in the back with a private client, but I backed up. Prospects.

"No, but my sister is looking for a place since her divorce—tired of her small apartment, I guess." She tapped a pen on the desk.

I leaned on the counter and gave her my full attention. "Really. What's she looking for?" I knew what I liked in a home—but if I wanted to buy and sell, I'd need to think about the customer.

She thought about it. "She loves a big kitchen since she likes to cook." Her eyes brightened. "Oh, she has three grandkids, so a big yard and extra bedrooms would be great."

I nodded. Hmmm. "Give me a few months to get it fixed up and I'd love to show it to her." I pulled a white business card out of my gym bag that Declan had suggested I have made at a local printer. Stamped in black was my name, the address of the house, and cell number. Simple but it got the point across. I smiled as I handed it over to her.

I said goodbye and headed inside the gym. Organized chaos, Front Street was crowded already, and I weaved between the mats and sparring ring for the running room. I'd already seen Declan working with one of his private clients near the back. Waiting for him to wrap up, I hopped on an elliptical and ran a quick five miles. With the endorphins and adrenaline coursing through my blood, I immediately felt better than I had last night.

Declan ambled over soon after, but wanted to reschedule, saying that Elizabeth wanted to meet him for lunch. He smiled when he told me, and I figured "lunch" was in their small apartment in the back of the gym. We chatted a bit longer, mostly him giving me advice about my upcoming classes. I listened, but it was tough because everything had always come easy for him.

After he left, I moved to the leg presses. Using my heels, I pushed the weight up slowly then let it fall. I'd gotten in about twenty reps when I noticed a girl coming in the door dressed in bright-pink athletic wear.

Eva-Maria. The little sister who'd bullied Remi.

I let the weight clang to the footrest, jumped up and wiped my face with a towel, and strode over to her.

She was leaning over talking to a girl on the butterfly machine when I came up behind her.

I halted a few feet away. "Eva-Maria."

She flicked her eyes over her shoulder and then completely pivoted, a huge grin on her face. "Oh my God. Dax Blay. I have been missing you at the house. Where have you been?" She wiggled over to me and threw her arms around my shoulders.

I untangled her.

She pouted. "Aren't you missing me? I hear you got a house now. Why don't you let me plan a big party for you?"

I studied her. She was pretty enough with pale blonde hair and nice curves, but for the life of me, I couldn't remember a specific thing about her under those clothes. I couldn't tell you if her skin was soft, if her nipples were big or small, or if the carpet matched the drapes. At best, she was second rate, and I'd been with her more times than I cared to recall my sophomore year.

She'd never really cared about me.

And that was exactly what I'd wanted.

Because love equaled pain.

"Dax? Are you listening to me? I was just telling you about the bonfire the brothers are putting together."

I waved her off. Of course I knew—but that was not what I wanted to discuss. "You know Remi Montague, right?"

She arched her brows. "Yeah. I've seen her at mixers. She's been dating Hartford forever—although the rumor mill says they're not engaged anymore." She laughed.

"They are engaged," I spat.

"Okaaay."

"Do you remember egging her dorm room door or putting sticky notes all over her car with *slut* written on it? Maybe you recall the lies you told about her to all your girlfriends."

She swung her ponytail back, a haughty expression on her face. "Whatever. I did those things, but I didn't tell lies about her. I only told the truth. She *was* naked in your bed, and she did end up pregnant—"

"What?" My stomach dropped.

She frowned and looked around the room as if people might be listening. Uneasiness crossed her face. "Um, I assumed she told you."

My head pounded, and I rubbed it. "She didn't tell me anything. What—how do you know for sure? She'd never tell you that."

"Her suitemate told me she'd been sick as a dog and throwing up every morning. A bit later, she found a positive pregnancy test in the trash in the bathroom, and Remi had been the last one in the room. The entire dorm floor knew something was up with her because she missed a ton of classes that month and never came out of her room. Lulu told everyone she had mono, but we all assumed that was a cover story." She grimaced. "Maybe it wasn't yours. I—I just figured it was since I'd seen you two together."

The room spun. I stumbled over to one of the chairs in the waiting area as far from the front desk as I could get.

She. Had. Been. Pregnant.

Was it true? I shut my eyes. Fuck. It explained so much. Why she'd hated me for dating other girls right after her. Why she'd never so much as made eye contact with me.

Eva-Maria took the seat next to me. "Are you okay?"

"What happened to the baby?" I pushed out, feeling out of breath.

She lifted her shoulders. "I don't know—but she met Hartford soon after that."

I leaned my head back against the wall, trying to get under control.

She said, "I'm sorry to be the one to tell you, but at least you don't have to deal with Remi and kid for the rest of your life. Can you imagine?" She laughed.

My eyes flew open. "Never say her name again. If you see her coming, turn around and walk the fuck away. Leave her alone."

Red rose in her cheeks. "I didn't realize you cared so much." She smiled uncertainly. "It's obvious you're wound up. Word among the sisters is you aren't very accommodating these days." Her eyes ghosted over my crotch.

A muscle twitched near my eye. My lips went flat. "I'm one step away from calling a meeting and getting you kicked out of the house. Now, get out of my sight and don't come back to my brother's gym."

She whitened. "Dax. I'm sorry—"

"Get out."

She licked her lips, sent me a final look, turned, and left the gym.

For half an hour, I sat in that seat, twisting different scenarios and outcomes from three years ago around in my head. I recalled every single moment I'd seen her.

But nothing—*nothing* hinted at her being pregnant.

Obviously, the baby never came unless she'd hidden it under baggy clothes and delivered in May, which would make sense if she'd gotten pregnant in September.

God.

I rubbed my face.

Did her mom have the baby?

Had she given it up for adoption? Abortion?

And Hartford—he wouldn't have dated a pregnant Remi.

Wait. Would he? Did he love her that much?

Why not?

You'd do it too if the baby wasn't yours. You love Remi.

My spine went ramrod straight from where I'd been slumped over the chair, raking my hands through my hair. Goosebumps rose over my skin.

That was not true.

Yet how did I explain my reaction to her and Hartford at the hotel? Why did I give a fuck if she was back with him? Why had I wanted her to live with me?

Right there in the foyer of Front Street Gym, I picked my life apart, digging deep for the bones I never let anyone see, even Declan.

I'd been a player for four years—further if you went back to high school. For years, I'd been a master at drifting in and out of girls' beds and lives, each girl a dance of one step forward and two steps back. I pushed real relationships away and had never looked back. Yet when Remi shut that door in my face three years ago, *I'd fucking flinched*—because the naïve boy in me who'd believed in love had craved her. My gut had seen something that weekend, our connection a live wire so hot that I knew if I took hold of it, I'd be fried.

In my head that day, I'd wanted to chase her down the Tau hall and drag her back like a Neanderthal. I'd wanted to tell her she was weird as shit, but in a good way that got me hot.

You should have, my heart said.

But I didn't.

Self-preservation had kicked in, protecting me from being

demolished. Maybe she'd figure out how shallow I was or that I'd barely passed Geometry. She'd leave me for someone with a bigger brain. Like Hartford.

Maybe she'd die like Mum.

My hands clenched.

Fuck that.

No matter what, I never wanted that awful feeling again when you lose someone, like an SUV has been dropped off a skyscraper straight onto your chest.

But this baby thing?

I had to get to the bottom of it. I had to know what happened; what she went through.

If it had been mine.

Fuck that. *You know it was yours,* my heart told me. She wasn't the kind of girl who slept with random guys one after another. You'd been her exception.

CHAPTER NINETEEN

Remi

MY MOM FOLLOWED Malcolm and me as we left her house and headed out to my car. She was mostly a good mom and wanted the best for me, but her micromanaging had driven a wedge between us over the years.

She tsked from behind me. "Your hair looks like it's on fire. What will your professors think? Don't forget you still need recommendations for Duke next year."

I sighed. She'd been picking at me on and off since I'd arrived at the house to pick up Malcolm.

Flip-flops? Really?

You're getting chunky.

I can't believe you're living with a man you barely know.

Oh, I definitely knew him.

Wonder what she'd think if I showed her my Union Jack tattoo? Probably have a heart attack then drag me down to the doctor's office to have it lasered off.

However—she *had* done something wonderful for me, and I attempted to keep that in mind rather than her harping.

While I'd been in London, she'd demanded a meeting with

the manager of the hotel where my wedding had been planned and somehow convinced them to give me back my ten-grand deposit. *Go, Mom.* Like me, she was tenacious and once she'd set her mind to something, you could be damn sure she wasn't going to give up.

She'd told me the good news as soon as I'd arrived back from London. I'd hugged her hard and for a long time. With most of my tuition paid for with a scholarship, that money would come in handy for living expenses. Of course, Hartford had offered to pay my expenses this fall—especially since he was part of the reason I had those issues—but it had felt wrong. I wanted to do this on my own, and having the money back that I'd saved from waiting tables meant something big.

Something in me had shifted in London, and having the extra money amplified it. Perhaps it was because Hartford had jilted me, maybe it was the attack, but for the first time, I was operating without a detailed plan except to get into graduate school and take care of Malcolm. By my standards, I was operating by the seat of my pants.

Marrying the perfect guy wasn't on my list.

Having the perfect suburban home wasn't on my list.

Kids weren't on my list.

I was on the list.

Who the heck knew what tomorrow would bring?

Rainbow-colored hair?

Maybe get a few piercings?

Mom put her hands on her hips as I threw Malcolm's bag in the backseat. She tucked brown hair behind her ears, her sharp eyes assessing me from the top of my red hair to my flip-flops. Tall like me with patrician features and wavy brown hair, she'd turned fifty-three this year, but you wouldn't have guessed it from the way she took care of herself. Even today on her day off as a night manager at the Pringles plant, she was dressed in casual pressed slacks, a boat-necked shirt, and a light sweater. If you looked closer, though, you'd see the brittleness in her eyes; the sadness that still lingered since Dad had died. He'd left us with life insurance, but we'd never been a wealthy family. Not like Hartford or Dax. Most of the money had gone to pay off the rest of our house, a large two-story colonial, while the rest had been used to help with my college fund, Malcolm's private school where he received extra attention for autism, and Mrs. Johnson, Malcolm's sitter who slept over on the weeknights Mom worked.

Mom exhaled. "Tell Hartford he needs to come for dinner soon. I'm glad you're giving him a second chance. You know, he'll always take care of you."

What she really meant was: *He's rich and loves you. Don't let him slip through your fingers.*

I opened my car door and slid inside. "I can take care of myself, Mom."

She leaned down to my open window. Confusion crossed her face at my comment. "Plain and simple, he's the guy for you—nothing like that boy from freshman year—"

"Do not bring that up," I said with steel in my tone as my hands tightened on the steering wheel. I didn't want Malcolm knowing the details.

"I'm just saying, your life would be easier—"

"Stop," I said, cutting her off. "This *is* my life, Mom. I like my red hair. I like my flip-flops. I'm completely in charge and it has nothing to do with Hartford. And you know what, I can do anything I want. Maybe I'll never get married. Maybe I'll jump on a plane and move to London. Maybe I'll raise llamas." I softened my tone. "Mom, you have to let me go."

Malcolm had stiffened next to me in tune to the mercurial relationship I had with Mom. He reached across the gearshift and took my hand. "Let's go now, Remi. I want ice-cream."

I smiled at him. Clearly I needed him way more than he needed me.

I cranked the car, my eyes flicking to Mom's. "Thank you again for taking care of the money thing. I love you."

She exhaled and stepped back from the car. "I love you both. See you tomorrow."

Putting the car in drive, I pulled out of my driveway and headed to Raleigh.

AFTER A QUICK trip to the grocery store and a stop at Sonic for ice-cream, we headed back to Dax's. Once there, I dug around my boxes, found my games, and we played a few rounds of Scrabble. Afterwards, we headed upstairs where Malcolm helped me organize my closet and dresser. I promised him dinner in return.

Around six o'clock, Malcolm was sitting at the kitchen table working on a puzzle of The Globe Theatre I'd gotten him in London while I stirred the spaghetti sauce I had on the stove.

The front door opened and my body tensed. Dax. I'd sent him a text earlier thanking him for my breakfast, and he'd replied with a *K*.

I turned as he walked in the kitchen, trying to keep my eyes off his body in a pair of athletic shorts and a fitted shirt that clung to every muscle in his abdomen. I noticed his face was softer than last night, his eyes hesitant, almost questioning.

"Smells amazing in here," he murmured, his gaze drifting over me, lingering on my hair. My lips.

My heart ached at the sight of him. *Stupid heart.*

"Thanks."

His shoulders dipped. "Look, Remi, I—I'm sorry for last night in the bathroom."

"Yeah."

"I'll let you hit me if you want—right in the gut." He grinned and patted his six-pack abs, and some of the tension from last night I'd been holding in melted.

Malcolm looked up at both of us, blinked. "You might want to rethink that. She has a mean right hook that Dad taught her."

"Thanks for the warning, man," Dax said, giving Malcolm a fist bump. "I've actually seen your sister in action, and it wasn't too shabby." He smiled at me—but it seemed off as he fidgeted from one foot to the other.

"No need for hitting," I said. "There's plenty of spaghetti here if you want some."

He smirked. "You won't try and poison me?"

"I never said I was a good cook. It might just kill you anyway."

He moved to the stove and stood next to me as I checked the noodles I'd put on earlier.

Keep your eyes off him.

"Homemade sauce?" From my peripheral vision, I felt his gaze boring into me.

"Yep—if you count Ragu with some spices and meat thrown in."

"Cool. Want me to do anything?" He inched toward me, the heat from his arm near mine.

"Uh, maybe set the table and get us some drinks."

"What would you like?" he asked.

I swallowed. "There's Coke and Newcastle in the fridge I bought today. Malcolm will want lemonade."

"Which do you want?" Another inch closer, and I caught the heady scent of sweat and man.

"What?"

"Which drink do you want?" he asked, a hint of laughter in his voice.

"Beer."

"Me too." He brushed past me, his fingers grazing the side of my leg.

I inhaled and kept stirring. Total accident. It was a small kitchen.

He set my beer down on the counter already opened and propped himself back on the counter to stare more.

Did I have a zit?

"You want to put the garlic bread in the oven?" I asked a bit later as I poured the noodles into the colander.

He paused, a strange expression on his face. "You want me to put a bun in the oven?"

Of course I got the joke, but it was out of place and odd. "Yes."

"Okay."

"Thanks." I poured the noodles back in the hot pot so they'd stay warm. I shrugged. "I guess I should have put it in earlier. Now our pasta will be cold."

"Nothing is ever cold when I'm with you," he murmured, putting the bread in.

Malcolm sent us a curious look, his hand pausing over a puzzle piece.

I started. Something was definitely wrong with Dax tonight.

A few minutes later, we carefully transported the puzzle to a place in the den to make room for our dinner on the table.

"It's our first cooked meal in the new house," Dax said quietly, his eyes on me. "Thank you."

My entire body tingled at his gaze. *God, would I ever stop wanting him?*

We sat down to eat and Dax kept sneaking little looks at me, the intensity of his attention making me self-conscious. Once, I'd even excused myself to run upstairs and check my appearance. I looked fine. My hair was kind of a mess, but I didn't see anything on my face. I sniffed my armpits. I didn't smell.

Later after we'd eaten and Dax had cleaned up, I hung out in the kitchen and baked chocolate chip cookies while Dax ran upstairs for a shower. I figured he had plans.

Malcolm plopped himself in the recliner in the den and flipped through the channels. He wanted to watch a movie, so I put the finished cookies on a plate and carried them into the den.

Dax was sitting in the middle of the couch with wet hair, dressed in loose sweats and a Tau t-shirt.

"It's Saturday night. Aren't you going out?" I asked.

He propped his feet up on the coffee table and spread his arms out along the back of the couch. "Nope." He patted the seat. "Come on, sit down. You worked hard at making us dinner. Malcolm picked a movie out already—*Four Weddings and Funeral*."

"He loves British movies," I commented as I sat down within inches of him, feeling like I was in high school again, nervous and jittery about what was going to happen next.

My phone dinged with a text. It was Hartford wanting to know what my plans were for tomorrow. I replied, turned my phone off, and tucked it under the cushion.

"Hartford checking in?" Dax asked.

I nodded, seeing his lips tighten.

Another hour and a beer later, I grew drowsy, my head nodding into my chest. I drifted off and dreamed that Dax was really Aquaman, only he was way hotter than any comic hero I'd ever seen. His hair was messy and sexy and he had dragonfly designs all over his blue skin-tight wetsuit. I was a beautiful mermaid only I had legs. With the sea crashing around us, he chased me in the sand until he caught me and carried me into his cave. He kissed me . . .

I jerked awake, the only light in the room coming from the glow of another movie that had come on. Malcolm slept in the recliner, his mouth open as he snored.

Dax stared at me. "Hey, sleepyhead."

I yawned. "Was I out for a while?"

"Not long." He touched my hair, his fingers ever so slightly brushing the ends.

Barely even aware of doing so, I sighed and leaned my head into his hand.

"What were you dreaming?" he asked softly. At my questioning gaze, he said, "You moaned."

Heat colored my face. "You remember in London telling me about your dream where I was a mermaid and you chased me on the beach and took me to a cave . . ." I stopped.

"I dream about you all the time, Remi."

My heart jumped. I licked my lips. "My dream was . . . like that." Feeling braver, I turned my head to take him in, questions burning in my mind. An idea had taken root earlier in the day as I'd had more time to analyze *why* Dax was so bitter about Hartford and me.

"Something's been bugging me, and I wanted to ask you . . ."

"Mmm." His hand pushed harder, the tips of his fingers digging into my scalp and working to the nape of my neck. Oh God. Felt so good. I bit back a groan.

"It's hard to think when you do that," I said.

"Do you want me to stop?"

"Never," I whispered.

"Good." His hand skated lower, massaging the knots in my shoulder. "What's been bugging you, Remi?"

My chest rose and I took a deep breath. "I—I have a theory about London on why you never answered my texts."

His hand stilled. "Oh?"

I swallowed, staring down at my hands. At my ring. "It's—it's because you *did* come back with breakfast but you saw me with Hartford when the door was open or you heard him through the door. You left—because you were hurt." My voice cracked at the end.

God, I was taking such a chance here. What if I was wrong?

I lifted my gaze to read his face. "Am I right?"

"Yes."

The bag of sand I'd been carrying around my neck dropped. "Why didn't you just tell me? We could have talked—"

"I saw you with your tongue down his throat. I don't think there's anything else to say. I was your rebound guy. You love him. He's good for you. I'm not." His voice was low. Matter-of-fact. Final.

I bit my lip. Nodded. Those things were all true.

He closed his eyes. Opened them, a void there.

"Don't—don't look like that." I slid over to him, and he wrapped me in his arms. I pushed my face into his chest, and we sat like that for a while. For some reason, I was terrified to look at him, and maybe he was afraid to look at me, because just one little movement from him, one little whisper of my name, and I'd be willing to jump off a cliff. I'd go down that rabbit hole.

He placed his hand on my stomach, his eyes questioning. "I have a question for you. What happened to our baby, Remi?"

CHAPTER TWENTY

"**W**AIT," HE SAID, grabbing my hand to pull me back as I jerked off the couch and stumbled in my haste to get away from him. The arm of the couch saved me from falling. My breath snagged, my body ice-cold as if a Siberian wind had blown in the room.

No. No. *Not this.*

His question triggered a wasteland of memories I didn't want to revisit.

Shaking my head furiously, I bolted for the kitchen and out the back door. The night air greeted me as I leaned over the rail that lined the patio.

Don't puke, don't puke.

Out of control. Need control.

I took deep breaths, inhaling. Exhaling.

How did he know?

"Remi?"

"Go away." Wetness fell from my face. "Leave me alone. *Please.*" My voice was a broken mess.

He touched my back. Soft little brushes as he traced my

shoulders. "I can't, love. I need answers."

"Stop!" I yelled at him, flinching away. I couldn't think when he touched me like he cared.

I ran down the steps to the yard, but it was dark and hard to see. I turned in erratic circles.

God.

I had nowhere to go, nowhere to run.

The sins of my past had caught up with me.

He'd chased me through the yard and caught my arm as I came to a halt in front of a large oak tree. He turned me around, peering down at me. Moonlight struck his face, accentuating his beauty, the sharp lines of his face, the shape of his mouth.

I closed my eyes so I couldn't see him.

He's going to be your ruin, my head said.

He pushed hair out of my face. "Shhh, it's okay. Don't be upset, Remi. Please. I just want you to tell me."

My entire body shook, and I shuddered against him.

He exhaled, and wrapped me up in his arms. "Please. Remi, forgive me for asking—but I have to know."

I rested against him, giving in, my chest heaving. "How . . ."

He rubbed my back. "Eva-Maria told me. I saw her today and told her to stay away from you, and then it just came out. She thought I knew." He paused. "I would have helped you. I would have done something. I don't know what, but please, talk to me."

I leaned back to see his face. Searched his eyes. "You want to know how I dealt with my blackest moment? You want to know what it feels like to be pregnant by a guy who was probably screwing someone else the next day?"

"Yes."

My throat caught.

Tell the truth, Remi. Let him see the emptiness you'd been left with.

I pulled myself out of his arms, backing myself up to the tree.

Swallowing, I said, "I found out I was pregnant when my period didn't come two weeks later. The campus clinic confirmed what my early pregnancy test had already told me. I—I was on the pill and you used a condom, but there were a few times—you didn't. I was so stupid! And I thought—I thought you felt the same way about me. I slept with you for three days—because I imagined myself in love with you! Love at first sight. Soul mates. So ridiculous." A bitter laugh erupted. "You were the only thing I did that was not part of my plan and it ended up nearly ruining my life."

"I'm sorry." Even in the darkness, I saw the torture on his face.

"Knowing I was going to have a baby changed everything. All my plans. Yet, when I saw those two blue lines, I *wanted* that baby. I made another plan—if I could get through fall semester, I was going to drop out, have the baby, and go to college later. Somehow I was going to make it work even if I had to live with my mom."

"What happened?"

A harsh laugh came out of me. "*What happened?* At eleven weeks, I was in my advisor's office and started . . . hurting. When I stood up blood was in the chair, on my pants. They—they called an ambulance. My mom came . . . She didn't even know I was pregnant until she got to the hospital."

I hugged myself, rubbing my arms. "They told me there was no heartbeat. It was simply gone. Someone I loved had died. *Again.* And just like my dad, I never even got to say goodbye. I never got to hold my baby. For weeks I grieved. I kept telling myself I'd get over you, that I'd forget about the baby." I furiously wiped my face. "I was a walking zombie—and every time I saw you on campus with another girl, I wanted to shatter into a million pieces all over again."

He exhaled and dropped his head, his hands pressing against his thighs. "God. You're killing me." His voice was ragged. Torn into pieces.

"I'd been careless and flighty. I made a mistake, and I promised myself I'd never do it again. My mom said it was for the best—God's way of giving me another chance. I needed to focus on what I needed instead of what I wanted. And then—I met Hartford, and *he loved me.*"

A shuddering breath came out of Dax. "*Fuck.* I can't take this."

Silence grew between us, stretching all the way to the stars.

The air seemed to hold its breath, heavy and thick with emotion; me brimming with grief and him with regret. I saw it on his face as we stared at each other in the moonlight, neither of us moving, neither of us speaking.

I wanted to run into his arms and let him comfort me.

I wanted him to hold me and tell me he loved me—but he didn't. *He never had.*

I whimpered. Distance. I needed it. Now.

Moving fast, I slid past him, the grass wet beneath my bare feet. Like a statue, he didn't move to stop me.

I slipped into the house and went back to the den. With shaking fingers, I threw a blanket from the hall closet over a still-sleeping Malcolm and went upstairs. I didn't stop to wash my face or brush my teeth or put on nightclothes. Falling into bed, I crawled up to the pillow, tugged it into my chest, closed my eyes, and wept.

Much later, as I lay awake, my door opened and he came in. Even though my back was to the door, I knew it was Dax because my body came alive, my skin aching for his touch.

He lifted the covers, slid into the bed, and formed his body to mine. His nose pressed into my nape as his arm encircled my waist as if he never wanted to let me go. His hand slid down to mine, and I clasped it tight.

"I can't know what you went through, but I'm here now," he whispered.

My breath hitched; I felt leftover tears rise up again, but I swallowed them down.

He kissed my hair.

And, eventually, we slept.

SUNDAY DAWNED. DAX was gone from my bed by the time I'd gotten up around nine. Part of me was glad. The other part didn't know what was going on.

I came downstairs after my shower and saw he'd been out

already and had gotten a new coffee pot and filters along with a bag of Starbucks coffee. Another bag of pastries rested on the table. He must have been up early. I pulled out a chocolate donut and ate it while looking out at the backyard.

He knew now. He knew about the baby. He knew that I'd believed myself in love with him after three nights together. For a reason I couldn't explain, relief filled me. The secret had been mine to carry for too long—and telling him, even if it was hard to revisit, made me feel lighter.

Malcolm and I spent the early part of the day hanging out with Lulu and getting her moved in her dorm. While Malcolm had been out of the room to get boxes from her car, I'd given her the lowdown on everything that had transpired between Dax and me.

"If living with him gets too hard, you can always apply to be my roommate next semester," she offered as we unpacked her clothes and put them in the closet.

"I'd hate to be mean to Carla if you dumped her for me before the year is up." Carla was her roomie and they'd been friends for a while.

She sighed. "Yeah. I keep hoping she'll decide to move in with her boyfriend, but she hasn't." Her eyes narrowed in on my face. "So, just noticing here, but you seem good."

"Malcolm is here, you are here, I'm going to graduate this year, and I have some money."

"And you have Hartford."

"Yes."

Needing to change the topic, I grinned and held up a shirt with white skulls and cut-outs everywhere. "Do you really wear this to class?"

She smirked. "Of course. And tonight, I'm wearing this!" A mini tank dress appeared, dangling from her fingers. Black with red roses and pin-up girls on the material, it was, um, eye-catching.

"Nice. Where you going?"

She pouted. "Don't you mean where are *we* going? Remember, it's the day before classes and ladies' night at Cadillac's. It's practically a tradition we go."

"We went one time our sophomore year," I said dryly.

She tsked. "And we're going tonight, so you best find something cute and flirty and come with. I promise to buy you drinks."

"Uh, they're free."

She snorted. "Okay, so I'll trek to the bar and be your errand girl while you chat and dance—"

"There'll be no dancing."

"Don't you want to wash your hair in front of everyone at Cadillac's?" Her lips twitched.

I threw a pillow at her. "It was the best I could do!"

She laughed. "And you looked good, I swear."

"Liar." I smiled. "Anyway, Hartford wants to see me tonight. He had family stuff all weekend."

She groaned. "Fine, invite Hairy. I'm desperate to get out and see everyone. Aren't you?"

I raised a brow, thinking. "I don't have a thing to wear."

"Wear that silk number from London, the one that made Dax's eyeballs pop out of his head. Maybe try some heels this time."

"No heels. Ever." I paused. "Besides, don't you think a dress is too fancy for Cadillac's?"

"Nope. Not where there's a blue-haired British boy popping in to see us." She squealed, her hands fluttering around. "Oh my God, I wasn't supposed to tell you. Shit! Spider's been texting me for days arranging to surprise Dax tonight."

"What are you talking about?"

She giggled and settled in on the bed, crossing her legs. "Spider's coming and we're having a party for Dax's new house. Declan is supposed to get Dax to Cadillac's, and I'm supposed to bring you."

"Me? I don't understand. And why you are suddenly texting a rock star? Is there something you're not telling me?"

An impish grin spread across her face. "He only texted a few times."

"How many?"

She shrugged.

"Spill."

She just grinned.

I pursed my lips. "I think you have some 'splaining to do."

"Whatever. It's nothing. We're just friends. He's still in love with some Mila girl."

"Uh-huh."

"Don't say it like that." Her face flushed a deep red.

"Fine, fine. But now I'm wondering what you two were up to while Dax and I were getting our tattoos . . . oh shit . . . my tattoo. Whatever I wear, it's got to cover it." I grimaced.

She ran to her closet and pulled out a short, lime-green dress with a mandarin collar.

"It's so bright." I held up my hands to shield my eyes.

"Nah. It's classy with a bit of slut, and the top is high enough to cover your Union Jack." She held it up to my frame and I peered down at it. It was short.

"You know I weigh about fifteen pounds more than you, right?"

She pushed it in my hands. "Here. Take it home and try it—and put something besides flats with it."

CHAPTER TWENTY-ONE

"**W**HAT THE BLOODY** hell is eating at you, bro? You're not even looking at my hands," Declan said. For the third time, I'd been distracted and had failed to shield a side-kick to the chest he'd given, ending with me flat on my arse on the sparring mat.

I shook it off and stood. Put my fists up. "Nothing. Come on, try again, knobhead. Let's see how far you get." I'd been here for an hour, helping him getting some training in. I wasn't good enough for him—not by a long shot—but his regular partner was on vacation and Declan was, well, driven. Missing a day of sparring was not an option so he took the next best thing. Me.

He slipped his gloves off. "Nope, we're done. Come on, let's head to the kitchen and get some lunch."

"Cool," is what I said, but internally I wasn't sure I could stomach anything. My gut swirled from last night and everything Remi had confessed.

We slipped through the back entrance of the packed gym, down a narrow hall, and entered their apartment.

Elizabeth met us in the kitchen and handed us both a cold glass

189

of water. "How's the roommate situation coming?" she asked as we pulled stuff out of the fridge to make sandwiches.

"Peachy."

She paused, sending me an odd look. "Oh."

"What does that mean?" I said.

"It's just, she's a pretty girl, and you're a guy, and maybe I'm wrong, but I thought there was a tiny bit of tension between you." She smiled and handed me a bag of chips for my sandwich. "Or maybe that was just the frat thing going on between you and her fiancé."

"He slept with her in London," Declan murmured. "Fake-married her too."

Her mouth gaped as she popped Declan on the head. "And you're just now telling me! What's wrong with you?"

"Bollocks, I'm sorry it slipped my mind. We came home and *we got busy* and then *the shower* and I guess I forgot . . ." He took a swig of water. "A man can't think straight around you, love."

"Mmmm. I guess so." She leaned in and kissed his cheek while his arm snaked around her waist hungrily and pulled her in closer.

I looked down at my sandwich. I mean, I was happy for them—always had been—but today . . .

After lunch, they convinced me to head to Cadillac's that night and I agreed, realizing I needed a dose of fun after my tough week. I headed to the house around five to shower and get dressed. Remi's car was gone, and I figured she'd taken Malcolm back home for the week. I parked on the street instead of the driveway, thinking it was safer for her if she had the parking closer to the house.

By six, I'd showered, shaved, and changed into jeans and a black Vital Rejects shirt Spider had given me in London. I spent a while around the house, mostly waiting to see if she came in, but she never did. I considered calling her and inviting her out, but in the end, I didn't.

I just didn't know where we stood.

At seven I headed to Cadillac's. It was a college hangout, and I figured it would be packed with all the students here over the weekend.

I walked through the door at Cadillac's—only the regulars weren't there.

"Surprise!" came the shouts from a room full of people.

I nearly fell arse over tit onto the marble floor. Grins and shouts met me as people crowded around me to slap me on the back and congratulate me on the house.

Everyone was here. Axel and some of the brothers, a collection of little sisters, Declan and Elizabeth, my father and step-mum, several other girls I knew from Whitman, and Spider—my eyes tracked back to him as he made his way over to me, wearing a baseball hat, black skinny jeans, and his gray leather jacket.

Declan wrapped a big arm around my shoulder. "Dude. Spider arranged this. He wanted to do a little thank-you for taking care of him this summer. By the way, everyone brought a housewarming gift. It's a Dax festival in here." He grinned.

Spider had reached us.

"Dude. What the hell?" I checked him out. He chuckled, eyes clear. Focused. "You did this? I don't know what to say—and that's not normal for me."

He shrugged. "You never left my side all summer, and you and Declan are the closest thing to real family I have . . . and bloody hell, I wanted to see you before I start touring." He pulled a thick envelope out of his pocket. "And . . . I never got a chance to give you this."

I opened it. Looked back at him. "I can't take this money. I lost this bet, plus I gave you your quid already."

"It's not about the winning—okay maybe a little, but why not? Consider it a housewarming gift and now you have more capital to invest wherever you want." He plucked at his leather jacket. "Plus, you'll hurt my little feelings if you give it back."

"Damn. Thank you, man." I gave him a quick side-hug. It was too much, but I could see how much it meant to him.

His eyes shifted to the door.

I followed his gaze and saw Lulu, Remi, and Hartford walk through the door. Jealousy lit me up like lightning, my temper spiking. I cursed under my breath and looked away from them.

"You good, mate?" Spider asked, checking out Hartford with critical eyes. His lip curled. "That's the boyfriend?"

"Fiancé," I muttered.

He arched a brow. "Want me to kick his skinny arse? Wanna bet if I can?"

I laughed. God, I'd missed him. "You're a nutter."

"Sod off," he said with a rueful grin. He pulled a small box out of his pocket. "Now, let's talk about this."

"What? No more gifts, okay?"

He shook his head. "It's for Remi."

My mouth parted, the pieces coming together. "You found it?"

The day after her bracelet had been stolen, I'd called every single pawnshop in London and the surrounding towns looking for her bracelet. I hadn't gotten a hit, but it hadn't stopped me from checking in with them until I'd left London.

He stuffed it in my hands. "Dude. You left strict instructions for me to call *every single day*. I did. Hell, it gave me something to do with myself. One of the pawnshops called back yesterday. They even fixed the broken clasp. I should have told you, but I wanted to surprise you . . ." He paused. "You okay? You look funny."

"No, I just know how much she loves it." I opened the package and there it was—her bracelet, amid a wad of tissue.

I looked back up at him. "She needs this. Thank you."

"You're the one who thought of it. I'll catch you in a bit." I nodded and he brushed past me to head toward an enthusiastically waving Lulu.

Someone pushed a beer in my hands, and I made the rounds to say hi to everyone. I talked to my father and step-mum first, since I assumed this wasn't quite their high-society scene and they'd want to get out before it got too late. They congratulated me, and my father looked pleased although he asked me a hundred questions about whether I was ready for classes to begin, if I had purchased my books, and on and on.

An hour later, after a few toasts had been had, I ended up on a stool chatting with Axel and Alexandria. I'd had a few drinks, and my buzz was making me antsy rather than relaxed.

"Any plans after this?" she asked, sending me a flirtatious grin. *Did I?*

That depended on Remi. I wanted to talk to her more—without Hartford in my face—but she hadn't left his side.

I flicked my eyes over to see them holding hands at the end of the bar. She towered over the other girls, looking gorgeous in some kind of green dress, her hair swinging against her neck.

I tried to catch her eye, but she never looked in my direction, her eyes seeming to avoid mine. It was intentional, I assumed, feeling my anger rise again. She was the girl who needed control, and I was screwing with it.

Hartford watched me though, his eyes narrowed as he caught me staring at Remi. Fuck him. I didn't care. I smiled at him and raised my glass. *You might have her now, Omega, but who knows about tomorrow . . .*

He gave me a haughty smile and leaned down to kiss Remi on the head. My fists clenched. Douche. I wanted to rip into him . . .

"Hello? Dax?" Alexandria asked.

I moved my eyes off Remi. "What?"

She giggled, pink lips sucking on her straw. "I was saying that Bettina and I are going to the Tau house later—but I don't want to go if you aren't there."

I slid a finger down her arm. "Maybe you can come to my place."

It was obvious Remi was with Hartford, so what was I waiting on?

A short time later, I saw from my peripheral vision that they'd joined the circle at our end of the bar.

Don't bloody look at her.

God, I hated seeing them together.

Most of all, I wanted a reaction out of her when she was near me.

Something. *Anything.*

I mean, how could she walk around with him and pretend like we didn't just have a big fucking moment last night?

She ordered a drink and the bartender set it on the bar next to me. Reaching to the bar, her arm brushed mine.

I flinched.

"Excuse me, sorry." She blinked rapidly, her face frozen.

I smirked. "Touch me anytime, *angel.*"

She'd been turning back to Hartford who was in a conversation with someone, but pivoted around to face me, a glare in her eyes.

"Oops. Bad habit." I grinned and turned to the blonde next to me. "Remi, do you remember . . ." I stopped. *What was her name?* Shit. I'd known it a minute ago.

"Alexandria," Remi said dryly.

I leaned over, took *Alexandria's* hand and kissed it. "Sorry. Too many drinks already, but I promise it won't happen later."

She giggled, and I leaned over and kissed her full on the lips, my tongue slipping inside hers. She moaned and just when her hands were snaking around my neck, I pulled back, glancing at Remi.

That was all for you, my eyes said.

You're a bastard, hers said.

I bit my bottom lip, my gaze raking over her dress, lingering on her legs. My eyes lifted and met hers. I cocked an eyebrow. *If you say the word, I'd kiss you instead,* my face said.

Her face flamed, and her hands shook.

But I was past caring if she was hurt by a girl *I* was with. *She was killing me.*

A side of me wanted to pick at the wounds I knew we both had, because goddamn, I just wanted *something* from her instead of the girl who wanted to pretend we were barely even acquaintances.

No way in hell was I going back to the game we'd been playing. I refused. REFUSED.

We *would* acknowledge we had a shitty past and only then would we move the fuck on.

I put my hand in my pocket and found the napkin I'd put there earlier. Standing up, I said, "If you ladies will excuse me, I have to visit the loo."

In the press of people, I had to slide by Remi, and when my hand brushed hers, I pressed the napkin in hers. "This is yours, angel. Contract is null and void. The next time you fall in someone's lap, remember . . . *you can't just be friends*."

Without a backward look, I stalked off toward the narrow hall that led to the restrooms. I went inside. It was a large room, but empty. Thank God. I needed to compose myself.

I kicked it shut with my foot and leaned against the concrete wall. I rubbed my face.

Spur-of-the-moment shit always get you in trouble, Dax.

And sure enough, Trouble walked in just like I'd wanted her to, blue eyes flashing fire.

We were about to collide at full force.

SHE MARCHED TOWARD me, legs swishing in her green dress. Her face was white, her lipstick a bright red. God, I wanted those lips.

I kept my eyes low and heavy. Waiting.

Halting in front of me, she threw the napkin in my face. It fluttered to the floor, showing me the large *X* I'd scrawled over it. "This meant something to me—even if it didn't to you."

I tossed my head back and laughed. "What? Like a sentimental value? It's meaningless, Remi. We don't need a contract to tell us we can't *ever* kiss each other. You're with *him*, and I'm going to screw that blonde tonight."

Her throat moved. "Stop."

"You stop. Stop getting in my head. Stop making me want something I can't have. Stop looking at me like you want me. Stop breaking my heart about the baby . . ." My head pounded and I pressed on it.

Her lips turned down. "You asked, Dax. You fucking asked."

My head dipped to my chest, remembering the emotion, the barrage of fucked up feelings from the night before. "I know, I know.

And I'm sorry you went through it without me. I'm sorry I was a dickhead to you. I'm sorry I suck at relationships. I'm sorry I can't be what you want. I'm sorry I stomped on your heart. I'm sorry you cried. I'm so fucking sorry. Just forgive me, okay?"

She whimpered at my words and pressed her hand over my heart. "I already have."

I put my hand over hers, ironically where her name was. My other hand went to her hair and threaded through the strands.

"You're shaking," she said.

"Because I want you so bad I can't breathe."

"I can't breathe either," she whispered.

I pulled her hair back and her mouth parted. I leaned down, ran my tongue up her exposed throat, and sucked on her neck. Inhaling, I groaned at the taste of her. "This is what I need," I whispered.

She sank into me, her tits hitting my chest.

I fused my mouth with hers. Hard.

Her tongue met mine, and we kissed like we were starving, our lips clinging to each other, our hands roaming everywhere. Touching.

I pillaged her mouth, her neck, her collarbone, unbuttoning her dress and shoving it down past her shoulders until I could see my name on her. I kissed her tattoo. "I wish you remembered how much you giggled when you got this."

She pressed her face into my chest. "I almost do. I don't regret it. Never."

I tilted her face up and kissed her again. Slowly this time. I never wanted to let her go.

Voices came from the hallway as someone walked by.

"The door . . ." she said between kisses. "What if someone comes in?"

"I don't give a fuck."

I unzipped her dress on the side, tugging it the rest of the way down until it pooled on the floor. I squeezed her breasts, pulling them out of her lace bra but leaving it on. My mouth zeroed in on one while my fingers played with the other. Repositioning us, I pressed her back against the wall, went to my knees, and pulled her knickers down. I inhaled her scent, my hands cradling her waist.

She shuddered as my tongue snaked out to find her clit.

"Dax," she breathed.

Need. Desire. Lust. *Love.* It all pounded. Put my mark on her. She was mine. Not his.

"Please," she moaned as I pushed her legs apart to get closer, my nose tracing along her legs, her thighs, and then back to her pussy. Her leg wrapped around my shoulder to get a better position.

"Look at me," I rasped out.

Her hooded eyes fluttered open, a different kind of fire burning there now.

While I stared at her, my hand replaced my tongue, settling into her wetness. Slow. Gentle. "This. This is where I want to be right now."

She swiveled her hips, working herself on my fingers.

"You want more?" I asked. "Harder?"

She nodded, putting her hand on top of mine and pushing.

I hissed, giving her what she wanted. "This is the real you, Remi. Hot. Ready. Needing *me* to make you come. Have you ever had this before? Have you?"

"No," she moaned, her chest rising rapidly.

"Good answer." I stood and kissed her, our tongues caressing each other. With my other hand, I tugged my shirt off over my head and threw it down with her dress.

"I need you," she whispered, rubbing her hand across my chest and down to my hips. "Take me."

"Say my name." I closed my eyes at the need in her voice and stroked her center again, my thumb brushing her bud.

She shuddered. "Dax, you. Always you. Forever you."

I bent my forehead against the wall, all the air sucked out of me at her words.

She pulled my hair back until our faces were level. "What am I going to do? I can't stop how I feel about you."

We stared into each other's eyes, deep into our past.

I'd been a failure the first time we'd met. What did I have now that she'd want?

Or need?

I did the only thing I knew I was good at. I touched her, owning her, pumping until her mouth opened and she writhed, her back arching as she cried out.

"Yes, love, yes," I whispered against her mouth.

She came undone, her muscles clamping down, her gasps like music, and I didn't miss a minute of it, imprinting her image in my brain.

Her eyes glossed over as she whispered my name. Once. Twice. Three times.

Slightly dazed, she rested against the wall.

Sliding my shirt back on, I picked up her dress and helped her step inside it. I zipped her up, my hands lingering on her shoulders. Aching. Still needing *something* and it wasn't just to get off.

She brushed her hair in the mirror while I did mine in the other mirror.

With shaking hands, she found her purse on the floor, opened it, and pulled out her lipstick. I watched her rub it on, eyes glassy.

She turned to me, a dead look in her eyes. "We can't do this again. I can't handle the pain that comes afterwards."

"I know."

Her eyes watered. Fuck. *I couldn't be what she wanted!*

I reached in my pocket and pulled out the box, gently easing out the bracelet. She gasped as she cupped it in her hands and then looked up at me.

"How . . . When?"

I kept silent as I wrapped it around her wrist and fixed the clasp.

I swiped at one of her tears.

She grabbed my hand. Kissed it.

"Go," I whispered.

I closed my eyes and counted to five. When I opened them, she was gone.

CHAPTER TWENTY-TWO

Remi

KNOWING THAT HE was going to be with Alexandria, knowing that he wanted me but didn't, made me want to crawl in a corner and weep, but my head wouldn't allow it.

Use pain to make yourself stronger.

Use heartbreak to make yourself wiser.

With that mantra, I made my way around the bar and forced myself to talk to a few people I hadn't seen all summer. There were questions about Hartford and me, but I fielded them by changing the topic or moving on when I saw someone else.

Dax eventually emerged from the hallway, his face a block of ice.

His eyes met mine and quickly bounced off. I watched him weave his way through the crowd, his head above most of the people there. He got within a few feet of me, paused for a moment as if debating, and then marched over to the pool tables in the back. He curled an arm around Alexandria as she was about to shoot with her cue stick, surprising her and making her squeal. She turned and giggled as he leaned over to show her a better way to shoot.

My body stiffened when his eyes flicked over to me. Watching.

Lulu came up to me. Her eyes flicked down to the tequila I'd ordered on a spur-of-the-moment decision. "Uh, we both know you shouldn't be drinking that."

"Yet, here I am," I said dryly. "Torturing myself. In more ways than one apparently. Good thing the bar doesn't sell tacos."

"Dax?"

I nodded, my eyes darting back to the couple in the back. Alexandria had taken her shot and now they stood against the wood paneling of the wall. She stood in front of him, her back pressed into his chest. I imagined her melting into him like I always did.

Don't think about them together.

I sucked in a breath, willing myself to not stare at them. But I couldn't stop. I wanted to march up to Alexandria and pluck every bleached hair out of her head. Maybe her eyeballs too.

Lulu had obviously seen them too. She gave my hand a squeeze. "Ah, Alexandria. You know, girls with five syllable names are all huge sluts. Always. We proved this theory freshman year when we met Eva-Maria."

I gave her a small smile. "I have three syllables."

"You're just a tiny bit of a slut," she said.

"I love you."

"Awe. Love you too."

We toasted our drinks, and I drained mine. I held up my empty glass. "Looks like I need another one."

Hartford found me near the end of the bar with another tequila in my hand. As he strode over to me, I pushed out a smile. Wearing a pale blue shirt that drew attention to his blond hair and a pair of preppy plaid shorts, he sat on the barstool next to me. His handsome face seemed tense. Dax's party hadn't been his idea of a great time. He'd only come because I'd asked.

"Hey, you disappeared for a while," he said.

"Yeah. Went to the bathroom and decided on a drink." I tipped back the rest of the shot.

"That doesn't seem like you." Earlier I'd told him I wasn't drinking since classes started tomorrow and I wanted to be at the top of my game. He swept my hair back so he could see my face more clearly. He sighed, the heat from his body warm and safe and familiar as his fingers touched my cheek and trailed down my jawline to my lips. "There are times when I feel like I don't know you at all, Remington."

There was an odd sadness in his eyes.

I started. "What do you mean?"

He slid his eyes from me to the hallway where the restrooms were.

Had he seen us?

"Do—do you mean since we took our break? Or since forever?"

He clutched the beer he held, took a long drink, and set it down carefully as if he was thinking through each motion. "Both. I don't know. I mean, you come back from London and you've got this wild hair and you seem—different. You're not soft anymore—you seem like you might break."

He paused. "You don't look at me the same way."

I faced him, my knees between his, not wanting any of the other people standing around to hear us. "There's a hole in us—somewhere—and *you* saw it, and now you want me to suddenly patch it up."

His hand cupped my nape. "But do you *want* me back?"

I wanted the guy who'd make me happy.

"So much has changed."

"I haven't." He pulled me in with his hand, and for a long moment, he stared at me, searching my face. "I still love you, Remi, no matter what you've done."

What did that mean?

He kissed me, his lips cold, his tongue bitter from the beer.

"Finish your drink. Let's get out of here," he said as we pulled apart. "There's hardly anyone here I like anyway." He tossed money on the bar to pay for my drink.

I blinked at the suddenness, my eyes scouring the room for Dax. "Isn't it rude to leave so soon?"

"I want to be alone with you."

Not now. Not after Dax. I couldn't.

"Hartford . . ." My voice was hesitant. I plucked at my bracelet, and his eyes widened.

"Remi! Where did you find it?"

I looked down. My chest ached. God, that moment in the bathroom. "Dax."

His eyebrows slashed down. "How did he find it?"

"I—he just gave it to me tonight . . . I don't know."

"Yeah?" His eyes went to my lips.

I licked them, knowing they were swollen. "He didn't say how."

"He just handed it over and walked away?"

I shrugged.

"When did this happen?" he asked.

"Earlier. In the hallway."

I was lying to him.

This wasn't right. I couldn't do this. I was an awful person.

He took my hand and helped me down off the stool, an urgency to his movements as we moved around the bar.

"Wait," I said. We'd gotten to the front door ready to head out. "Shouldn't we tell Dax goodbye? It's—it's his party."

Hartford's lips thinned, but he nodded, his eyes already scanning the room until they lasered in on the pool tables. Holding hands, we made our way to the back of the bar. But with each step closer to Dax, Hartford grew tenser, as if something inside him was building. Bubbling.

Dax watched us approach with hooded eyes.

Hartford came to a halt in front of him. "Came to say our goodbyes although we'll probably see you soon."

Dax arched a brow, his voice cold. "That so?"

"Your house? We're headed there now." He wrapped an arm around me. "You might want to give us a head start though. We've got some catching up to do now that Malcolm's gone. Remi's hot for it tonight . . . can't keep her hands off me." He leered at Dax. "If you catch my meaning?"

"I see." Dax paled, his hand white around his pool cue. Gray eyes found mine.

I gripped Hartford's arm. Appalled at his words. "Let's go. Please."

He ignored me, shaking me off. "And thank you for getting Remi her bracelet."

Dax tensed, his eyes flicking to my wrist.

"A bit odd to go to all that trouble for someone you just happened to run into in London. I mean, you must have been in contact with the police? And pawn shops?"

Dax's face was a mask, his body held in tight control. "I saw how much she missed it. She was hurting in London." He paused, a flush rising on his cheekbones. "Because of you, arsehole."

Hartford's face twisted. "I think you've got a hard-on for my girl. Stay away from her."

"She isn't mine. She's with you," Dax replied softly.

Hartford stepped into Dax's personal space, his voice like sandpaper. "I knew her moving in with you was a terrible idea, and you can damn well bet she'll be moving out of your house. Tonight."

I felt dizzy. Hartford was losing it.

Dax's control snapped, a dark look on his face as he glared down at Hartford. "You're on dangerous ground, Omega. Tread softly or I will hurt you. You're lucky I haven't already."

"Hartford," I called, my voice thin and shaky. "I'm leaving. With or without you." I pivoted and took long strides to the door. If he didn't come, I'd walk or call a cab or go back in and find Lulu.

I heard him muttering something to Dax, and then he followed me outside to his car.

I put on my seat belt as he got in the driver's seat.

"Reming—"

"No. Just take me home. Now."

He stared out the front windshield. "I saw you follow him in the bathroom. Your dress was messed up when you came out. I'm not stupid."

I blanched. "I—I'm sorry."

His teeth clenched. "What happened in London?"

I sucked in a ragged breath. "I slept with Dax."

"Goddammit!" He banged on the steering wheel with his fist several times, making me flinch. He stopped, his chest rising. "Fuck me, I knew something was off at his house. I can't believe you—and *him*—" He rubbed his face. "I have to get out of here."

He cranked the car, squealing out of the parking lot.

Neither of us spoke during the ride, the tension thick. My face was hot, my hands clenching the armrest as I stared out my window. As soon as he stopped the car at the curb, I unsnapped my seat belt and jumped out.

He got out just as quick, taking long strides to keep up with me as I practically ran to the front door.

"Don't leave like this. We have to talk," he said, his voice tight.

Shaking my head at him, I fumbled around for my keys. "No. I—I can't. We're both too upset. Just go home."

"You were with *him!*" he yelled. "You've always acted like you barely tolerated him. You've been lying to me since London. You've been screwing him since you moved in!"

I flipped around to face him. "You dumped me, Hartford! You wanted a break, and I gave it to you! I wasn't aware there were rules to go along with it." I shook my head and took a step back, wanting to calm down. The neighbors could probably hear us. "And you posted a picture of you and that girl *on our wedding night*. How do you think that made me feel?"

"I wasn't with her. All I could think about was you! I was just confused and scared." He groaned. "I made a *mistake*."

I believed him—but it didn't matter.

"Are you . . . are you in love with him?"

I inhaled. "I can't explain it, but we—have something."

God, there was so much I wasn't saying.

His face morphed to utter anguish. "Stop," he said, pulling at his hair. "You're fucking killing me with this shit."

"I'm sorry."

He spun away from me and paced through the yard. "We're *supposed* to be together. We're perfect. You've said so yourself a million times." He stopped and looked at me. "Don't you love me?"

"I do," I whispered. But was it the right way?

Long moments passed. My breath hitched at the growing pain in his eyes. "I'm so sorry, Hartford. I should have told you about Dax as soon as we talked in London."

He came in closer, his face vulnerable. "This is all my fault. I never should have broken up with you. I pushed you away and I just didn't think you'd . . ." He stopped and stared at me for a long time and then his warm hands cupped my face. "I still love you, Remington. We have something good." He kissed me sweetly but with urgency, as if trying to get me to understand.

We parted, and his eyes were feverish. "I'm the one that put you in this situation. This is my fault."

I frowned. "Hartford. I have feelings for him—"

"He's not a good guy. You know it."

I closed my eyes. Opened them. "There's more I need to tell you. You don't know everything." The heartache I'd nursed. "We slept together before I met you. Freshman year. He—he got me pregnant. I lost the baby."

He looked shocked but wrapped me in his arms. "Jesus," he breathed. "I don't know what to say. That must have been horrible."

I nodded, burying my face in his chest. He held me tighter, stroking my hair, his anger seeming to dissipate as the moments ticked by.

Later, he said, "You're upset. Come home with me. I'll sleep on the couch, and we'll talk once things have settled down." He squeezed my shoulder as if to reassure me.

"I can't go home with you," I whispered, yet part of me didn't want to be here if Dax brought Alexandria home.

He nodded. "Okay, then let's go to Minnie's Diner and get some coffee like we used to when we first met. We can talk—as friends—and you can let it all out."

A long sigh came out of me. That sounded good. I owed him that much. The truth. "Okay," I said.

CHAPTER TWENTY-THREE

I WATCHED THEM leave from where I'd parked my car down the street. Earlier, when they'd driven past the bar and I'd seen her face through the windshield, I'd gotten worried he'd hurt her. I shouldn't have lost my temper with him, but it was Remi . . .

I'd said hasty goodbyes and thanked everyone profusely and left, driving to my house like a maniac.

I didn't care that it was my party. There'd be other parties.

Like a horror movie, I watched them hug, and my gut twisted. *Fuck.* Seeing them in a tender moment cut me in half.

I'd missed some of their interaction, but it was obvious from their body language they cared about each other. And now she was leaving with him—holding hands. My hands clenched the steering wheel as he opened the passenger car door and helped her in.

Once his taillights disappeared, I pulled up in the drive and hopped out of the car. I went inside, clicked on the den light and made my rounds around the house.

Feeling like hell.

I dropped down on the couch and turned on the telly, not really noticing as I flipped through the guide looking for something.

My mind kept jumping around.

Antsy, I jerked back up, went into the kitchen, grabbed some water, and guzzled it. Wiped my mouth. Debating.

Fuck it. Maybe I should go to his place.

Back off. That's stalker territory, I told myself.

God, but when it came to Remi, I didn't care. She made me into someone I didn't recognize. She made me crazy. She made me fucking ridiculous.

I toyed with my keys. It would be easy to find his address on Google.

But she isn't yours. Stop interfering with her happiness.

I took another shower, a long one. I got out when my phone kept going off. I checked it—Alexandria. I tossed it back on the bed. No interest.

I went back to the den, turned off all the lights, and plopped down on the couch to watch the late show.

At midnight, Baz Luhrmann's *Romeo and Juliet* came on.

Stupid movie. There had to be something better on; even the news was better than this.

But I watched. Remembering London.

Remi unlocked the front door and entered the foyer. She came to an abrupt halt when she saw me. Her hands rubbed her eyes, leaving black streaks of mascara on her cheeks. She gazed around the room, looking dazed. "All the lights were off. I assumed you were asleep."

I nodded and paused the movie. "Where's Hartford?" I flicked my eyes down at her ring. *Still fucking there.*

"He went home."

I straightened. "He didn't hurt you did he?"

She shook her head, her expression sad. "Where's Alexandria?"

"Not with me."

A few ticks went by.

"Are you moving out?" I asked.

She started. "No."

I nodded. I wanted to ask her more about what had happened

with Hartford, but I was afraid of her answers.

She moved, coming around the couch and sitting down a few seats away.

"Wanna watch with me?" I asked, hearing hope in my voice. Not caring.

She sighed. "Yeah."

"Come here." I motioned with my hand and she slid next to me, tucking her legs under her body.

"I've seen this one a hundred times with Malcolm," she said, resting her head against my shoulder as we watched Romeo kiss Juliet at the masquerade party. "The beginning is always my favorite part. When he sees her and wants to know who she is."

I put my hand in her hair, playing with the strands. "They're going to fall madly in love," I said, keeping my eyes on the screen.

"And have a secret wedding at a church . . ." Her voice halted, a little catch in it.

"But they can't see what's about to crash into them."

"What's that?"

"She leaves . . . dies. Then he dies because he can't live without her. Love sucks."

"I know." She closed her eyes and leaned back into my caress. I'd long given up watching the movie, my need to look at her too great.

She snuggled in more, her hand over my heart, tracing the lines of my tattoo under my shirt. Leaning down, I adjusted her until we lay side by side, our heads on a couch cushion together, her back to my front. My arm snaked around her waist. She laced her fingers with mine.

And the movie played on as the scenes played out, two star-crossed lovers—fated by the universe, but separated by the world.

The movie ended. Remi had fallen asleep somewhere in the middle, the soft rise of her chest apparent against my hand.

I rubbed her shoulder. "Love, you need to go to bed."

God, I didn't want her to go. I could hold her forever.

"M'kay," she murmured but didn't move.

I whispered, "You know you want to be bright-eyed and bushy-tailed for the first day of class."

I got nothing, but a soft snore.

Her face was serene, her lashes dark against her face, and I allowed myself to kiss her on the lips. Just a touch. Then I eased away from her, maneuvering up to my knees and away from the couch. I stood.

She stirred and turned back over, confusion flickering across her face. "Is it over?"

I nodded, bent down, and like at the club in London, I scooped her up in my arms and lifted her off the couch. She hid her head in my neck as I carried her up the stairs and into her room.

I eased her down to her bed, pulled the covers back over her, and left.

THE NEXT DAY, I got up at six, ran to the bakery for Remi, came back, and showered. My first class was at eight, and I was out of the house by seven forty-five.

My morning classes were good—two upper-level psychology classes that I thought I could handle with some serious class attendance. My noon class was a science credit I needed, and I'd opted for zoology. As a senior, I'd been able to get early registration, plus my choice of teacher, and I'd chosen the easiest one.

I made my way to the Fanfield Science Building. I eased into class and Remi was there in the front row, scribbling notes that the teacher had already written on the board. It was early still and most of the seats were empty, and the professor had yet to walk in.

I sat down across from her in the next row over. "The view from the front row looks different—odd."

She looked over at me in surprise, a slow blush rising.

I cocked an eyebrow, feeling glad to see her. "Miss me?"

That's right. Pretend like you didn't tuck her in bed like a pussy last night.

She stammered. "No—I mean, yes, I didn't see you this

morning. Thanks for my breakfast—and, again, for the bracelet. I'm not sure what you did to find it, but knowing you did it for me means something. And thanks for putting me to bed last night. I guess I crashed."

"You're welcome."

She smiled, and I blinked. There was something different about her.

But I got distracted as the warm scent of vanilla and sugar hit me when her arm stretched between us to pick up her book bag. Today she wore a pair of yellow skinny jeans and a low-cut flowery shirt. A small strand of pearls glistened around her neck, hanging down. She rummaged around in her bag with her head bent, giving me a clear view of her white lace bra. Her tattoo. I bit back a groan and shifted around in my seat, my jeans suffocating me. A cold shower might be necessary after class.

She sat back up. Glanced at me. "What's wrong? You look . . . weird."

"You're supposed to say I look hot." As long as we kept the banter up and nothing else, we were fine.

Her lips twitched. "Uh-huh. What were you thinking about?"

I looked at her with heavy eyes, not caring if she was Hartford's. "Sex, vanilla cookies with sugar on top, sex, a sandwich for lunch, sex, more sex—on the kitchen table, on my couch, on my patio." I wet my lips. "You."

Her face flamed.

The professor walked in and immediately began calling the roll. He handed out the syllabi to the ones in the front. I took several and passed them back to the class that had slowly filled up, although I'd barely noticed.

How was I going to get through this class with Remi beside me three days a week?

CHAPTER TWENTY-FOUR

HOW ON EARTH *was I going to get through this class with him?*
During class, I kept sneaking looks at Dax as he listened to the professor. I doodled in my notebook, completely distracted by him. Wearing a heather-gray shirt that perfectly matched his eyes and a pair of jeans with leather flip-flops, he looked drop-dead beautiful.

He glanced up and met my eyes, making my heart pound.

We were in a weird place, and I didn't know how to fix it.

Yet we'd watched a movie together and he'd tucked me in bed.

We were a goddamn mess.

I sighed, wishing I'd stayed awake long enough last night to tell him I'd broken up with Hartford.

But . . .

Would it make a difference?

He's a temporary guy, Remi. He wants your body but not your heart.

But . . . was that right?

The professor droned on, and my thoughts drifted to Hartford from the night before. We'd gone for coffee, and I'd told him about the pregnancy and London, leaving out the more intimate details that might hurt him needlessly. He'd listened to me with a carefulness I appreciated.

I told him we were over—which is what I should have done when he showed up in London. From the moment he'd jilted me and I saw Dax, we were done, but it had taken until last night for me to figure it out. In the end, perhaps it was good that we'd had our blow-up and hashed everything out. There were no secrets. He knew how I felt. It was closure.

The professor ended class, and I stood up and waited for Dax to get his things together. He looked up at me, and I smiled. "I was thinking of getting some pizza at the Student Center. You want to join me?"

He hesitated, but nodded, an earnest smile growing on his face. "Really?"

"I want to talk to you. It's important."

His eyes softened. "Yeah. Sure. I'd like that."

I smiled, feeling shy. "Maybe we can even go to Panera if you don't want pizza."

He laughed, the warm sound sending tingles over my body. God, I wanted to be alone with him. Maybe after lunch we could go back to the house and—

"Remi," a male voice called from the door. I turned to see Hartford there.

"Hey, I was just walking past—" He noticed Dax and stopped, his face tightening. "Is this a bad time?" His eyes swept over me, assessing.

Dax exhaled, a muscle popping in his cheek. "Nope. I was just leaving."

I opened my mouth to say something, but nothing came out. I was in completely strange territory.

Dax bolted from the room, keeping his face averted from me.

I walked over to Hartford, who grimaced.

"I had no clue you guys were talking. I just saw you and wondered how you were today. We had a late night . . ."

I smiled tentatively. "It's fine. What's going on today? How are classes?"

We made small talk for a few moments, neither of us sure about what to say.

It hit me. I rummaged around in my purse and pulled out his ring. "I completely forgot to give this back to you last night."

He blinked, his eyes sad. "Keep it."

I frowned. "I can't do that."

He met my eyes. "I don't want it. Toss it away or at least sell it and get some of your other wedding expenses back. I'm sure your dress was nonrefundable."

I bit my lip. "No. You keep it and trade it in for another ring when you meet the girl you're really supposed to be with."

Because I wasn't that girl.

I pressed it into his palm and he grasped my fingers, taking the ring.

He nodded, and I watched him walk away.

In the end, Hartford wasn't mine.

Dax wasn't mine. Not really. He'd said so at the bar.

But I still had *me.*

And I'd be okay.

THE EVENING ROLLED in, and I met Lulu at the Student Center for dinner. After that, we went to the Tiger Bookstore and picked up last-minute supplies and books that we hadn't already purchased.

"Watch it. Number One Whitman Bitch headed our way." Lulu poked me in the arm and pulled me to a standstill in the spiral note-book section as Eva-Maria waltzed by us with a group of her co-horts, all dressed in their sorority jerseys and skinny jeans.

Glancing around, Eva-Maria's eyes drifted over me—and then came back. She said something to her girlfriends, and they looked over at us.

Lulu flipped them off.

I laughed. "Stop, Lu."

But Eva-Maria didn't bat an eyelash. I'm sure she'd seen worse from girls who didn't like her. With a swish of her hips, her petite frame sashayed over to us, leaving her friends behind.

"Remi," she called as she approached, coming to a stop in front of us.

"That's my name," I said.

"What do you want?" Lulu snarked, her eyes glittering.

She exhaled, a conflicted expression on her face as if she was unsure how to begin. "I've been thinking about freshman year. Actually, Dax and I spoke—well, he told me off to be truthful. Anyway, I wanted you to know that I'm sorry about everything that happened. Dax has never been mine—or anyone's. I was just a kid really, and I'd like to think I'm better now."

"Yeah, right," Lulu muttered.

"Shh," I said. "Let her talk."

She twisted her lips. "About Dax—everyone adores him, especially the little sisters. Heck, everyone on campus wants him—but he's never wanted anyone. But, the day you left he was . . ."

My throat caught. "Yeah?"

"Different." She sighed, lifting her eyes up to me. "We were never together again after that."

She shrugged and made her way back to her friends.

"Once a slut, always a slut," Lulu said, watching the group of girls strut across the courtyard like they owned the place.

"Wow. That was . . . totally out of nowhere," I said.

"You don't buy that crap, do you?"

I thought about it.

"She was such a bitch to you, Remi. You can't possibly forget that."

"No, I won't forget it, but I appreciate her words . . ." I stopped, thinking. "But it's funny. She doesn't matter. Not anymore. She's a zit on the face of the earth, and I see her for what she is. Insecure. Needy. Dax never cared about her."

Her eyes softened. "Does he care about you?"

I couldn't answer that.

THE NIGHT CAME and Dax never came home. I waited up to talk to him, but at two in the morning I gave up and made my way upstairs and crashed. He was probably at the Tau house. *With someone.*

Tuesday dawned, and I got up, hoping to catch him in case he'd gotten in after I'd gone to bed, but there was no sign of him. Breakfast was on the table again, telling me he'd at least stopped by, but because I was ornery, I didn't look inside. I grabbed a breakfast bar instead and headed out to my car.

Tuesday was my light day with only two classes, and after they were done, I hit the library with Lulu to pick up some reading material for one of my upper-level biology classes. Lulu dropped down in the fashion section on the lower level while I headed upstairs.

It was only when I'd gotten a few paces in that I happened to glance down one of the hallways to see Dax at a study table with a few others. They had books open, talking quietly. His head was bent low, his pen scribbling in his notebook.

It didn't feel right to bug him while he was studying—but dammit, I walked over anyway.

Axel looked up and saw me first. "Hey, Remi. What's up?" His voice boomed, and I bit back a smile. If he didn't keep it down, the librarians would come hush us.

"Good," I said, my eyes on Dax as we exchanged pleasantries.

He'd raised his head up, along with two girls I recognized as little sisters, but not the bitchy ones. In fact, I'd had a class with one of them and she was kinda nice and brilliant to boot. Jealousy ate at me. I clutched my book bag to hang on and ground myself.

I looked at Dax. His hair was tousled, the strands a mess as if he raked his hands through it a dozen times. "I just wanted to say hi. I didn't hear you come in last night."

He leaned back in his chair. Cool. "Stayed at the frat. You know how it is. Lots going on."

"Oh, a party?" I asked, trying to appear unconcerned.

"Yeah. Off the chain. You should have been there."

Axel shot him a quick look, as if surprised by his answer.

So did the little sisters. They shrugged and went back to writing.

"I wasn't invited," I stated.

Dax shrugged. "Just Taus—no one else."

Oh.

A few beats of silence went by, and slowly but surely I realized it was becoming weird—me standing here and no one talking.

Axel jumped in. "We, uh, we're studying for a psych class. Already got a term paper assignment. Trying to get a jump on things before things get crazy."

"Oh, that's smart," I said, my eyes searching for something to land on. Anything except Dax. He didn't want me here.

Everyone stared at me expectantly. Waiting.

Was it my turn to talk?

No. I couldn't do this. I couldn't pretend with him anymore. Not now.

Giving up, I swallowed, said a hasty goodbye, and fled.

Reaching the end of the hall, I turned the corner and leaned against a wall of books, feeling out of breath for no good reason.

Dax was breaking my heart. He was beautiful and broken, not able to see what I could see. And just glimpsing him at a table with other girls, obviously studying, made me bonkers. It was freshman year all over again, only magnified by a million.

Steadying myself, I walked downstairs, found Lulu, and dropped down next to her with a groan.

She flicked her eyes up at me from over a magazine. "What's eating you? I thought you loved it upstairs with all the musty old books."

"Dax is up there."

"And this is a problem?"

"He didn't come home last night. He had a party at the frat."

She grimaced. "That's what he does, Remi. You knew this about him a long time ago."

I nodded. "Yeah."

I fiddled with my phone. "Hey, you wanna get out of here?

Maybe get a beer at Cadillac's."

Her eyebrows went sky high. "On a Tuesday? It'll be dead."

"Not the first week of school. Come on. I need to blow off some steam."

She slapped down the magazine. "As long as there's no tequila involved, I'm down with that."

ON WEDNESDAY, I woke up with a hangover.

I took a long shower, praying the hot water would work its magic on me.

Coming downstairs, I plodded into the kitchen wearing my nightdress. Nothing had changed. No glasses in the sink. No dishes on the counter. I peeked in his bedroom and the bed was still made. No evidence that I had a roommate.

Dax showed up for zoology, but instead of taking the seat next to me like he had on Monday, he aimed for the middle next to a couple of pretty girls. He sent me a polite nod, and I wanted to scream at him.

He bolted from class when the professor dismissed us, and I followed him out in the hall. "Dax?"

He halted and turned to face me. "Hey."

His casual words didn't fool me. The barrier he carried to protect himself was already in place.

"You haven't been home much."

Concern etched his face and he came in closer. "You're not scared there alone are you?"

"No." I nibbled my thumbnail.

"What's wrong?" His eyes searched mine.

"I miss you." I said the words honestly, not caring.

He whitened. "Please don't say that. You can't."

Blood left my face, and I closed my eyes, digging deep to find a tiny piece of strength to walk away from him.

Why are you still standing here, Remi?

Don't you have any pride?

How much will it take for you to leave him alone?

The answer burned in my head—so simple and easy, like beautiful things usually are. *I loved him.*

There are no coincidences in life, only fate pushing you toward one another.

He was my imperfect soul mate, and every tiny thread in the universe had stitched my heart to his, piecing us together, fashioning us into something that was, in my mind, absolutely perfect.

The broken ticker in my chest knew it.

My bomb-ass brain knew it.

I suspected he knew it.

I was crazy for him, always had been, and it was never going to change. Even when I'd been with Hartford, the majority of my heart had belonged to Dax. Oh, I'd ignored it for three years, shoving it down deep, constantly reminding myself of how he'd hurt me. He'd been too young then. He hadn't been ready. Maybe he still wasn't ready—but my love?—it was wild and crazy and wicked with a filthy need for him. I craved him, body, soul, and mind.

I don't think I'd want to live if he died.

I don't think I could carry on without knowing he was breathing.

Like a piece of carefully folded paper that's been hidden away but is now opened, I saw everything clearly. The truth had been right in front of me the entire time.

He was mine; I was his. Nothing would ever change that.

I opened my eyes when the sound of a phone vibrating brought me back. It was Dax's.

He didn't notice, his eyes on my face, as if mesmerized by what he saw.

"That's your phone," I finally said as it continued to shake, the sound coming from his backpack.

He opened his backpack and checked it. Looked back at me. "It's Declan. He's waiting for me to come to the gym. I have to go." He didn't look like he wanted to go, a torn expression on his face.

"Then go." I pushed a piece of hair out of my face, and his eyes widened.

He dropped his book bag. "Where's your ring?" he barked.

"I gave it back to Hartford. I—I wanted to tell you, but there hasn't been a good time. You're never home—"

"Remi." His voice was low. Gravelly. "Why didn't you tell me? Text me? Something?"

"I'm telling you now. Here."

He sucked in a shuddering breath and swallowed, his throat working to form words. "I'll—I'll be home tonight."

AROUND TWO, MALCOLM texted me a pic of him holding a can of Ragu.

> **I want spaghetti. Mom says she'll bring me and the groceries if you'll cart me back tonight.**

I grinned.

> **We just had it a few days ago. Don't you get sick of it?**

> **Look who you're talking to. I have a one-track mind. I like what I like,** he typed.

> **You know how to get what you want that's for sure,** I said.

> **Send me a pic of you.**

I took a selfie of me with a crazy expression on my face and my tongue hanging out.

> **You look like dad.**

I laughed.

> **See you soon.**

Mom and Malcolm arrived around four. She hadn't seen the place yet, so I gave her the tour. She asked where Dax was, and I told her he was rarely around. She didn't know Dax was the guy from freshman year, and I didn't tell her. There was no reason to.

But I did tell her about Hartford. She let out a long sigh, but accepted it along with the promise she could hook me up with her boss's son.

I laughed.

She left to head to work, and Malcolm and I played a quick game of Scrabble while the sauce and noodles cooked.

Dax came in the back door. He was sweaty, wearing athletic shorts and a white wife-beater. Obviously he'd been working out. He ran his eyes over me, his gaze lingering on my bare left hand, a strange intensity in his eyes.

"Hey, bro," he said to Malcolm as they greeted each other.

"Is that my sister's name on your chest?" he asked, cocking his head as he peered at Dax's chest.

Oh. I hadn't noticed you could see part of his tattoo, too caught up in the fact that *he was here.*

Had he worn that to the gym? He was showing people?

My heart fluttered.

I busied myself checking the stove.

Malcolm walked over and got in Dax's personal space to get a better look, taking in the top of the flag and the bottom of my name that disappeared under his shirt. Dax didn't seem to mind.

"Will you take off your shirt?" Malcolm asked.

Dax looked at me, shrugged, and pulled his shirt off.

Like mine, the redness of the image had healed leaving only a vibrant flag, and my name written in black.

My eyes popped at the hard muscles of his pecs, the tanned skin of his six-pack, the deep V that tapered down to his hips. He looked even bulkier than in London.

Malcolm glanced at me. "Did you know this?"

"She has one too," Dax said, stalking around the kitchen and grabbing a bottle of water from the fridge. He chugged it, eyes on me, making me squirm.

Malcolm cocked his head, studied me, and then checked out Dax's face. A flicker of understanding dawned. "Oh. I get it. You two like each other. You're probably having sex."

Dax spit out a mouthful of water then grabbed a dishtowel to get it up off the floor.

"Malcolm, remember those conversations that aren't your busi-ness? This is one of those," I said sternly.

Dax rose back up from cleaning the water.

"Are you mad at me for saying inappropriate things?" he asked Dax, a dip in his shoulders.

"No, dude. Not at all."

Malcolm nodded. "Good. Then tell me what it's like to get a tattoo."

"Sure." They sat down at the table as I stayed at the stove, lis-tening as Dax described the process, how long it takes to heal, and if it hurts. Malcolm had a million questions, and Dax answered each one, describing the shop where we'd gone and the different images he'd seen people get. He showed him his dragonfly, turning his bicep so Malcolm could peer down at it and trace over it.

"Remi loves flying things," he mused, glancing at me. "She tried to beat me at Scrabble with *quail* but I got her with *Xerox*."

"Good job." Dax laughed. "Once I beat my brother Declan with *Xylol*. He claimed it wasn't a real word, so I pulled the dictionary out and proved it. It's some kind of volatile hydrocarbon apparently. I won, and to this day he still doesn't know that it was a total Hail Mary. Now I refuse to play with him, so I can say I won the last game."

Malcolm laughed and wandered off to watch television while I finished everything up on the stove.

"Do you want to eat with us?" I asked, at the sudden silence in the kitchen.

He walked over and stood next to me, leaning against the count-er with his arms crossed. He studied me intently like he always did.

"Stop staring at me," I said. "You're making me paranoid and it's kinda creepy."

He spun me around and pinned me against the counter. "Is it really over?"

I didn't have to ask what he was talking about.

"Yes."

"Why?" His voice was raw.

I touched his lips, wanting them on mine. A few beats of silence went by.

He groaned. *"Remi, just say it."*

"Because he's not *you*. I want you."

He inhaled sharply, fear on his face. "Remi, don't you see—*you don't need me.* You need a guy like him. I can't be what's on your list. I don't have a plan after college. I'm not responsible. I live from day to day. Hell, I don't even know if I can sell this house."

My eyes softened. "For you, I don't have a list. I don't need one. You check all my boxes, Dax."

He let me go and stalked around the room, his hands all over the place as he spoke. "Every fiber of me *wants* to believe what you say. I've pictured us a million times, but in the end you leave me for someone who's got his shit together—like fucking Hartford. I can't watch someone I—I . . ." He stopped and exhaled. "You're the only girl who's ever walked away from me. *Ever.* You went out my frat bedroom door, and you never looked back. *You were pregnant and you never looked back."*

"We aren't those people anymore," I said, watching him pace.

He strode back over to me, eyes flashing. "The thing is, I don't think I *could ever* leave you, Remi."

"Dax, please." His voice was breaking me. I didn't understand.

"Since your dad died, you've gotten it in your head what kind of man you need to be happy. *I'm not it.*" He paused. "And now you decide I'm the one. I can't . . ." He let me go, grabbed his shirt off the counter, and slipped it back on. "I—I need a break from this."

I clutched the counter. He needed a *break?* The word pinged around in my head. God. Hartford had wanted a break, too. My chest rose.

"Dax, don't . . ." My voice croaked, and I stopped, afraid I'd cry.

His expression was torn as he gazed at me, his eyes excruciatingly vulnerable. He opened his mouth to speak but slammed it shut. "I'm scared, Remi. Fucking scared. You. Can. Hurt. Me."

And he was gone.

I held onto the counter as he left out the back door.

I was free to love, and all he had to do was claim me—but he hadn't.

Malcolm walked in the kitchen slowly, and by the look on his face, I suspected he'd heard us. He wrapped his arms around me.

"You'll always have me, Remi. I'll even let you win at Scrabble."

I squeezed him tighter.

CHAPTER TWENTY-FIVE

Remi

I DIDN'T SEE him Thursday.

I ignored him in class on Friday.

He looked like shit.

I ~~didn't~~ *did* care.

I jumped up to leave right as class ended, determined to not glance back. I looked—*dammit*—and his eyes were on me. Focused in. Raking over each inch of me.

After my classes, I got an excited call from Lulu, who said her roomie Carla had decided to move in permanently with her boyfriend, thus leaving me with the option of contacting the housing department and checking if I could fill her spot. I called immediately, and it was a done deal.

That night, Lulu and Malcolm came to the house to help me pack clothes and necessities. I'd be leaving the bedroom furniture until we had more time to arrange for the heavy lifting. Malcolm offered to help, and he was strong, but I wasn't sure he or Lulu would be able to help me without the proper equipment. Moving completely out would take some time.

"You could ask Hartford?" Lulu suggested, but I nixed that

idea. We were done, and me asking favors would confuse things.

I was determined to do this on my own.

"Good thing there's already a bed in the dorm room," Lulu mused as she took in my queen-sized headboard and chest of drawers.

"Yeah." I wiped sweat off my forehead and pulled my shirt away from my chest to get some air. "I think we can get the end table in your truck though. Wanna try?"

The table was made from pressed wood; Malcolm insisted he'd do it, so we moved out of his way as he picked it up and eased it down the stairs carefully while I walked in front of him in case he stumbled.

We'd just gotten the last box of my clothes in the back of Lulu's truck when Dax's car came to a halt on the street.

He jumped out of the car and strode toward us.

"Oh, shit. Here comes some bloody British trouble—dammit, he's hot, even sweaty. You think he's dangerous? Want me to stay or go?"

"He won't hurt me. You guys get in the truck and give us a moment."

"Too bad I don't have any popcorn in the cab." She motioned for Malcolm to get in on the passenger side while she got behind the wheel. Both of them turned around to watch.

"What's going on?" He looked in the back of the truck, taking in the contents.

Once again, he'd just come from the gym, wearing a tank and a pair of black nylon shorts. His tattoo was out there for everyone to see.

"I'm moving."

"Where?"

"Dax, look—"

"Sonofabitch!" he yelled. "You're moving in with Hartford, aren't you?"

"Never. There's a spot open in Lulu's room."

He raked a hand through his hair. His chest rose. "Fuck."

I let out a breath. "Dax, look, you've barely been here all week. I feel like I'm the one pushing you away from something you should be proud of. You just bought this place."

"I'm here now."

"Not the way I want," I said softly, my heart aching. I sucked in a breath.

He paced around me. Angry. "So, this is it? No warning. No note. No call. Not even a text—just you sneaking away while I'm gone."

I rubbed at my wrist. My bracelet was packed away. "I was going to leave you a note."

"I don't care about a note, Remi! You're leaving me." He shook his head, his voice cracking. *"Just like I said you would."*

"No, it's not like that," I whispered.

I was leaving him for my own sanity. I felt unhinged here without him, walking around his house, waiting for him to appear like some mysterious ghost. This house was nothing without him here. And someday—*someday* he'd walk in with a pretty coed, and I would lose my fucking mind. I'd crack wide open.

I forced evenness into my voice, trying to rein in the emotion. God, it was so hard to walk away from him, but I had to get some backbone. "I'm in the way of you having a home. We can't keep pretending we want different things. Someday you'll bring a girl home and—"

"I haven't been with anyone but you, dammit. *You.*"

"Neither have I!" I yelled, my nails digging into my palms. "I only want you. Did you really think I could sleep with Hartford after us?"

His eyes softened like a morning mist. "Remi . . ."

"This isn't easy for me," I whispered, weakening at the sound of his voice. "It's nearly impossible to walk away from you even when you aren't really mine. I'd much rather wait around for you to figure things out, but it's hurting me—it's breaking me inside. My heart is destroyed. I—I can't put myself through freshman year again. I can't watch you party and drink and screw around—when I—I'm in love with you. I always have been—*and you know it*." I whimpered. Tears pooled and I battled them back.

His eyes closed.

"Goodbye, Dax." I touched his arm, and he flinched, eyes flying open.

He studied me, his eyes lingering on every part of my face. "I'm not saying goodbye. I can't."

WE DROVE AWAY in silence. I clenched my fist to my mouth to keep from screaming.

A few tense moments passed and Malcolm grabbed my hand. His big eyes took me in. "I'm sorry things got screwed up."

"It's okay," I said, barely keeping it together.

He gave me a sad look. "Dax's a little intense, but it's because he doesn't know how to tell you he loves you. He's never loved a girl, I think. His head's all messed up. He reminds me of those skinny dogs at the shelter, the ones that are scared of their own shadow, but they want you to pet them really bad—" he paused, thinking. "I don't mean he's a *dog*, dog. I'm using a metaphor here, and a damn good one I think. Not bad for an autistic guy."

I sent him a watery smile and hugged him. "You're amazing." My voice was shit.

"Will you be okay?" Lulu asked.

"I don't know. It doesn't feel right leaving him," I whispered. "Not at all." I rubbed my chest. I felt empty. Lost. As in really lost. Like I might never know which direction to go in.

I clutched my pillow that someone had thrown in the cab and buried my face in it.

How was I going to live without him?

CHAPTER TWENTY-SIX

SHE DROVE AWAY, and I let her.

In a grief-induced haze, I went in the house to shower and get the gym sweat off me. In between classes and studying, I'd been working out with Declan, and it gave me focus. At nights, I'd been crashing in a recliner at the Tau house, trying to get a hold on myself. There'd been no parties. No girls. All I wanted was her.

I stood in the shower with my back against the wall to hold me up.

I felt like I was dying.

After my shower, I put on jeans, a Tau shirt, and Converse. Nothing too nice since tonight was the bonfire at Myer's Farm about five miles outside the city. The farm was owned by one of our alumni; it was an annual party with a bonfire, tug-of-war by moonlight, and lots of beer. Thank God.

I hadn't planned on going.

But no way was I missing it to sit here and cry like a baby.

An hour later, I drove down the gravel road that led to the clearing out in the middle of a huge field. The biggest weeping willow trees I'd ever seen lined it on one side near a stream, and pine and oak trees dotted the rest of the perimeter.

I sighed. This would be good. I needed people tonight. Friends.

Axel, Alexandria, and Bettina were standing near the kegs, and I made my way over to them. I grabbed a glass and filled it up.

Here's to many more, I told myself.

Someone cranked up the music and the dancing started, reminding me of Remi at the Masquerade.

I got another beer. And another.

As it grew late, we lit up lanterns around the part of the party where the fire didn't illuminate. Sitting in pop-up chairs in a circle of people, we played drinking games. Alexandria planted herself next to me, her hands resting on my thighs, her fingers inching closer to my inner thigh the braver she got.

I didn't fight her off. I didn't encourage her either.

I was empty, nothing without Remi.

Remi.

She was all that played through my head.

Fucking hell. I stood up. *I had to get out of here.* People weren't helping. Alcohol wasn't. I needed *her.* She was it. Everything. My life.

I clutched my head. God, I was going to find her tonight and tell her, no, *beg* her to come back—

Bright lights swung into the clearing as another car parked in the designated area near the tree line. There had to be about a hundred people here, and before the night was through there'd be more.

Two girls walked into our circle. My eyes flared at one of them.

I stumbled and thankfully managed to fall back in my chair.

Wearing that short-as-fuck dress from Masquerade and heels— *what was she thinking*—Remi walked into our circle. The cream-colored dress showcased her *Dax* tattoo and was almost see-through with the lanterns behind her. Her hair was like fire, her pearls draped around her neck.

No bra. No panties.

Someone whistled.

My beer fell out of my hand and spilled on the ground.

Everyone hushed in the middle of a game of Never Have I Ever. I don't know if it was because they saw my livid face or if they were gawking at her body.

I was a statue, couldn't even twitch as I watched her sashay over to me, teetering a little when she stepped on a rock.

She stopped in front of Alexandria. "You. Whatever your name is. Up."

"Excuse me. *No.* You don't own him." She squinted, letting out a nervous laugh. "Wait. Aren't you his roommate?"

"*Get up.* I do own him. And take your hand off his leg."

Alexandria looked at me for help. The best I could eke out was one of my trademark shrugs. My heart was freaking out. My mouth was dry as cotton. "She's the boss," I pushed out.

Sputtering, Alexandria stood and flicked her hair over her shoulder. "Fine. He's boring as shit anyway."

I burst out laughing just to relieve the awkwardness; plus the idea of *me* being boring was ludicrous.

Remi took her seat, politely covering her ankles so no one could see up her dress.

"Don't you think you're a bit overdressed?" I said curtly.

She smiled, showing me the little space between her teeth. "You're lucky I wore anything at all."

I hissed.

"I wore it to piss you off."

My lids lowered. "It's working," I growled.

Lulu took a seat on the other side of her, which had been vacated when Alexandria stormed off.

The conversation began to grow again, but I could feel people's eyes on us.

I knew what they were thinking.

That chick is practically naked!

Wasn't she engaged to Hartford?

She just claimed Dax Blay as hers. Is it the end of the world?

I laughed as warmth buzzed in my brain, and it wasn't from the beer.

Someone handed the girls cups of beer, and we got back to playing the game. I tore my eyes off Remi and kept them focused straight ahead. Maybe if I didn't stare at her, I'd get some sense, because right now, all I wanted to do was scoop her up and carry her off.

No one could remember whose turn it was, so Remi said she'd go.

I leaned back in my chair and watched her stand. She looked damn beautiful—even if I did want to grab a blanket and wrap it around her.

She raised her glass. "Never have I ever had a one-night stand."

Everyone murmured or chuckled and most of us took a drink. She drank. I drank.

"May I go again?" she asked sweetly, and of course, all the brothers said *"Sure, babe,"* eyeballs all over her. My fists clenched.

"Never have I ever had a one-night stand that turned into a three-night stand because you'd fallen in love and couldn't bear to leave that person. Ever."

She tipped her glass up and took a swig. I didn't see who else did, because my eyes were only on her.

I drank.

God, I loved her. Deeply. Intensely. Completely.

She smiled around at the circle and did a little curtsey. "Thank you for letting me hijack your game."

"Anytime," a male called suggestively, and I sent him a *go to hell* look.

I stood. "My turn," I announced. Nerves hit me. My hands shook.

It's now or never, Dax. Tell her how you feel. Own it. Embrace it.

"Never have I ever loved someone so much that I'd get down on my knees and beg her to forgive me for being too young to know that what we had was the most beautiful thing in the world, and all I had to do was let go of my fears and love her forever."

I gulped down the rest of my beer, watching her.

She picked up her glass, saluted me, and took a drink.

The group grew quiet. Again. Eyes on us.

Hell, we were a soap opera. I'd just confessed my love for Remi in front of the entire frat and probably some random people I didn't even know.

Something had fried my brain because I wasn't done.

I gazed around at my brothers. "And just so you blokes know, this girl here"—I pointed at Remi—"is *mine*. I love her, so chill with the flirty comments." I leaned down to her, my arms on either side of her chair, tipped her chin up, and kissed her. Nothing crazy, but my lips and tongue telling her she was going to pay for showing up in that dress.

I sat back down and made a show of it, stretching out my arms over my head, cracking my neck, and getting loose. Fuck. I felt incredible.

Her eyes glittered as she took in every movement, her top teeth digging into her bottom lip.

A few minutes went by and the game continued. My body was amped, ready to snap at the slightest thing. Waiting for what trouble came next. It came.

"I'm headed to the keg for another beer. You want one?" she asked Lulu.

"Nope," Lulu answered. "Watching you and Dax is enough of a buzz for me."

Remi shrugged and took off into the darkness for the keg area.

Go after her!

I let her get about fifty feet before I jerked up, blood pumping.

I jogged, and she must have heard my footfalls because she kicked off her heels and dashed for the tree line.

Like a streak of lightning, she dodged the parked cars, weaving in and out as she headed for the weeping willow trees. Jumping a tiny stream, she landed with a little grunt, her legs disappearing under the draped foliage.

At this rate, she'd kill herself before I reached her.

The light from the bonfire and lanterns didn't quite go this far, so by the time I pushed aside the grass-length branches and got inside, I was greeted with darkness. The only thing visible was a faint outline of her as she pressed herself against the trunk. The sounds of laughter and music from the party drifted inside the tree's sanctuary, but the only sound I homed in on was her breathing.

I stalked toward the trunk.

She whimpered when I put my hands on her collarbone and stroked down to her wrist, fingering her bracelet.

"I see you," I said. My hands picked hers up and pinned them above her head against the tree, careful to not hurt her.

"You caught me," she whispered and arched toward me.

"Mmmm." Inhaling, I ran my nose up her throat to her ear and whispered, "Whether I can see you or not, I always smell you. Every time I walk in a bakery shop and get a whiff of sugar—on a donut or a damn cookie—I get hard."

"Is that why you bring me breakfast—"

I kissed her. The best kiss I'd ever had. Soft and languorous, my lips played with hers, giving her tiny kisses and then longer ones.

My kisses went down her neck to her collarbone and to her chest. My tongue outlined her tattoo, tracing the lines of my name as she squirmed, trying half-heartedly to get loose from being pinned. Using my teeth, I nibbled on the front of her dress, aiming for her nipples, my mouth soaking her dress until I could see rosy tips through the dress.

"Dax." She rotated against me. "Let me touch you," she moaned, her voice thick with heat.

"No." I wanted to punish her until she begged me to let her do what she wanted.

Using one hand to secure her wrists, my other one reached behind her back, grabbed the zipper, and yanked it down. Her dress fell to the ground, leaving her nude, and I latched onto her breasts, my tongue, teeth, and lips devouring her.

"I'm burning that damn dress," I said into her neck. I bit her shoulder.

She cried out in pleasure, and I went back to her mouth. Kissed her. "Do you want everyone to hear us?" I asked between kisses.

233

"I don't care," she said and sucked on my bottom lip, her teeth tugging, making me ache. I groaned, liking the way she knew me. I wanted her to do that to me for the rest of my life.

I licked her throat. "I'm going to let you go, and you're going to stand there and not move."

"Yes."

With care, I let her hands rest, and she collapsed against the tree, arms dangling at her sides. Taking my sweet time, I kissed down each arm individually, to her elbows, to the palms of her hands. I went to my knees. Kissed her stomach. Sucked on her hipbone.

Emotion tore at me. Regret. Lust. *Love*. Real love.

"I'm so damn sorry," I said against her skin. "I'm sorry I couldn't commit to you in the kitchen when you told me you were done with Hartford. I'm sorry I'm terrified of losing you. But I want to try. I want to be yours and you be mine. I want to wake up next to you, put my nose at your throat and just . . . breathe. I want to hold you in my arms. I want to carry you up to bed when you fall asleep. I want to kiss you wearing a mask where we pretend like we don't know each other. I want to live in my house with you." I pressed my forehead against her. "Just . . . don't . . . hurt . . . me."

She pulled my head up, stared into my eyes, and sank to her knees. We faced each other. "I will never hurt you. It's why I came here tonight. When I left your house, it dawned on me that maybe I needed to be the one to fight harder for you if you couldn't."

I kissed her. "I was just getting ready to leave here, hunt you down, and take you back to my house. Seeing you leave today—I can't ever lose you again. I'll die without you," I said, cradling her face. "We are meant to be, Remi."

Her blue eyes gleamed. "*Fate always knew*. She tried three years ago to get us together and failed. She tried again in London and failed. But here and now, we're listening."

She kissed me, her hands cupping my face and sliding into my hair.

I shivered against her, melting into her. "God, I love you, Remi."

"I love you," she whispered.

We kissed, our arms wrapped around each other, and nothing could tear us apart.

I didn't intend to ever let her go.

Grabbing her hand, I pulled her back up. "I haven't been able to forget London—or Cadillac's. I want to own you, body and soul."

She shuddered. "I'm ready for you."

Reaching behind my head, I tugged off my shirt, stepped out of my jeans and kicked my shoes off. She watched. Bending down, I fished a condom out of my wallet and slipped it on my hard cock.

"Let me put my back to the tree," I murmured, my gaze heavy and low.

"Not sure I can move. I—I think it's the only thing holding me up."

"Love, I'm gonna hold you up."

I picked her up and she straddled me, her legs tight around my waist. I backed up against the tree and her feet clung to it. Using every muscle in my body, my hands cupped her bottom as I eased into her wet sheath, dipping in and then backing out, groaning.

She tossed her head back and shuddered, her muscles clinging to me.

I teased her mercilessly, going slow and getting used to the stance of holding her, sliding inside her heat, then coming out to rub across her nub.

Yes, baby, yes. I could go all night like this.

"Please," she whispered, clinging to my shoulders and writhing, her mouth sucking on my neck. "All the way, Dax."

Finally, I slammed my cock home.

"Fucccckkk," I roared, leaving the gentleness behind and taking her with powerful strokes, oblivious to the tree marking up my back.

I cupped her arse and owned her. She moaned when I adjusted my angle, biceps quivering as I worked to press down on the most sensitive part of her skin.

She tugged on my hair until I kissed her.

235

"Yes, love," I murmured. "Lean up a little. Get closer to my mouth." She arched into me, and I went for her tits, laving her nipples. Sucking. Biting.

We devoured each other, our bodies syncing together, knowing innately how to make the other feel good. Sweat dripped down my face and onto her skin.

She was the best sex I'd ever had. *Always had been.*

She yelped as she went over the edge, her muscles pulsating around me, legs locked around my hips as she spasmed.

I didn't stop.

With my mouth deep over hers, I eased down the tree until I was lying on the grass and she straddled me. I tugged on her pearls, bringing her to my mouth. "Ride me."

She sent me a heated look and took all of me, her eyes finding mine as we moved together.

Soft. Slow. Easy.

I cupped her face, my heart full. "I've dreamed about us for so long. I just didn't know how to say it—didn't know what it was."

She leaned down and kissed me, her face radiating love. I ran my fingers down her spine. *She was mine.* Beautiful Remi.

"Here, let me," I said eventually when she grew tired. I took over the hard work, my hands lifting her hips to get her where I wanted.

I hissed as I moved inside her, grinding my skin against hers, the top of my cock brushing against her clit.

"Dax . . ." she cried.

She was close.

With intense need driving me, I pulled her hair back, the arch of her neck a beacon as I latched onto it and sucked hard. *Yes. This.* Getting into a steady rhythm, I hammered into her ruthlessly, my mouth at her throat. I'd never get enough of her. Never.

The sounds of our sex, wild and rough, made me crazy. Sensation built in my spine, my strokes fast.

"Dax, yes, please," she called, as if my name was a benediction. Her nails dug into my shoulders, tugging me closer, even though we

couldn't get any closer.

She screamed out her orgasm, her body clenching me. I told her I loved her, whispering it against her shoulder and came right after, yelling into the night. My heart pounded like a train. Fuck. Would it always be this crazy-hot with us? I suspected so.

Panting, I pushed hair out of her face. "Are you okay? Did I hurt you?"

"Never," she murmured.

A few minutes later, I crawled around, found our clothes, and spread them out on the grass. I carried her over as if she were fragile, laid her down, and we held each other.

She cried quietly—happy tears—and I held her, my own emotion clawing at my chest.

My fingers idly traced her arm, and she traced the tattoo on my chest.

"This is the best night of my life," I said later, softly, into her hair. "And we owe it all to fate."

She grinned. "And tequila."

I laughed. Tightening my arms around her, I pulled her until she was lying on top of me, her head on my chest.

She was my light, my breath. She was my Juliet.

Only we'd have a happy ending. I'd make sure of it.

CHAPTER TWENTY-SEVEN

W E WOKE THE next morning to the sun shining through the cracks of the thick, sweeping branches. It was our own private haven.

"Is everyone gone?" I whispered.

He eased away from me, stood, and stalked over to glimpse between the foliage. I bit my lip at the red marks on his broad shoulders and muscled back. His perfect ass.

How would I ever get used to such a man?

I grinned to myself. I'd come up with a few ways . . .

He turned, saw my smile, and smiled back.

He loved me.

He wanted us.

"I see a few cars and a couple of people are still here watching the fire burn down."

"I guess Lulu left?"

"Why? You're leaving here with me."

I rolled my eyes. "I know, but I just want to check on her."

He peeked out again and turned back to me. "Don't see her

truck . . . which reminds me . . . let me get dressed and run to my car. I've got something for you."

What?

He'd done so much for me. Rescuing me in London, fake-marrying me to make me laugh, letting me live with him when he knew it was a horrible idea, the bracelet.

"Okay, but be fast. I'm feeling lonely." I wiggled my eyebrows at him and he chuckled.

"Woman, my back and arse are so bloody right now, the next time I take you, it will be in a soft bed with no rocks or trees." His lips tipped up in a cocky grin. "But if you insist, I wouldn't say no . . ."

I shooed him and he pulled on his clothes and shoes, stepped out from the heavy leaves, and took off at a run. Getting to his car, he pulled out a bag and dashed back to me.

He entered the area under the tree, threw down the bag, and pulled out a *Front Street Gym* shirt and a pair of slick athletic shorts. "Put this on."

My brow wrinkled. "Why? I have my dress."

"You really want me to get pissed off when you put that dress back on and march in front of my brothers?"

Heat went through me. *Yes?*

I saw his point; I'd only done it to get his attention and obviously it had worked.

"Put on my clothes," he murmured softly, his eyes vulnerable yet coupled with his domineering attitude.

He helped me pull the shirt on, and thank goodness the shorts had a drawstring so I could cinch them.

"I look homeless."

"You have a home. Mine." He pulled my pearls out to rest against my chest.

I sighed, brushing his tousled hair off his face. "Tell me how you came to know you loved me?"

He stared down at me. "When you slammed the door in my face at the Tau house, I knew I'd screwed up. When I heard you were engaged to Hartford, I was certain I'd screwed up." He stopped. Closed his eyes. Opened them. "The night you kissed me at Masquerade and I *instantly* recognized your scent, the taste of your lips, and how you felt in my arms—I knew you were the only girl I wanted. I'm an idiot, and I just didn't know how to do it right."

"You're doing it right, Sex Lord," I murmured, running my fingers down his chest and down to the hard shaft in his jeans.

He groaned. "Don't start something you can't finish."

"Oh, I can finish it. It's your back that can't take it."

He laughed, grabbed my dress, and we took off for his Range Rover. At the last moment, he veered toward where a few of his brothers were standing by the fire. They appeared as if they'd just woken up, judging by the sleeping bags and cots strewn around the field.

Dax said hiya, sent some nods, and made his way to the low-burning fire.

I'd thought he was ready to go . . .

What was he doing?

He held my dress over the flames.

"Dax Winston Blay, if you drop that dress, there will be trouble," I called loudly.

He lowered his eyes. "I can make you get over it soon enough."

"Don't do it," I growled.

A smile played at the corner of his mouth. "Give me one reason."

I bit my lip. "I promise to only wear it for you. No one else."

He pulled it back slowly, eyes on me. "Promise?"

"I promise," I said and snatched the dress and dashed for his car, calling over my shoulder. "Unless you make me really mad and I have to teach you a lesson."

I giggled and ran backward—scary for me—just to watch his face. He glowered at me, but in his favor, he gave me a few moments before he ran after me and chased me down. He scooped me up by my legs, making me yelp, and carried me the rest of the way to his Range Rover, kissing me the entire way.

I sighed, happiness exploding inside every atom.
Mr. Beautiful. He was mine and I was his.

The End

EPILOGUE

One Year Later

DAX WALKED IN the Masquerade around ten, his black domino mask conforming to the perfectly chiseled planes of his face. Declan was with him. They both wore low-slung designer jeans and an *I am hot* attitude. At first glance, it was nearly impossible to tell them apart, except one was a bit bulkier and they had different tattoos.

I sat at the bar watching them, and even with an entire dance floor separating us, I knew exactly which man was mine.

I smiled as I tipped back another shot of tequila.

He hadn't seen me yet, his head turning to search the crowd.

Declan was eyeing everyone too, his arms crossed, an inscrutable expression on his handsome face. He was the tough guy. The protector.

I leaned over to Elizabeth who was sitting on a stool next to me. "Our guys are here. They haven't seen us yet."

She smiled, pink lips curving up as she followed my eyes to the foyer of the club. "And, look, the women are fawning over them already," she said with a chuckle.

True. A pack of giggly girls were pointing them out to their other girlfriends.

We weren't worried. Our guys only had eyes for us.

I turned around to ask for more limes, putting my back to the door. "Let's give them a minute to find us. I still need another drink."

Excitement ran over me, thinking about how hard it would be for them to find us, especially since we'd chosen the biggest masks we could find, fluffy with lots of feathers and fabric. We'd also both worn our hair up in loose knots, with soft tendrils hanging down.

Mine had grown out enough to make it work.

Since we'd had a girls' day today, we'd splurged and gotten new dresses. I wore a slinky black number that contrasted nicely with my red hair, and Elizabeth had gone for a white halter dress.

I'd even put heels on. I know. Amazing.

We flagged down a bartender.

The four of us had come to London a few days ago for three reasons. First, we were celebrating that Elizabeth's attacker, Colby, had pleaded guilty to a lesser charge of one count of first degree attempted murder instead of facing the other two charges against him. His sentence had been life in prison with the possibility of parole later. That was fine. She'd gotten closure, and Declan was mostly satisfied. He liked to say that if Colby ever got out, he'd kill him, but mostly I think Elizabeth has tamed him.

Second, Dax and I had both graduated Whitman this past semester. He'd pulled out a 3.0 GPA with diligent studying and lots of alone time with me. We liked to study in bed mostly, although our focus wasn't always a college class. His plan (yes, I'd helped him) was to get his real estate license this year as well.

The housing market had worked well for him. He'd sold his first home after living there for six months and had promptly bought two additional properties. I'd started a YouTube channel for him where he took people on virtual tours of the two houses and talked about the renovations. I popped in on the video to talk about birds, eighties trivia, tattoos—anything really to make people laugh. The fans, who were in the millions, ate it up. They loved us—mostly because he was gorgeous and had that sexy British accent. HGTV had even contacted us, inquiring if we'd be interested in filming a pilot in Raleigh about redoing older homes in the South.

As for me, I was taking it slow with graduate school. I was enrolled in online courses through Duke, and for now, that was perfect. I refused to rush my life and plan out every single detail. Malcolm still stayed with us some, and he and Dax were like tea and biscuits. They adored each other, and I sent up a prayer each day, thanking the heavens that put Dax and I together. My soulmate.

Fifteen minutes later, they still hadn't spotted us, and I was tempted to turn around and make eye contact—but I knew Dax liked this.

He knew I was here somewhere, and part of the hunt was finding me. Anticipation.

Elizabeth, who'd been dying to visit the ladies' room, finally gave in and left me to go pee.

I toyed with my shot glass, running my fingers around the rim.

If he didn't find me by the time she got back, maybe I should go look . . .

Warm hands settled on my bare shoulders as a steely voice whispered in my ear. "Want to dance, love?"

I stiffened and didn't turn around. "No, thank you. I'm waiting for someone."

He didn't go away, but stood so close I could smell him and feel the heat emanating from his skin.

His breath skated across my neck, a light finger tracing my flying black birds tattoo I'd gotten a few months back in honor of my dad. "I like your birds. Does it mean you're just as wild and free as they are?"

I sighed and turned around to face this person.

I raked my eyes over him. "I'm so wild you wouldn't be able to keep up. It takes a real man to satisfy me. Are you him?"

He leaned in closer, his massive shoulders forcing me to ease back in my stool. With a gentle brush, he flicked his finger over my pearls, letting them fall back to my cleavage. Goosebumps flew everywhere.

"Indeed, you are gorgeous," he said softly, hot eyes taking in my strapless dress.

I smirked. "Don't "indeed" me with your haughty English accent. It takes more than that to get me to dance."

"Then how about a kiss?"

I blinked. "You don't waste any time do you?"

Dark eyes narrowed.

I swallowed, getting nervous. Excited? God, I didn't know.

My eyes went over his shoulder, looking at random faces.

"Who are you looking for?" he asked, reaching across me to take my tequila bottle off the bar and look at it.

I smiled. "The hottest guy here—hotter than a billy goat with a blow torch."

He tossed his head back and laughed. I watched fascinated as he poured himself a shot—*in my glass*—and then drank it down.

What game was he playing?

"Iris" by The Goo Goo Dolls came on, and I started, recognizing the song Dax and I had danced to. Memories of London a year ago flooded me.

"You like this song?" He stared at me, eyes searching my hidden face.

"Yes."

A silence fell between us, thick and heavy. I got antsy.

So did he, judging by the way his chest rose up and down. A muscle flexed in his cheek, and I sensed he was barely keeping control—

He broke character. "Are you going to give in?" Dax finally growled, a tinge of authority in his tone.

"No," I managed to say, even though I wanted to fall to my knees for him.

"You want me to dance with someone else?"

"You won't," I said softly.

"Fuck. You're right."

I pretended to ignore him, pouring myself another drink and shooting it back—all while he watched with a hungry, vulnerable look in his eyes.

One that I recognized well.

He was on the edge. Teetering.

So was I—but I held on, doing what any good player would do who was involved in a bet for a quid.

Would he kiss me first? Or would I kiss him?

Yes, he'd told me all about Spider's bet, and tonight we'd made up our own version.

"Stand up," he said.

"Please?"

He sighed. "Please."

I stood and we faced off at the bar. A few patrons noticed the tenseness between us, their eyes bouncing to us and then away.

I put the strand of pearls in my mouth, and moved them over my teeth, my tongue dipping out to taste them. "Too bad this isn't your mouth."

He groaned, his hips moving forward and pressing me into the bar. I should have felt claustrophobic with the bar behind me, him in front, and all the people watching, but I didn't.

This was him. This was me. This is what we liked.

"You're trying to kill me here," he said, his voice ragged, his lips perilously close to mine.

I snaked my hand around his neck and pulled his head down until our foreheads were touching. "You kiss me first and let me win the bet, and I promise to dance with you to our song."

He hesitated. "Can we dance like we did last time?"

I bit my lip and smiled. "Maybe."

"You little minx," he whispered. "You win." He took my mouth slowly as if we had all the time in the world, as if there weren't tons of people watching. I got lost in him, like I always did.

"I love you," he said in my ear when we pulled apart.

I melted even more into him, my hands clinging to his shoulders. "I love you, too."

He took a step back and pulled me out to the dance floor. Once we got there, I saw that Declan and Elizabeth had apparently found each other in the time Dax had found me. They were already dancing, their arms tight around each other. I waved at them, but they didn't notice, too caught up in each other.

Dax pulled me to his chest and touched my face, almost reverently. "Almost a year ago—you fell in my lap. I can't imagine one day without you."

I smiled up at him with absolute certainty.

Romeo and Juliet may have been star-crossed lovers, but we

were not.

"We have forever," I said as he kissed me.

Really The End

DEAR READER,

Hearing from you is very important to me. Honestly, it makes my day because I love to talk about my characters like they are real people (they are in my head!). So please drop me a line on my website or on Facebook. Book reviews are like gold to indie writers, and you have no idea how we relish each one. If you have time, I'd appreciate and love an honest, heartfelt review from you. Thank you for being part of my fictional world.

Ilsa Madden-Mills

ABOUT THE AUTHOR

NEW YORK TIMES and USA Today best selling author Ilsa Madden-Mills writes about strong heroines and sexy alpha males that sometimes you just want to slap. She's addicted to dystopian books and all things fantasy, including unicorns and sword-wielding females. Other fascinations include frothy coffee beverages, dark chocolate, Instagram, Ian Somerhalder (seriously hot), astronomy (she's a Gemini), and tattoos. She has a degree in English and a Master's in Education.

Sign up here (http://eepurl.com/TN2X1) for her newsletter to receive a FREE Briarwood Academy novella ($2.99 value) plus get insider info and exclusive giveaways!

For more information about the next book and to order signed books, please visit my social media sites:

www.ilsamaddenmills.com

Ilsa Madden-Mills Facebook
(www.facebook.com/authorilsamaddenmills)

Ilsa Madden-Mills Goodreads Page
(www.goodreads.com/author/show/7059622.Ilsa_Madden_Mills)

Ilsa's Instagram
(http://instagram.com/ilsamaddenmills/)

Ilsa's Twitter
(https://twitter.com/ilsamaddenmills)

MY OTHER BOOKS

BRIARWOOD ACADEMY SERIES
Reading Order:
Very Bad Things
Very Wicked Beginnings
Very Wicked Things
Very Twisted Things

Dirty English

ACKNOWLEDGEMENTS

THERE ARE SO many fantastic people in the indie world that made this journey possible. Please know that my gratitude in no way lessens as the list continues.

First of all, this book was ONLY written because my readers demanded it, and for that I eternally grateful. I didn't even realize Dax had a story until you told me he did. Writing him was tough, because I'd loved Declan so much, but once I figured out who Dax was and what drove him—I fell hard. I hope you did as well.

For my husband who has stood by me every step of the way. You and me, babe, against the world.

For author Lisa N. Paul—thank you for all the giggles and lunch dates that we've never even had in person. Most of all thank, you for being my dear friend and being there every single day. Let's go smoke.

For author Tia Louise, my twin brain, my signing buddy—thank you for the friendship, advice, and encouragement. I can't imagine a unicorn without thinking of you. Someday, my friend, we will ride one together.

For all the girls in FTN, I appreciate each and every one of you! Thank you for making me giggle every single day.

For the girls in Tribe who have encouraged me and lifted me up. We are new friends, but I love you already. I'm here for you, and all you have to do is ask. Mwah.

For Rachel Skinner of Romance Refined, my awesome and sweet editor who is extremely tough on content and exactly what I need. For Katherine Trail of KT Editing for the fast copy edit.

For Jimmy and Jenn Beckham, Pam Huff, and Julie Deaton—thank you for proofreading and helping me polish.

For Christine Borgford of Perfectly Publishable for doing a phenomenal job with formatting.

For Miranda Arnold of Red Cheeks Reads: my wonderful and talented PA. HOLLA! Haha! So happy we connected through our love of Very Bad Things. Thank you for being a go-getter for me. Race to the end, baby!

For the admin girls of Racy Readers: Erin Fisher, Tina Morgan, Elizabeth Thiele, Miranda Arnold, Stacey Nickelson, Sarah Griffin, Heather Wish, Lexy Stories, Pam Huff, and Suzette Salinas. You ladies are responsible for the great reader group we have. It's one of the best ones ever, and I thank you for your constant support, ideas, and love.

For the ladies of The Rock Stars of Romance who worked tirelessly and answered all my questions and offered advice: Lisa and Milasy…you are the best!

For my Ilsa's Racy Readers Group: you may be last on this list, but you are the BEST. You picked me up when I got knocked down and made me laugh when I needed it the most. Thank you all for every shout out and each review you posted. Thank you for sharing a part of yourself in our group.

Made in the USA
San Bernardino, CA
03 August 2016